THE PRESIDENT SHOW

COSTANZA
CASATI

THE PRESIDENT SHOW

ISBN 978-1-913713-41-6
First published 2021 by Compass-Publishing UK

Edited by Tina Morganella
Typeset by The Book Refinery Ltd
www.thebookrefinery.com
Author Photo © Arianna Genghini

A CIP catalogue record for this book is available from the British Library.

For my mother

CONTENTS

To achieve victory in reality TV "you must lie, form alliances, stab others in the back and conspire to get the strongest players voted off the show. In order to win you must really set aside your compassion, your kindness and your sense of fairness."

– Ronda Scharf, "The Danger of Reality TV," *HuffPost*, 2016

"A lot of us were in very vulnerable situations and in extreme poverty, circumstances where we didn't have anyone on our side."

– Survivor of Jeffrey Epstein during a federal court hearing, 2019

"You wouldn't have your job if you weren't beautiful. It's very sad, isn't it?"

– Donald Trump to reporter Maria Ngo, *VegasNet TV*, 2010

"Nations never build apparently radical forms of government on foundations that aren't there already."

– Margaret Atwood, "Haunted by The Handmaid's Tale," *The Guardian*, 2012

THIEF

Chinatown, 2087

My mother told me there were too many guards around town to steal tonight, but I didn't listen. Now I'm fucked.

I'm running as fast as I can, the pocket of my jacket heavy with the stolen watches, my boots slipping on the thin layer of snow that covers the sidewalk. Chinatown at this hour is a mess. The bright signs with green and orange writing throb all around, blinding me. There are heavily made-up girls smoking and women overloaded with plastic bags. Shopkeepers linger by the dirty curtains that hang in place of shop doors. An old woman smiles at me, toothless. I run past her, panting, as the smell of fish and burning plastic makes me feel sick. I almost knock over a *tanghulu* stall, the candied fruits skewered on sticks that look like tree branches; the vendor yells at me but I ignore him.

I turn left into a narrow street and quickly enter the first door on the right. The room is stuffy, and the ceiling is low. Tiny dumplings are arranged on a counter, and, behind it, an old man looks at me, confused. His nails are broken and dirty, covered in flour. Before he can say or do anything, I put my forefinger to my lips. He must be quiet.

I take the steep spiral staircase at the back of the shop. The steps are slippery and I'm almost climbing, hands against the cold metal. On the roof of the building, I lower my body so that no one can see me from the street, and peep. Three guards in silver uniforms are entering the shop. I hear menacing shouts, then the old man's fearful voice. I hurry and climb onto the roof of the adjacent building.

The guards' voices become closer. I throw myself over the wall, land on my back, gasping for air. I push myself up and start running across the roof. When I hear the gunshots I turn, even though my father always told me to never look back, only run forward... I see the guards running, closer and closer. One lifts his gun and takes aim.

I hold on to the drainpipe of the building and let my body hang in the air. I look for toeholds on the walls, but I can't find any. My body drags me down; my palms bleed against the rusted iron. A few meters down there's a green metal staircase. I let go of the pipe. The impact with the stairs makes me gasp with pain. I'm barely on my feet when the guards start shooting at me from the roof. I rush down the stairs, missing some steps.

Back in the half-deserted streets, I run until I cross the border between Chinatown and my district. My feet splash in puddles of half-melted snow. Some men are walking back home from their nightshifts in the factories, their faces sunken, their cigarettes burning in the dark. I avoid the path that leads me straight home, in case the guards are still following me. I need to protect my mother, my sister. They will be waiting now, their faces flattened against the cold windowpanes, their eyes looking for a gray shadow in a white landscape. I have instructed them to never leave the building at night if I don't come back. But I always come back.

I catch my breath in a corner, away from the feeble light of the lamp posts, burying my hands in the snow to stop the bleeding. There is silence, except for the gusts of wind that make the snowflakes dance in the sky. I breathe out, relieved, and take my shaking hands out of the snow before they freeze. I walk around the corner, thinking about the upcoming warmth of our apartment.

A sudden blow to my head makes me fall to the ground. My face is wet with snow and tears. There is my heavy breathing, and the smell of garbage and mud.

"You're fast, aren't you?" A man's voice. My head hurts, all I can see are my red fingertips in the snow. Other steps. Hard, gray boots around my hand.

"Search her pockets," another voice says.

A man pulls me by the hair and throws me against the wall of a building. My back scrapes against the rough plaster. The man is short and looks young, about my age. Before searching my pockets, he looks at my face.

"She's also pretty," he laughs. "Maybe this one has a chance on the show."

"Get those watches." Another man, with the tattoo of a snake around his neck doesn't even look at me. The short man unbuttons my jacket. His hands linger on my body before taking the watches from my pocket.

My voice comes out as if I'm being strangled. "Please."

The slap is quick and painful; it makes my eyes water and my nose bleed. The snake looks at me from the man's neck, its mouth open, ready to bite me.

"Shut your mouth."

My voice dies in my throat.

"Hit her again before she runs away," he adds.

Before I can think, my head is bashed against the wall. As I lose my senses and everything becomes blurred, I see the creepy smile of the short man, his teeth chipped, his lips cracked.

THE PALACE

New Town, Golden Palace, 2090

I'm having sex with a man, but it won't matter tomorrow. He is a Visitor, or that is what they call him around here. A politician who doesn't live in the Golden Palace, but comes to work here every now and then.

When I entered his guest room, he was standing in front of a foldout double bed smoking a cigarette, his white shirt unbuttoned at the top. I thought that his face was handsome after all, symmetrical. He didn't even tell me his name. He skipped every preliminary and undid my robe. I looked past him at a colored poster tacked to the wall—the image of the president, our Great Leader, depicted in bright shades. Red lips, pearly white skin, pale blue eyes, a sickening orange shirt. He's still smiling at me from the poster. It's supposed to be a benevolent smile, but it looks more lascivious to me.

The Visitor's beard is stinging my cheekbones, like a harsh sponge rubbed on my skin. It smells of aftershave and smoke. I move my face slightly away from him, exposing my neck. Politicians often like my neck; it is long and thin, my vertebrae exposed when I bend it. It makes me vulnerable, breakable to their eyes, and thus precious.

I look outside the tall window, at the city lights swaying in the night sky and let my mind linger on good memories. My mother's voice, the smell of coffee warming in the pot, my sister's breath on my face as she sleeps, the sound of my laughter. They are all in the back of my mind, not chaotic and blurred, as memories should be, but in strict order, one leading to the next. When I was brought to the Golden Palace, I decided that the only way to remember things properly was to find connections between them. I would go to sleep listening to my mother's words, wake up in the morning to the smell of coffee and laugh as my sister's breath tickled my cheek.

The Visitor's gasping suddenly gets louder so I try to breathe hard as well. The sound feels weird to me, fake, but he doesn't seem to notice. I wonder how I look on camera. I'm a performer, a Lover on *The President*: if I don't think about such things, I might as well be kicked out of the show. I risk a glance toward the cam stuck to the wall right next to the poster of the president, thinking about which shots they will use tomorrow. Probably my face, maybe even a close-up of my lips. I don't like my lower lip, so I bite it. I want to get this over with, and run somewhere and shout. But he is moving faster now and I can hardly breathe. Or I *pretend* I can hardly breathe.

With a satisfied gasp, he stops and moves away. How long should I wait before standing and putting my robe back on? I'm eager to hide. Sometimes my skin feels like plastic wrap, my pain visible through it like rotting food.

"I should go," I say.

He looks back at me as if he'd forgotten I was there.

"Of course," he says. "You must be busy." I don't know if he's making fun of me, since I have plenty of free time here.

I smile, just in case. "Goodbye."

I don't need to fight for his attention. He will leave soon and can't give me marks, so he is useless to me. Then tomorrow I will convince myself that this was not so useless. People would do anything to have a life with meaning.

Tomorrow is Evaluation Day. The six Lovers with the highest scores on the show will be chosen to entertain the president, the vice president and the European ambassadors who are coming to the Palace. I wonder who the politicians' favorites are this year. It's usually easy to guess who the audience will vote for, but the politicians can be unpredictable. This is my third year in the Golden Palace and my score has never been high enough to be part of this "elite." I've tried to keep my head down, to avoid being in the spotlight. Lovers are jealous, desperate women, capable of just about anything.

The day before Evaluation the producers of *The President* show always send us to Counseling, which is meant to be a safe space, one of the few where we are not monitored by TV cameras and where we can freely talk about our past, other contestants, and even complain about the show. Or so we are told.

Dr. Brooks has been my therapist since the very beginning. She has a wrinkly face that makes me think of a crumpled leaf, and brown hair always pulled back in a tight bun. I envy her, in a sense. She is a woman in a man's position. She has a job I didn't even know existed before coming here. In her office, next to the poster of the president, there are pictures of her family. A younger Dr. Brooks in a gown, smiling at the camera as she holds her diploma. Her two boys. Her husband, the CEO of some bio-tech company.

As I sit opposite her with my hands folded, Dr. Brooks reaches for a cup of tea on the desk between us.

"Can you recall how you felt during one of your past anxiety attacks?" she asks, her voice serene as always.

"I'm in a room and it suddenly feels too small, as if everything was shrinking around me. I can't breathe so I leave if I can, and go somewhere else. That makes me feel better for a while. But I know that it's my mind that feels too small, because the panic always comes back."

Dr. Brooks nods. "Are you experiencing more anxiety now that Evaluation is getting closer?"

"Maybe. I don't know."

"Do you wish to be chosen?"

"I'll never be chosen."

Dr. Brooks doesn't comment. "But what would you hope for?"

"I hope to be chosen if I deserve it."

Dr. Brooks sighs. I must be one of her most difficult patients, always impossible to read. Every time I go to Counseling, I feel like a nutshell, sheltering my kernel. I picture Dr. Brooks as a patient nutcracker, who sooner or later will get what she wants.

"Do you want some medicine for tonight?" She means anxiolytics, which Lovers gulp down as if they were water.

"No."

Dr. Brooks smiles. "Of course not. Then go, Iris. And good luck for tomorrow."

She knows that our conversation has become useless by now, so she makes me sign a form on her tablet and lets me go.

I usually don't sleep much, and tonight is no exception. Because I'm tired of staring at the president's face on the poster smiling at me from the wall, I put on my slippers and leave my room as silently as I can. The long hallway that leads to the Lovers' suites has the quiet of empty corridors at night. Everything is still, resting in the dim light. I walk quickly, my steps muffled on the crimson carpet, until the Lovers' Area is well behind me. The corridors all look the same here. In the recesses of the white painted walls, screens display computer-generated sunsets and night skies.

Before turning right at the end of a corridor where the screens don't work properly—they flicker and buzz like flies—I check that no one is following me. There are no shadows on the carpet except my own, so I open a white door, close it behind me, and walk down the stairs that lead to one of the forgotten rooms of the Palace, a place that used to be a service entrance, until the door was walled up. The air is a bit stuffy and a thin layer of dust covers the posters and photographs hanging on the walls. The president is in most of them, his pulled black hair held with hairspray, his forehead too high, his neck too fat, the grease paint too thick. At times, it seems that his face is about to melt, like ice cream in the heat.

I hold on to the white banister, cold to the touch of my hands. Once, I saw two Lovers kissing on these stairs, one pressing the other against the handrail. I recognized them; they didn't see me. I ran away and never told anyone. Months later, one of them was found murdered in her bathtub. Blood was dripping on the white floor, her head was tilted as if she was resting. A whole episode of *The President* was dedicated to her death. Some blood always boosts the show's ratings. The official version of the events—which the president kept repeating to the press—was that "she had passed away because of her mental disorders and harmful use of alcohol," while we all knew she had been killed because she had gone against the rules. *We must not fall in love with another Lover, we must not leave the Golden Palace, we must not get pregnant, we must not reveal any classified information we overhear in the Resting Rooms.* Most of the other things, we can do. We could even kill one another and the producers wouldn't really complain as long as they could manage to cover up the truth. Instead, the rules are simple and there is no forgiveness for their transgression.

The audience doesn't know about the rules, of course. That is one of the first things I learnt when I came here. *Don't rely on the audience. Don't ask them for help.* People believe what they're told. So they believe that our lives are all glamour, parties and desirable men. At least that's what the rich people want to think as they watch us on TV, otherwise how would they entertain themselves? As for the poor families from districts like mine… they know how girls are taken from their homes and they don't expect they'll be treated better once on the show.

At the end of the staircase, there is a poorly lit room with a small, round table, a lamp and a mirror. On the table, old newspapers are piled up, dusty and crumpled.

I remove the lampshade and turn off the camera stuck onto the base; no one in the Surveillance Room checks the cameras of this hallway anyway, they have better things to watch. I glance at the newspapers. The president has acknowledged the Eastern nuclear threat. An Eastern spy has been captured and sentenced to death. Some Leader's son talks about his life of privilege. Citizens all across the Great States place their bets on Lovers as Evaluation approaches.

My mother used to tell me about a time when politics and entertainment were different things. Now if you don't appear on a screen in the Great Cities, you're no one.

I look at the person reflected in the mirror. All the colors seem faded on me, like a color drawing half rubbed out. I used to look different, *fiercer*. "You're like the sun," my sister would say. "Too bright to look at." And she would laugh.

I feel a pain cutting across my chest. I remain still, then I remember no one can see me, so I hurl the lampshade against the wall.

Back in my bedroom, I curl up under the soft blankets that cover the double bed. On the nightstand, there is a big glass container filled with tablets. The label on it says: "Love Pills." I take one, preparing myself for the stomach cramps and the lack of appetite that will follow tomorrow morning. *We can't get pregnant. We must not leave the Golden Palace. We can't reveal any classified information.*

As always before falling asleep, I force myself to remember. I tell myself the same story, over and over, the story of my past and how I got here. If I can remain focused, maybe I will get out.

It's 2090, and I'm twenty-two years old. I spent the first nineteen years of my life in a Southern district of New Town, which we called the Silver City because of the gray skyscrapers that sparkle like silver during hot summer days. I lived with my mother and sister Lily on the top floor of a dark brick tenement building. To get to our flat, we had to climb steep fire escapes that got icy during winter and sticky during summer. Our district was poor and most of our neighbors worked either in the shopping malls of Chinatown or in the textile factories near the harbor. Still, when I think back to it now, I know I was happy. In summer we ate ice cream cones and went down to the harbor, which was packed with kids screaming and playing with dirt in the blistering sunlight.

Our apartment was small like all the others, but because there were only three of us, we could manage. There was a single bed next to the door, where Lily and I slept, as my mother used to say that the sofa was better for her back. We knew this was a lie of course, but we never insisted because mom could be stubborn as a mule and fighting with her was the last thing you ever wanted. In front of the bed there was a window that overlooked other tenement buildings, the stairs zigzagging, the windows like eye sockets. There were often posters on those walls, of the president and other popular politicians, some of them faded, others covered in graffiti. The most common captions beneath them read OUR GREAT LEADERS and POWER AND PRIVILEGE. The latter was intended to make the people feel special and privileged but what it truly meant, everyone knew, was that the men on the posters had the power, and everyone else had none.

I used to look outside the window when the sun was setting, as only the upper halves of the buildings were illuminated, the lower already shrouded in darkness. The tips of the bare tree branches would come into the light, casting shadows on the brick walls, desperately trying to benefit from the last rays of warmth. My sister once said that the branches were like us, living in the dark and stretching our arms to get more food, more warmth, more money. She said it in a whisper, afraid that mother could hear, as she worked hard for us and never complained.

Despite the endless hours of work as a cleaner in the mall, my mother was a beautiful woman. Her hands were rough and dry but her hair was still blonde, her eyes bright. Lily and I have always looked like our father, but no one ever said that out loud, not in front of mom anyway.

The last time I saw Lily she was almost as tall as me, her dark wavy hair as long as mine, her eyes as deep. She was lying still on our bed, her hands resting on her stomach. I closed the curtains while my mother was washing the dishes, afraid that Lily might wake up and complain about the light, as she always did. This is all I remember from that day: Lily's hands, the smell of soap and my mother's warning, her back to me.

"Don't come back late," she said.

I didn't come back at all.

This is enough for tonight. I think I'll sleep.

THE SIX LOVERS

1st week of Evaluation

Thirty women, lined up. That's how Evaluation starts. Soon, only six of us will be chosen. We stand in front of large windows, bathed in golden light, in a room that politicians normally use to watch the news. But every year, when Evaluation approaches, the room is cleared and cleaned for the show. White sofas and fancy chairs rest under a frescoed ceiling. The room gets warmer by the second. I'm in the third row, my feet crushed in low, tight heels. On my left, a skinny Lover with freckles bites her nails. On my right, Aura, a brown-skinned girl with sweet black eyes, yawns. When she sees me looking, she winks.

Aura sleeps in the room opposite mine. I think we're friends, but with Lovers it is hard to tell. My first day in the Palace, we observed each other, weighing similarities and differences, like two animals locked in one cage. Her skin is a beautiful light brown, like milk chocolate, but apart from that our bodies look eerily similar. We are the same height and have a tiny birthmark at the base of our neck. Our hair is the same dark brown, and wavy, reaching to our backside. But hers was rich and glossy that day, a sign that she had been living in the Palace for a long time, while mine was frizzy and dirty, fresh out of prison.

"Are you alright?" I ask her.

She smiles at me. "Just hungry."

I grin. I'm hungry too.

Aura has been one of the most popular Lovers for quite a while, yet she has never been chosen for Evaluation. I suspect that Nelson Price, the vice president and executive producer of the show, doesn't want her to win and go home. He's had a weakness for her in the past two years.

Someone whines about the heat. A maid comes in and turns the air conditioning on, while on the TV right in front of us a blonde journalist is doing a recap of all the contestants.

"Aura, a sweet girl from a foster home, keeps the vice president's attention; Helen, a nineteen-year-old from the South, believes she's destined to be a TV star; Caroline, one of the newest Lovers, adapts to life in the Palace; Paris, a blonde from the Coast, would do anything to be with the president…"

The producers talk to the cameramen about getting the light right, then walk around us to check if we look good enough. The girls clear their throats, straighten their backs, fix their hair. It's like being in a market, only I'm not the one doing the shopping. The president is, and he will be here any minute. Meanwhile, every man, woman and child in every Great City of every Great State is ready to watch us on TV, if they have one, or on the shared screens of their districts. *The President* isn't compulsory viewing but special events such as Evaluation are treated like some kind of mandatory festivity, a celebration of the generosity of the Great Leader, who helps struggling women live a life of ease.

"Good morning."

The president enters the room, followed by Nelson Price. He's sipping his morning brandy while Price whispers in his ear. The sight of the drink, combined with the side effects of the pill I took last night, makes me want to throw up. The two of them sit on the sofa. The president reminds me of some of those men from my district who used to sit on plastic chairs in the summer heat, smoking, their tank tops slick with sweat. Price must have been handsome back in the day, or maybe he's just one of those men who age well. Whatever the case, I find him frightening.

Someone turns the TV off. The producers hurry around the president, speaking loudly, as if we weren't there.

"Paris seems a bit shabby this morning—"

"We thought it best to keep the windows in front of them, to make sure the lighting is good—"

"Helen and Bella are looking gorgeous, so we put them front row—"

Out of the corner of my eye, I see Bella turning to the Lovers behind her and smiling, proud. I shake my head and try to focus on the pain in my feet. We were friends during my first years on the show, Bella and I. Then she hurt me, and now I hate her. Not that it matters to her, of course, as long as she's popular on the show. Bella grew up with her alcoholic mother in a small town of the Midwest, watching reality TV and longing for a glamorous life. She's needy, mean and occasionally patronizing.

"This is Bella's year," Aura whispers. "She'll be chosen."

I don't have time to answer because the president downs whatever is left of his brandy, then nods to the technicians. The cameras are rolling.

Nelson Price orders us to smile. I rearrange my face to look as confident as possible; insecurity doesn't read well on camera.

The president clears his throat and starts talking. He says pretty much the same things every year. He talks about the recent history of the Great States, of his predecessors and their achievements. He praises the success of the show and the importance of entertainment in times of international tension. His bright blue suit, at least two sizes too small, is about to explode.

"Our pilot aired more than twenty years ago," he says. "Every year, our audience keeps growing, with a current average of more than 80 million viewers in the Great States only. On our show you can watch the Leaders of today and the Leaders of tomorrow. You can watch their goals, their fears, their stories. Meanwhile, you can see your favorite Lovers fighting for their attention, for their love."

He takes a pause and clears his throat again. The sound is like someone choking on his own saliva.

"As you know, after four weeks of Evaluation we will choose one favorite among the six talented contestants with your help and support. She will win a cash prize and be free to either go home or remain in the Palace as a privileged guest. Past Evaluation winners have made their careers in TV. Some of them have been given their own shows. *Cook with Chloe, The Art of Makeup, The Island of Men*, these are all dreams that came true. What else can a girl wish for?"

Everyone cheers. What the president *doesn't* say is what happens to the other five chosen contestants. They're sent home and no one hears from them anymore. They literally disappear. Some say they are killed, because they know too much. Most of us think this is a joke, but I've learnt that as far as I don't know something for sure, it's better to be cautious. Also, it's much better to go home with money for my family, rather than go back empty-handed.

The air conditioning is making me shiver. Someone on my right coughs and the producers glare at her. Price hands the president a tablet. He grabs it and speaks again.

"When I read your name out, please step forward."

Aura gives me another wink, but when I look down at her hands, I see that her fists are clenched, her nails sunk into her palms.

"The first Evaluation contestant is Victoria," the president announces.

"Such a cliché," Aura whispers.

There is a shuffle and a gorgeous girl with long black hair and light blue eyes appears. The daughter of European immigrants, Victoria is the holy embodiment of the perfect Lover: effortlessly beautiful, loyal to the Leaders and even educated, because her father was fairly wealthy before he lost everything in the last financial crisis, when Victoria was sixteen. Producers often like to use her as an example of how Lovers should behave: "generous and well-mannered, poised and grateful." But once I spotted her in a corridor, writing *whore* with spray paint on the bedroom door of another Lover. When she saw me, she shouted, "What are you looking at?" staring at me with her cold blue eyes. Not so generous then.

Victoria takes her place next to the producers, glowing in her flowery dress. I bite my lip until I can taste blood, bracing myself for the next name.

It isn't me. It's Aura. She steps forward quickly, and Lovers make space. After shaking Price's hand, she lifts her fingers to her mouth to bite her nails, but then reconsiders and lets her hand down. Everyone is looking at her now, and she mustn't look anxious—oversensitive Lovers don't last long in the

Palace. The president compliments Aura for her "grace" and "talent" then calls another name.

"Margaret."

There is a moment of silence, when no one moves. Then the president repeats, "Margaret?"

A girl with straw-colored hair and slight signs of acne on her cheeks walks to the front of the group. Margaret isn't as pretty as all the others but has always been a favorite because she is the kind of woman men always want around: the cool–fun–attractive girl, the one who enjoys dirty jokes, hamburgers and oversized sweaters. Basically, a girl who trains herself to be exactly what the men around her want—funny, hot, enthusiastic and always willing to give a blowjob happily. Margaret preaches things like "be whoever you want to be" and "women supporting women" but is actually manipulative and desperate to take out the competition. I guess she thought I was "competition" the first time she saw me, because she said aloud that I "looked like slum trash."

The president is getting bored, I can see it. He doesn't even wait for Margaret to take her place next to Aura, when he speaks again.

"Our fourth choice is Iris."

I feel a sudden pain in my stomach that makes it hard to stand straight. I wasn't ready for this. I see the camera zooming in on my face, while the technicians push Lovers aside to film me better. When I step forward I feel Aura's gaze on me. She must be happier now, the happiness we all feel when we're not alone in a great misfortune. I force myself to smile in her direction, but then the president calls the next name and the smile drops.

"Bella!"

Bella takes her time, even though she is already standing

in the front row. She shakes the president's hand a bit longer than she should and, when she takes her place next to me, she whispers in my ear, "Congratulations."

I turn my head away.

Caroline is the last choice. She doesn't seem much of a threat, but I don't know her too well. She's a newcomer. She looks very young, with a confident smile and hair dyed platinum blonde. She joins Bella, looking around with a who-cares-about-any-of-this expression. Clearly being chosen for Evaluation isn't a big deal for her. The president stresses that she's barely of age—here politicians often want to know how wrong it is to go with teenagers and underage girls; the more taboo something is, the more it turns them on. But Caroline doesn't seem bothered. She looks as if this whole ceremony was a big waste of her time.

Now we're all lined up, the six of us. An unlikely group of girls who would never be friends outside the show. But that is why we have been chosen. Reality TV doesn't work without drama.

"Thank you for tuning in," the president says looking straight into the camera. "As European leaders are coming to the Palace for the annual International Political Forum at this very moment, we will make sure our Lovers welcome them at dinner in the ballroom…"

But I can't listen anymore. The cameras keep zooming in on us and I'm getting anxious. I feel like I'm sweating, the lights are too blinding. I don't know what to do but Aura takes my hand and, for a moment, I feel less lonely and scared.

Before I was caught and forced to join *The President*, I had escaped once already, though I didn't realize it at the time.

When I was fourteen years old, a group of men and women in rich suits visited my school. I had never seen such precious clothes and shiny jewelry, except on TV. One of the women had golden earrings and hair bleached blonde. The school of my district was near the border with Chinatown, and it was as devoid of color as Chinatown was bright. The building was gray, with small, whitewashed windows. The only color was on the poster of the president right next to the entrance, with its red and orange propaganda signs. From the school windows, I could see the backstreets of Chinatown, where sounds and colors were loud and mismatched, alleyways lined with food chains and love hotels advertising the rooms by the hour.

Any girl from the Great States is eligible for *The President*. And every female child from the age of fourteen is eligible for reality show training. That means that producers can just visit every school and select soon-to-be Lovers. Only, rich girls are never really taken. Their families pay large sums of money to the show as compensation.

When the men and women in golden suits arrived, our teacher introduced them as TV producers, scouts for the most successful reality shows of the West. They were looking for the prettiest girls in every school. If selected, the girls would be sent away, though no one said where. They would be "entertainers," the blonde woman said.

The scouts walked between the rows of desks. They slowed down when they came to mine to take a closer look. I raised my head and saw the blonde woman from up close. Her skin was orange with foundation and she smelled like smoke. We stared into each other's eyes for a long moment. I felt self-conscious of my dirty hair, the spots on my forehead. Then the woman walked past me, a disgusted expression on her face. Maybe she didn't like that I stared back at her, because she said that they were also looking for "a graceful and respectful attitude."

No girl was chosen that day. We weren't pretty, or respectful enough. Who would have thought that nearly ten years later I'd be here, in this very Palace, being the "entertainer" those rich people wanted us to be.

I'm thinking about that day as I sit, undressed, on the toilet seat cover in my bathroom, my arms around my knees. Aura is testing the temperature of the bath with her fingers, humming to herself. She didn't want to be alone after Evaluation, and I felt the same.

The water is a little too hot, but we enter anyway and soap ourselves from head to toe. The steam fogs up the mirror, and we draw faces on it. Aura draws a sketch of the president and we giggle.

When the bathroom grows too warm, I pull out the plug and the water quickly drains away. Aura curls up next to me, her head on my shoulder, our feet leaning on the edge of the tub.

"Are you scared?" I ask her.

"No. And you shouldn't be either," she says. "We'll be alright."

At lunch, a long table is laid with all sorts of delicacies in the Lovers' Dining Hall. There are only the six of us, because the other girls will eat in another room during Evaluation month. Two maids, one with dark skin, the other pale and freckled, stand next to the table, checking the poached salmon, re-filling chafing dishes with egg-drop soup and jars with green shakes.

Mia, the brown-skinned girl, smiles at me. I have grown to care about her in my years in the Palace. She once told me her mother came from a land of burning sands and scented air before the president built the Wall. I thought that was sweet, as if she was speaking of a lost paradise, but actually Mia has lived in the Palace her entire life, as it often happens when maids get pregnant and raise their children in here. Still, she's a good girl. She is the one who found me when I was punching my bedroom wall, crying, or when I was flushing Dr. Brooks's anxiolytics down the toilet. She never said a word.

I'm observing the way Caroline stuffs an entire muffin into her mouth—it is quite impressive—when Aura nudges me.

"Cameras aren't working," she says.

I frown. Politicians have complete freedom in handling cameras in their own quarters; we don't. Still, cameras don't work twenty-four hours a day. They're turned on every morning at ten, turned off at two in the afternoon. Then on again from five to three in the morning.

I look at a large clock next to the poster of the president. It's one thirty. I'm just thinking that some producer must have turned them off for a private announcement when Price walks into the room. We all instinctively stand, surprised. Usually, we don't get to see the politicians before late afternoon.

"Sit down, sit down," says Price. He grabs a cup and Mia hurries to pour some coffee for him.

"So," he starts, x-raying us, "the lucky ones have been chosen."

"Never misses a chance to give his little pep talks, eh?" Caroline whispers in my ear, making me jump. Price doesn't seem to notice.

"You're all popular, young, attractive enough," he continues. "Well done, I'm proud of you lot." He pauses to take a large sip of coffee and I realize my body is tense. "But the show has been a bit too boring for my taste lately. So I'm here to warn you that things are going to be different. You need to make things happen, give the audience some drama."

Bella nods vigorously, while Caroline starts eating her muffin again, unbothered.

"Because *boring* is a problem. People don't watch a *boring* TV show with *boring* people. It's called the entertainment industry. You have to entertain." He looks at Aura. "What does that mean?"

"We provide amusement and diversion for the audiences at home," Aura replies mechanically. We all know this line by heart. We were forced to learn it when we got to the Golden Palace.

Price slams his hand on the table and Mia flinches. "Yes! Provide diversion! That is your job. You're celebrities for God's sake! Every girl out there wants to be you!" He pours some more coffee for himself, waving Mia to stay away when she tries to help. "You can't be boring. You have to be exceptional! Come up with something and *provide diversion*. Don't give me the usual show this year, everyone has already seen that." He wipes his mouth on his sleeve. I want to ask which kind of diversion he wants this time, but I understand it's better to keep my mouth shut.

Margaret doesn't. "What do you want us to do?" she asks.

"Whatever the fuck you want! Just give me a show!" he shouts. He leaves without another word, and we all keep sitting in silence, staring at the door.

After a while, I notice that Mia is shivering; her eyes are wide open, fearful. For a moment, I think that maybe she's afraid of Price because he has hurt her somehow. But then I dismiss the thought and remind myself that in the Palace we're all afraid of one another.

Extracts from the newspaper *The Silver Times*

"Evaluation is Back (and what to expect from TV's most loved competition)"

by Nicholas Cole

The most anticipated special of the year is back and the lucky contestants have been announced today. The prize for the winner: $500,000 and a contract for a career in TV. Home viewers are already placing bets and choosing their favorites. Not many believed that 22-year-old Iris would be among the six chosen contestants, especially after the video of her panic attack that was leaked last year. After the incident, Iris has struggled to get high grades and has been labeled by some of her fellow Lovers—most famously Bella, who is also among this year's favorites—as "aggressive." Still, the show is known for its Evaluation surprises. In the next four weeks, the six contestants will do everything in their power to charm our Great Leaders and the Palace's guests. May the best Lover win.

"Former Lover Missing in Chinatown District"

by George Graham

A former contestant of *The President* show, Sophie Watts, has seemingly disappeared last week from the district of Chinatown. Sophie was forced to leave *The President* two years ago after being diagnosed with bipolar disorder. Her disappearance seems to be linked with the recent complaints against the reality show that the industry is not doing enough to protect its contestants. Days before her disappearance in fact, Sophie released a statement saying that: "TV audiences really think that reality people live the best life possible. But they don't know how awful and manipulative it can be." *The President*'s producers pointed out that Sophie was mentally unstable during her final weeks in the Palace, and also "dangerous for others." As vice president Price remarked, Sophie's disappearance might be related to the district gangs she used to associate with before being rescued by producers and selected for the show.

THE WORST MEMORY

I feel a sudden, sharp pain in my shoulder. Lara, the fashion stylist of the Palace, has stung me with her needle. We're in the corridor that leads to the ballroom, and she's trying to sew up the strap of my emerald dress.

"We're late," Aura points out, calmly. "Everyone else is inside already."

Another prick. I catch my breath. This time, a small drop of blood appears on my arm.

"For fuck's sake," Lara complains.

The skin of her face is so stretched that her cheekbones are too sharp, her nose too flattened. I've been told she was beautiful once, but plastic surgery certainly hasn't done her any good. She was a model and then a recruiter for the Leaders, which means that she would select girls from fashion shows and send them to the politicians' villas and properties to keep the men entertained. Then a couple of years ago she got hired here as a fashion stylist, her life-long dream finally fulfilled thanks to our Great Leader. So she always says.

"We really need to go," Aura insists.

Lara glares at her, but then she opens the double doors to the ballroom and pushes us inside. I stumble and hold on to Aura. She grips my wrist tight.

The ballroom is on the top floor of the Golden Palace, overlooking the entire city. Everything looks glossy and spacious, and a grand piano glimmers in one corner.

Nelson Price instantly sees us walking in. He comes over, a cold expression on his face.

"You're late," he says, grabbing us by the arms.

"Lara had to fix our dresses," Aura replies calmly.

"Of course she did." He flashes his shining smile. "Help yourselves."

His fingers leave a reddish mark on my elbow. Aura follows Price towards the long table that has been laid in the middle of the room, where the president is talking, wearing a pale green suit and a lot of foundation on his face. Around him, Victoria and Caroline stand out in their glorious dresses and impeccable makeup.

My sister used to tell me that rich people could afford to reinvent themselves every day wearing new outfits. Today they are brunette and mysterious; tomorrow they will be blonde and sexy. In my long dress, my hair tied in a braid, I don't feel different. I might be glowing outside, but inside I'm empty like a shell.

I pick up a champagne glass and sip quietly, looking around while the maids finish setting the table. Unintentionally, I catch Bella's eye. She smirks and walks in my direction. Her eyes are big and green, sometimes bright like water springs, other times as murky as a pond.

"So someone finally voted for you," she says with a little laugh.

I knew this would come. Ever since we stopped being friends, she has done everything to make my life a nightmare.

"I heard some Lovers talking today in the restrooms," she continues. "They said you didn't deserve to be chosen."

"Maybe they're right."

Bella shrugs, looking away. I follow her eyes and see a young man wearing a white shirt slightly open at the collar.

"Apparently he's a big deal," Bella says. "His name's Sebastián, he's one of the new European delegates."

I step away from her. The maids are silently backing off and lining up against the wall, like obedient ants. Dinner is ready.

"World leaders, ambassadors and distinguished delegates," the president says. "It is an honor and privilege for me to welcome you here, in the heart of the Great States." Some politicians nod and smile, others simply stare. A brown-skinned man with a simple black suit is frowning. Maybe he senses me looking, because he turns in my direction. I hastily look down.

"In the following weeks," the president continues, "we will talk about the crisis with the East, the progresses made by the Wall, the accomplishments of my administration. But tonight we leave politics aside." He points at us Lovers and we all smile, knowing cameras are doing close-ups at this very moment. "Tonight we relax with our wonderful Lovers. Tomorrow, we go back to business. Enjoy the dinner gentlemen."

Everyone applauds politely, Price leans towards me and Aura.

"Let's entertain these guests, shall we?" He winks and looks towards the piano. Then he stands and addresses the table in a loud voice, "Just a moment of silence, please. Aura and Iris have something they want you to hear."

I join Aura as she sits in front of the piano. There is a

moment of silence, when everyone stares at us. Out of the corner of my eye, I see Bella whispering in Sebastián's ear. As soon as Aura starts playing, I sing, staring into Sebastián's eyes until his attention, and everyone else's, is on us.

I used to embrace the night
Stars were candles in the dark
I used to dream of you
of us in the sunlight

Midday is midnight
Dreams are hollow
I wish I'd remember
a path to follow

Candles in the wind
are lights to get through
the essence of love
myself dreaming of you

On the show I often sing the songs that my mother hummed, as she washed the dishes, rocked Lily in her arms or walked me to school when I was little. Sometimes I forget some of the words and have to make up new ones.

As I sing now, the light of dusk comes through the windows and falls on the floor in shades of amber and purple. For this time only, I hope mother is watching back home.

We eat and drink as the sun sinks behind the skyscrapers. Because Aura and I are sitting next to Price, it's easier to make conversation. We pretend to laugh at his jokes and listen as he asks questions about the families the politicians left back home.

After glasses and dishes have been emptied, a few guests leave with the excuse of being tired. Truth is, they don't want their families to see them with us. Some countries in Europe have different customs, from what I understand. Here, the more women you have, the more popular you are. The dark-skinned man lingers for a while, watching me, then joins his colleague and leaves.

But other European men stay, more than half of them. After all, a good relationship with the Leaders of the Golden Palace and the visibility *The President* gives can take their careers to the next level. Which is also why the annual international forum is scheduled right before the European elections.

I hear Price talking with two men who both want to spend the night with Aura, while Margaret takes a tall guy and guides him out of the room. As the ballroom slowly empties, Bella joins me.

"Do you mind if I take Sebastián?"

"Why would I mind?"

"Playing dumb doesn't suit you. You were staring at him before, when the two of us were talking." She gives me an annoying look. "Don't be jealous."

I force myself to laugh. "You wish." I stop talking because Sebastián is approaching. To take Bella with him, surely.

But when he is close enough, he says, "Iris, do you want to help me find my way back to my room?" As he speaks, his elbow touches my arm, and I feel blood flowing into it.

"Sure. This palace is a maze," I reply, smiling at Bella. She doesn't smile back. As she walks away, I look at the tattoo between her shoulder blades. It's a sketch of a pink flower, the petals facing up as if praying, longing for help.

We walk side by side in the long corridors, the sound of my heels muffled by the crimson carpets. He looks at me from time to time, but doesn't say anything.

When we get to his room, he takes the keys from his pocket and lets me in first. The place smells nice. Next to the painting of a naked woman lying down, the poster with the president's face watches us. Sebastián looks back at it, smirks, then sits in an armchair.

"So, how does this work?" he asks.

His eyes are of a blue-gray that shuts you out. I set my features into a pleasant expression. Before saying anything, I turn around, pretending to admire the furniture, while looking for cameras: there are small, round ones next to each painting, and a bigger one above a vase of orchids.

"We do whatever you want," I finally say.

Sebastián loosens his tie. "What about a bath?"

"That sounds good," I say.

He stands and I follow him through the L-shaped living room into a large bathroom. He gets the bath running, while I rest my head against the cold ceramic tiles of the wall.

"This is it then?" Sebastián asks.

"What do you mean?"

"I sleep with you and then we spend every day together until I leave?"

There's something cold about the way he talks. I feel like crying but that would be completely out of place.

"You don't have to. *You* have a choice."

He seems puzzled, but quickly blinks and his face goes back to normal. "What could I do, for example?"

"You could sleep with someone else, *for example*."

He laughs and I smile even though I don't understand what's funny, really.

"I guess you could do that too," he says. He clearly doesn't know what he's talking about.

The bath is ready, and he watches me undress. I douse my feet into the water. Sebastián stretches his arms as if his back was hurting, then he takes off his clothes and joins me in the tub. We sit, facing each other. His hands open and close in the soapy water like the jellyfishes that we often found dead in the harbor of the Silver City.

"What do you want, Iris?" He has closed his eyes; his neck is resting back and his Adam's apple is sticking out. I could rip his throat with a razor right now, if I wanted to.

"You mean, now?"

"I mean in general."

"I just want some company." This is not a lie. I think.

"Are you alone?"

"Just lonely."

"What about the other Lovers?"

"I feel lonely especially around people." Once, I was afraid to speak like that, but I have learnt that sometimes you can exploit weakness to get what you need. He stares at me. I cross my arms over my breasts and say, "Tell me about your job," because men often like to talk about themselves.

"It's a good job," he says. "Back home, we're not as famous as your politicians here, so that's good."

"Why?"

"I don't really like being in the spotlight." He's lying, obviously. Every politician wants to be in the spotlight.

I sink into the bath, feeling the water lap my neck. He turns serious quickly and takes my neck in his hands. I can see that he's like every other man, and for him, I'm probably like every other Lover too. We have sex in the tub, and when he's done I leave, feeling lonelier than ever.

Back in my room, I find Aura on my bed fast asleep, her long blue dress still on, her heels abandoned on the floor.

I undress quickly and shower, soaping myself and using the scrub brush on my thighs. "They become thinner if you scrub them every night," Lara said to me during my first days in the Palace. I thought that her interest in my thin thighs was determined by her own pathetic obsession with diets and workouts, but then I found out that fatter girls can be sent to entertain the production team, or worse, guards, if no politician requests their presence anymore.

When I'm clean and comfortable in my pajamas, I pull the dress away from Aura's body. She mumbles something in her sleep. Next to her is an empty packet of pills—Dr. Brooks's downers. I take it, crumple it and throw it away.

I wrap Aura into a soft robe and wipe the makeup off her face. Her black, thick eyelashes remain wet as if she were crying. I lie down beside her and stare at the small scar she has on her nose. She told me she got it when she was little and fell down the stairs but I'm not very inclined to believe any story Lovers tell about their past.

I'm falling asleep. I stare at the ceiling, desperately trying to stay awake, to make sure memories don't turn into nightmares. But it's too late. My lids are heavy and before I can stop it the past comes back to haunt me.

I dream of the day I was caught.

It was the floor that gave me away, that stupid slippery floor of the hotel. I'd stolen the watches already and I was walking back towards the side entrance, as silently as possible. Usually floors in the Chinatown hotels are carpeted but when I turned into the last corridor there were no carpets and my shoe slipped. I stumbled, and in a stupid attempt not to fall I knocked a statue over. Some lady from the reception popped her head inside and asked, "What are you doing here?"

I jumped up and started running. The lady screamed as I dashed out of the door and into the cold night.

But in this dream there are no guards following me. I make it home safely, the precious watches in my pocket. When I reach my district, I make my way to the tenement building and start climbing the stairs. I'm already thinking of calming my mother down, telling her, "You see, you worry over nothing as usual," when I stop at the top of the stairs. In front of the door of the apartment there is the guy with the chipped teeth. I freeze.

"You're fast, aren't you?" he asks.

I scream and he hits my head against the wall.

I wake up gasping, tears streaming down my cheeks.

"You okay?" Aura is looking at me in the dark, her head propped on her elbow.

"Just the usual nightmare."

She cups her hand around my cheek and I close my eyes.

"It will go away," she says.

I nod. I would rather spend a thousand sleepless nights than dreaming about the day of my capture, but, no matter how hard I try, I know this memory will never leave me.

BEWARE OF ANGRY MEN

When I wake up the sky is bright, with cotton-like clouds. In the bathroom, Aura is splashing some water on her face, probably trying to get rid of the drowsiness from the pills she took. But when I go in there to brush my teeth, she is going through the pills in my own cabinet, each container lined up and filled to the brim. She picks one and gulps it down with tap water.

Without bothering to change, we stumble into the Chatting Room, a large space with sofas and comfy chairs adjacent to our Dining Hall. The others are already there, drinking coffee, waiting for the scores to be announced. Every Monday of Evaluation Month a ranking of the six chosen Lovers is officially announced on *The President*, based on the scores given by the audience and the politicians. This is helpful in order to have an idea of who among us will be the winner. It also increases the competition, pushes us to do more to outrank the others.

Victoria and Margaret are laughing about some useless celebrity gossip, while Bella is talking to an unbothered Caroline about her father. I sit as far from them as possible; I already know what story she's telling anyway.

Bella's father sold her to *The President* because he liked to gamble and had debts to pay. That is the word Bella used when she told me: "sold." We were friends then, and were lying on the yoga mats in the Exercise Room. I propped my head up with one hand and said I was sorry. She had tears in her eyes. After that, I heard the same story many other times, as Bella told it to a politician, a maid, another Lover, a producer. I started suspecting that this was her way into people's hearts. She tells them about her sob story and the importance of forgiveness, and there she has them. In truth, Bella always wanted to be on TV. She hated her alcoholic mother for choosing the wrong men and thought the only escape possible from her shitty life was to be famous and marry a rich man.

The President's title sequence starts playing on screen and everyone falls silent. Margaret chews her nails, Victoria fiddles with her rings. I look at Caroline as she lights a cigarette and stares out of the window. I wonder what she's thinking about.

The rankings and our scores appear, accompanied by what the show runners call "a profile" on *The President*, where we can see our grades, our pictures and the people's comments from home.

Aura is first with an eight, which, surprisingly, is also the grade that Caroline gets. I wonder how Caroline managed to get such an impressive score, having been in the Palace only a few months. Margaret comes up with a seven, and so do I. Victoria and Bella get a six.

That's not such a bad beginning. My body fills with something like relief. Bella opens her mouth to complain, so I stand and leave the room before I start feeling the need to slap her.

I knock on the Counseling door. There is no answer but I open it all the same. Dr. Brooks is typing on her tablet. She doesn't seem surprised to see me.

"Good morning, Iris. This wasn't scheduled."

"I'm sorry, Dr. Brooks. I was wondering if you had some time to talk before lunch."

"If every Lover just came in without an appointment, how could I manage?" She sighs, but puts her tablet aside. "Sit, Iris, you look tired," she adds. She stares at me with her pale eyes and says, "First of all, congratulations."

"Thanks. I didn't expect it."

"You said so. Why didn't you expect it?"

"Because I'm neither good nor interesting enough for Evaluation."

"Why do you say that?"

I shrug.

"What do you think makes one good and interesting for Evaluation?" Dr. Brooks asks.

I should have expected this question. "Being quiet and compliant, flirting, pretending."

"Let's talk about these things a bit more."

I nod, even though there is something excruciating about her patience, about her composure.

"Last time you were here you said that you were losing your real self. That it was hidden in the dark."

I don't see where she's going but I nod.

"If your true self is in the dark, what is in the light?"

Now I see. "Lies," I say.

"What lies?"

"The ones others tell me, the ones I tell them," I reply. "Also, the ones I tell myself."

"What do you tell yourself?"

"That I'm happy. That I'm not losing my mind. I also tell myself stories of my life."

"And those are lies as well?" She seems very pleased with my answers and writes everything down in a brown leather notebook. This surely feels like a small victory to her, cracking the nut, making the difficult subject speak.

"No, not lies. I think I just alter the stories a bit to feel better."

"I see. And how do you feel now if I ask you to think about sex?" Dr. Brooks asks.

"I don't know."

"Try. Tell me the first words that come to mind when you think about it." She often does this, asks me to express my feelings by associating them with words. I find this helpful, as if by linking an unspeakable emotion to a word the weight of it becomes more bearable.

"Apathy, intimacy, submission, fear, consent, pills."

"That's a lot. Now, can you write down a thought or moment that you associate with each of these things?" She hands me her notebook, where she has listed the words I told her. Her neat handwriting makes me sick. I write:

1. *Apathy. You reach a point when you can't cry anymore. Something has been taken and you are empty. How do you reclaim yourself, fill yourself up again?*

2. *Intimacy. Falling asleep next to Aura, the sheets rolled around your legs keeping you both warm.*

3. *Submission. He tries to kiss you. You turn your head but he grips your wrist and you give in.*

4. *Fear. Beware of angry men, beware of nervous men, beware of sharp objects around men.*

5. *Consent. Be kind and generous. You are privileged and a privilege.*

6. *Pills. Why is everything you have to do harmful?*

I give the notebook back to Dr. Brooks. She takes a look at it, then closes it, a sad expression wrinkling her features.

"Where did you learn to write like this?" she asks.

An image of my mother's face, weary but intent, pops up in my head. I remember watching her closely as she listened to my teacher. I was fourteen. He had come down to our place to tell her that I was gifted, that she had to give me a chance because I couldn't stop going to school like all the other girls. I remember mother working double shifts in the mall to pay for my night classes in a school in Chinatown. The street was filled with drug dealers who would scream obscenities at me, but the school looked nice inside, better than the one in my district. It even had clean carpets and heaters. I remember the evenings spent there reading and writing. My mother hoped I would become an accountant, like a young man she knew from our building.

But these are no memories to share with Dr. Brooks. These are mine.

"I stopped going to school when I was fourteen, like every other kid in my district," I say. I'm angry with her now, because she had a chance and I didn't.

"You write well, Iris," Dr. Brooks speaks softly. "Now, that's enough for today. You must be late for lunch."

"Yes. Thank you for your time."

There is nothing else to say so I walk out of the room.

Once, Aura, Bella and I were watching TV in Aura's room. It was one of the usual shows about rich, powerful men and the beautiful women they fell in love with. We were cuddled together on the bed, Aura's head resting on my legs. Bella was leaning against the wall, right next to the president's face on the poster. It was three in the afternoon and the cameras were off so we could say pretty much what we wanted. I was eating little cubes of watermelon, staring at a blonde, blue-eyed girl waiting for her businessman to come home on *The Perfect Housewife.*

"How could a man fall in love with someone like that? She's pretty, that's all. She barely speaks," I said.

"This is exactly why men fancy these women," Aura replied. "It's because they're not threatening, because their lives are just accessories of the men's lives."

"Men aren't like us," Bella sighed, as if she was explaining something obvious, something we were too stupid to see. "They need things. They need women's attention, they *need* women living *for* them. It's not their fault."

This reminded me of one of those newspaper articles about the importance of having "women who care for men" that my mother hated so much. Such sentences were everywhere when I grew up, sometimes even on billboards that depicted the president smiling at a group of women crowding around him. CARE FOR YOUR GREAT LEADER, those signs said.

"You don't really believe that," Aura was saying, when we heard the strong sound of someone beating on the door of the room next to us. An older Lover with short black hair slept there. Someone yelled and I dropped the cup I was holding. It broke into two and the cubes and watermelon juice spread all over the carpet.

"For God's sake," said Bella. Aura gestured us to stay silent and we lowered the TV volume. A man was whispering outside, in the corridor; it was a threatening whisper, "Open up now, girl! Open the fucking door!"

Aura was about to open the door and see what was happening but I stopped her. The man was let in and the door was slammed shut. There was the sound of broken and overturned furniture. I listened to it, looking at Aura, who had hugged her knees and closed her eyes, waiting for it to be over.

After a while it stopped. We stood in front of the door for a long time, unable to move. Then we heard the Lover crying next door, and when I raised my eyes I saw that tears ran down Aura's cheeks too. I picked up the watermelon and cleaned the floor with a wet cloth, then I turned the volume of the TV up again, even though none of us felt like watching anymore.

THE CLUB

Tuesday goes by, and no one calls us to entertain. Aura looks tired and quite stressed, so when she asks me if she can rest in my bed, I tell her to do as she wants.

"Wake me up if anything happens," she says before disappearing.

Sure enough, when I go back to my room, I find her asleep on the bed, packets of pills all around her, one of them still clutched in her hand. Seeing her like this always makes me want to shake her until she wakes, but I know better than to say anything.

Aura's relationship with downers started back in the foster home where she grew up. Apparently the women who "took care" of the girls crushed tranquilizers in their milk. Aura told me that one time at the home she stole too many pills and overdosed.

"What happened?" I asked.

"I was out for a couple of days but then I was okay."

I couldn't understand it; I've always been too freaked out about losing control.

"But that's what's so peaceful about it," Aura told me.

I didn't say anything until one day she woke up with her room's furniture completely rearranged. Apparently, in her drugged blackout, she had moved her bed far away from the poster of the president, tore some of the fancy clothes Lara had given her, ran a hot bath and asked the maids to give her some junk food—her nightstand was covered in unopened pints of ice cream. I had to cover for her with the producers, and told them that we were just playing around because we couldn't sleep. As a result, Dr. Brooks gave her even more pills.

After that episode, I told Aura that she had to stop. She looked at me with crazy eyes and grabbed her packets of downers. The grip was so tight that her knuckles went white.

"And what I'm going to do, eh?" she said with a mean, low tone. "Kill myself to sleep?"

I had never seen her like that. I let it go.

To avoid having to see Aura in her drugged state now, I go around the Palace scavenging for some peace. I walk past the endless rooms that stretch between the Lovers' and the Guests' Areas, past the lounge and the terraces, up the spiral staircase winding at the center of the Palace. In one Break Room next to the National Security office two maids are cleaning, mopping the floor. A group of Lovers are stretching in the Exercise Room, lying on pink mats while a blonde, fit instructor checks on them. In the News Room, Price is talking to a lanky middle-aged man whom I once entertained and who has recently been promoted to Secretary of Defense. I hurry past them before they can notice me.

When I'm back to the Chatting Room, Caroline is smoking, reading a newspaper. She doesn't even look up when I come in. I stare at the paper, wondering where she got it from. Technically we're allowed to read. Trouble is, all the books and newspapers are usually in the politicians' quarters and Lovers rarely ask if they can have them. Reading feels slightly subversive and subversive doesn't really get you a good score.

The headline on the front page of Caroline's paper says: **"Our Great Leaders take care of the revolts in the city."**

"Where did you get that?" I ask.

She looks up.

"Someone gave it to me." It's the first time she talks to me. There's something about her, about the way she stares that I can't quite tell. It's blunt and intimidating.

"Who?"

"I can leave it here when I'm done if you want to read it after."

I shrug, and she raises her eyebrows. Then she goes back to her paper.

I pick up a tablet and check my *President*'s profile. It appears with my picture, perfectly lit and beautifully framed. I scroll the page upward and look at the latest comments.

> I live for Iris! and this new European guy? He's f***g hot!
>
> Is it just me or does Iris grow more beautiful by the second?
>
> All those hot girls and IRIS is chosen for Evaluation? She's average!
>
> Iris keeps talking but no one's asked for her opinion.
>
> A strict diet would do Iris nothing but good. Her thighs are like pigs.

I swipe the screen and the comments disappear. I smooth the hem of my dress, walk to the Dining Area. Butter cookies are spread on tiny plates. I take one then put it down. I look at my thighs.

Fuck me.

On Wednesday Lara takes us to the Beauty Center to get us ready for a night at the Golden Club. I hate the Center—it is a large room where everything is strangely white except for pictures of women with very small noses and plump lips. If you get close enough, they look as if they're filled with Bubble Wrap.

I go and sit on the table that Mia has prepared for me. She makes me lie down and removes some of my leg hairs with tweezers. An older maid with frizzy hair sanitizes the cots and tools, and the room fills with the scent of alcohol. I close my eyes and listen to them talk. The older maid is telling Mia that she must never smile at the politicians.

"If you smile, you're wrong," she berates her, spraying sanitizer onto the waxing tray. "And you're young and pretty. So you're always wrong, darling."

Mia says that she didn't mean to smile, she was only bringing coffee to the European guests and she couldn't knock 'cause the door was already open and her presence had to be acknowledged somehow. She removes one last hair from my knee and looks up at me, timidly, as if looking for my support. I don't know what to say to her.

"You got lucky no one complained," the older maid says shaking her head. She mops the floor and leaves. Mia goes to the sink and washes her hands.

"We have to do your nails," she says, wiping her hands on a towel. Then she looks up at me hesitantly.

"Can you talk about life outside?" She often wants me to talk about life in my district, my life before. It is something her mother used to do with her when she was little. Her mother died recently, she told me. But Mia hadn't seen her in a while, because she'd been moved away from the Palace into Price's villa in the city.

"Not today, Mia," I say.

She looks down and starts doing my nails in silence, her small, delicate hand on mine as though they were part of the same body. As though we were not alone, each in her own patch of unhappiness.

When my skin is smooth and my nails done, I slip into the glittery purple dress Lara has chosen for me. Silver hoop earrings match my eye shadow, and my hair is tied into small braids that fall onto my shoulders.

"Dazzling, you are dazzling!" Lara's mouth twitches into something that should resemble a smile. She makes me turn around and claps her hands enthusiastically. I wish her attention was flattering, but it isn't. Behind her, Caroline is fixing her rose pink, low-cut dress. Her legs and arms are sparkling with glitter. Aura is resting, sitting as comfortably as she can, given her tight leather dress. All the others have left for the club already.

"I have to go now," Lara says after fixing a braid behind my ear. "I'll make sure they bring you dinner in here. You're late, as usual."

"Can you get us some fat food?" Caroline asks. "Not those tiny carrots you gave us last time. Unless you want me to faint."

"You're hopeless, Caroline," Lara says, a disappointed expression on her face. She leaves the Center shaking her head, mumbling something about "composure" and "skinny girls."

Aura slides onto the floor, watching commercials on a tablet. I can tell her mind's still foggy from her pills.

"You shouldn't do that," Caroline tells her.

"What?"

"You shouldn't watch that stuff. It fucks with your brain."

Aura looks up at Caroline, then back at the screen, where blonde girls brush their teeth white, and pauses the commercial. I think that there are many other things that fuck with our brains but keep quiet.

Three cheeseburgers are left outside the door. I pick up the tray and leave it on a table. Caroline sits on the floor, crosses her legs. She bites into her burger, and mayonnaise stains her fingertips.

"I'm staying in here because all the other girls do is talk shit about one another," she says. "I hope you don't mind that."

Aura glances at her. "Of course we don't mind."

"It's like they don't even feel the need to hide their own jealousy," she says swallowing a big bite of her burger. "It's sad."

"Maybe they think it works with the audience," Aura says.

"The audience likes confidence. You don't win a show with pity."

"Is that how you're going to win?" I ask her. "With confidence?"

She shrugs. "I'm never going to win."

"That makes two of us," I say. "According to most comments on my profile, I should keep my mouth shut and disappear."

Caroline chuckles. "Well, *The Silver Times* did say you were an unexpected contestant for Evaluation."

"That's because they think I'm weird. They believe I don't *work hard* enough to be on the show."

Caroline looks back at me, a faintly amused expression on her face. She cleans her sauce-stained hands with a napkin.

"You *are* weird. No wonder the hot European guy wants you. Europeans are into weird."

He's not that hot, I want to say, but Caroline lies down on the floor with her eyes closed and starts moving her arms up and down like the wings of an angel.

"What are you doing?" Aura asks. Because Caroline ignores her, she looks at me, confused.

I smile. In the coldest winters my sister used to do that on our bed, and this thought makes me suddenly happy, so I lie down next to Caroline and do the same.

Half an hour later, we're walking along a corridor whose walls are covered in graffiti, following the loud music and the smell of sweat. We're in the underground maze of the Palace, where rooms are softly lit and where we often shoot promos for the show. The sound of our heels on the floor is shrill. I look down at my sandals, my feet pushed slightly out of the shoes, my toes wrapped in invisible plasters.

We reach a door guarded by two sturdy men in golden uniforms. Behind it, the music intensifies. Caroline sways a little and her hair bob bounces on her shoulders.

The men let us in. The green and blue lights bubble up and down with the music. This place used to be a small theatre, but the chairs have been removed, and vines and lights hang down from the balcony railing. There is an older woman singing on the stage, a cascade of silver hair shining down her back, the tattoo of a spider web covering her wrinkled face. Her voice is raw, beautiful.

Most Lovers are already dancing around the club, a few men watching them. There are seventy politicians living in the Palace and thirty Lovers, but some people don't come to the club anyway. The men are young and middle-age politicians but also journalists, bankers, TV personalities, producers. The younger ones are assistants or the politicians' sons, ready to follow in their parents' footsteps. They're the ones I hate the most: spoilt monkeys, they act as if they own everything they touch.

Victoria is standing with one of *The President*'s casting directors, two fluorescent drinks in hand. Her eyes are blank, bored as he talks to her excitedly. Not far from them, Bella is sipping her drink. She looks at us walking in, her eyes light and shimmering, her lips red as if blood-dipped. Next to her are the president in a cherry-colored suit and a tall, blonde man: Michael, Price's son. Michael is handsome, fit and confident. He thinks the whole world owes him something, especially women. I've heard he was accused of raping an underage girl a couple of years ago with two other guys, but he got away with it thanks to his father's lawyers. He looks annoyingly entitled in his white loose shirt, its upper buttons open to reveal the tattoos on his chest.

"I'm going to get a drink," I say.

"I'll come with you," Aura says. "Caroline?"

"Sure, whatever." She's glancing around, her eyes narrowed as though looking for someone.

We walk to the bar, where bottles of alcohol are arranged among potted plants. The bartender is a woman in her thirties with a pink ponytail and purple lipstick. We wait while she mixes alcohol from fluorescent glass bottles.

I move my hips to the music, feeling the dress swaying around. As soon as the bartender hands me the drink I down it. My throat burns. Aura looks at me in alarm.

"I'm okay," I say. "Just thirsty."

Caroline laughs, amused. She takes hold of my hand and moves to the center of the dance floor. Aura follows. Caroline is a great dancer, energetic and sensual. Everyone stares at her. The bubbling lights illuminate her thick lashes, her platinum hair, her freckles. Aura sips her drink, moving her body in time with the music, smiling at me. Out of the corner of my eye, I see Bella laughing with the president and Michael leaving them, his eyes on me. He comes closer and slips an arm around my shoulder. I've never talked to him.

"Here, drink some," he says, handing me the bottle he's holding. I drink and the air grows heavier. He smells like cologne. I slip out of his arm, stumbling on my feet.

On the dance floor the bodies are glowing and grinding on each other. Other people have joined us but Aura isn't here anymore. Feeling drunk, I turn to search the room, wondering where she's gone. Caroline joins me and props an arm on my shoulder, running her fingers through my hair. I notice a young man at the bar staring at us while he talks with the pink-haired bartender. Caroline is staring back at him, an annoyed look on her face.

"Who's that?" I ask.

She doesn't reply, but takes my hand and leads me away, towards the restroom. We wobble across the room, leaning our sweaty bodies against each other. On the entrance to the women's restroom there's a tag with gold script: *Lovers*. It reminds me of the Chinatown hotels from which I used to steal, whose toilets had tags too. Only their tags said: *Ladies*. There is an older Lover inside, with heavy silver eye shadow glittering on her face. She is sitting on the floor, alone, sipping from her glass.

"You okay?" I ask. She nods, staring vacantly into space.

Her image reflected in the long mirrors looks fake, not human.

"Fuck this," says Caroline. I don't know what she is referring to so I enter one of the cubicles, leaving the door slightly open to see Caroline examining her image in the mirror.

"Oh fuck this," she repeats, untying her hair. The pins don't seem to come out so she makes an annoyed sound and lets her head rest against the cold glass of the mirror, her hair half tied up. The older Lover leaves, mumbling something inaudible. I flush the toilet and join Caroline in front of the sink to patiently unpin the rest of her hair.

In the mirror, I see the guy who was staring at us from the bar. He's short but quite handsome, with arms and hands covered in tattoos of what look like snakes and knives.

"This is the Lovers' restroom," I say, staring at him.

"Yeah, ladies only," adds Caroline lifting her head. She stops when she sees him reflected in the glass, but doesn't turn around. For a moment, no one says anything. Then I ask, "And you are?"

"Adam," he says. He has a sort of troubled and unkempt look that reminds me of the drug dealers from my district.

"Adam's in the propaganda department," says Caroline. "He's working with the producers on the show." She looks at him with an indecipherable expression on her face and adds, "As an assistant."

I raise my eyebrows. "Charming," I say.

He smiles. "Not really."

"Go on Iris," Caroline says. "I'll catch up with you."

I look from her to Adam, then walk past him, out of the restroom and back into the loudness of the party, determined to drink as much as possible.

The music's still playing but it's muffled now. The room dances around me and I see Caroline's and Bella's faces like momentary flashes. I'm sitting on the floor next to Sebastián, his knee brushing against my arm. When I found him before, he was talking to Bella at the bar with two other men. As I was approaching them, the men stopped talking and stared at me until Sebastián was forced to look too. "Wow, look at you," one man said. It wasn't clear whether he was being serious or mocking. Bella ignored me and kept asking about Sebastián's wife (what does she like, how does she feel being married to such a powerful politician, and so on). I was a bit lost for words. I kept drinking and looked down at my ankles.

Now, in front of Sebastián and me, Caroline is kissing Adam's neck, a bottle of wine in her hand. She was the one who dragged us to this room. Adam referred to it as "the cloakroom" and Michael laughed, winking at him. They must have taken Lovers here many times in the past. There are no cameras in sight.

I wish I could take Sebastián out but I'm too drunk. Adam and Michael share the wine from a bottle, rating some new Lovers on a scale of 1 to 10. Caroline joins them. When she bends to take the bottle, I gather her hair in my hands so that it doesn't go into her face. She drinks, then lies down on my thighs with a sigh. Sebastián stands up.

"I'm leaving."

I try to stand too, but Caroline's head on my legs feels heavy. Bella jumps up in a second.

"I'll come with you," she says and fires me a look, which I can't really interpret because my sight is a bit blurry.

Michael laughs. "Why? The fun hasn't begun yet." He takes a small plastic bag filled with white powder from his pocket and holds it up for Sebastián to see.

"You should be more careful with that," he says. "Your father wouldn't approve." Then, without even looking at me, he walks away with Bella.

"Boring," Caroline says, and Michael and Adam laugh. I rest my head against the wall, the world spinning around me.

When I open my eyes, the room looks empty. I slide back into my heels and I stand, drunk. Someone coughs behind me. Michael is lying on the floor, his shirt unbuttoned, his eyes bloodshot. I attempt a few steps towards the door, and the heels echo in the silence.

"Where are you going?" Michael asks, his voice hoarse.

"To bed."

"Come here."

I find the wall, straighten myself and open the door. My hand is still on the knob when Michael grabs my foot and drags me down. I fall, hitting the floor with my knees. I tug my leg free and the heel remains in his hands. He throws it away and takes my ankle, pins me down. His breath smells of vodka.

"I don't want to," I say.

"Yes you do." I feel his excitement, his impatience. I have to leave.

I take off my other heel and thrust it into his neck. He jumps back.

"What the fuck—"

I quickly stand and run to the door, but in a second he's also standing, one hand on my hair, the other one on the knob.

"What are you doing?"

"Leaving. Let me leave."

He laughs, his grip tight on my hair. I want to scream but no sound comes out of my mouth. If I could push him back a bit, then I'd be able to open the door and run down the corridor, but how long before he catches me? I doubt anyone's still around and if there are guards, they won't help me. He starts unzipping my dress and for a moment I think that I can handle it, I just have to wait until it's over. But I can't. Then I hear voices. Someone is having a fight outside.

"I'll scream," I pant, jerking my face back from his hand. "I'll scream, they will open the door and the camera will get you."

He stares at me, confused.

I go on, "What will your father say? You going around raping girls in front of the cameras—"

He puts his hand on my mouth but I bite him hard.

"Fuck!" he screams. "You're mad!" He throws the door open, pushing me back, and runs away.

I catch my breath. I try to breathe in and out, but it feels impossible. The sweat on my chest disgusts me; I need to wash it away. I feel panic rising in my body like a wave, but the fighting voices are closer now.

The door opens again. I turn the lamp off and crawl back in the darkness.

I bend and peep through the hanging coats and furs. The moving shapes of Caroline and Adam. They look for the lamp switch, turn it on. Caroline's face is wet; streaks of tears drag down her makeup. Her lips are tight, held in disapproval.

"You promised," she says.

"I did not."

"Yes you did."

"It was a mistake. I was drunk."

"It was not! You were not!" she cries hysterically.

Other voices come from across the corridor. Adam steps forward and cups his hands around Caroline's cheek, gently.

"You don't give a shit about me," she says. "Just say it."

I'm unable to see his expression, he's moved beyond the light. Now he steps back, towards me, in the deepest corner of darkness, and Caroline follows him, unwilling to let him out of close range.

"Say it, Adam. Ever since I've come here, you've behaved like nothing happened before."

I shrink on the bare floor tiles, hiding my face among the furs. He kisses her and Caroline produces a soft, wet sound. I see two little dents at the top of her shoulders, caressed by shadows, and the glimmer of the whites of her eyes. He puts his hands on her neck and draws her even closer to him. The kiss doesn't last more than a few seconds. Then he walks away.

A long moment passes, the silence so thick I'm afraid to breathe. Then Caroline lets out a sob. She looks around with tearful, helpless eyes. Her fingers tremble and she clutches her fists tight to make them stop. For a moment only, I think about reaching out and touching her.

But then she leaves, slamming the door behind her.

In order to fall asleep I need to imagine my sister's body in front of mine, two crooked spoons facing each other on the bed. I imagine a conversation about mom, about the shopping mall, Lily asking endless questions while playing with my hair, me patiently answering. Maybe we had walked together back home, among the naked trees and the tenements standing in the frozen air. Maybe she was shivering and I'd wrapped her in my coat, I'd rubbed her hands with mine.

"How colorful the ground is," she'd said, looking at the garbage spread on a carpet of gold and scarlet leaves. I'd smiled; it is a gift to see the beauty in the most desolate places. And she had run in the misty air, a joyous child in a sleepy land, her arms outstretched like wings, her hair dancing like a fire tongue. And I had followed, to never let her out of my sight.

My breathing becomes regular; the panic freezes. I drift off.

WHERE CAN I FIND THE BETTER ONES?

I wake up alone in my room with a headache. My hair looks dirty so I tie it up in a bad-looking ponytail. I keep my pajamas on and reach the empty Dining Area, keeping the lights low to ease the pain in my temples.

I pick up a tablet and look at the photos uploaded on my profile from the club. There are a couple of pictures of me and Caroline in the restroom, me unpinning her hair while she looks vacantly into the sink, and others of us dancing, our faces sweaty and happy. Then there's a whole photo set of us talking around in groups. Victoria laughs with the president; Margaret dances with a young European politician. I notice there's a pale bruise on her back, which hasn't been edited out. I wonder why; maybe the editors just missed it. In the next few pics, Michael dominates the scene. He appears in every photo while Bella is always looking at Sebastián, who, in a picture, looks back at her while stroking my hand. Bella has a naughty look, while I just seem an appendix of Sebastián's body.

I drink some coffee and take a single buttermilk pancake, thin and perfectly round. Bella comes into the Dining Area. Her hair is wet and she has a bad pimple on her forehead, but she looks radiant. I reach for the syrup and pour it. Bella grabs a banana and takes a seat at the head of the table. The sound of her chair scraping against the floor makes my head hurt. She casts a quick look at the tablet, left unused next to my coffee.

"I'm sorry I stole your man last night," she says.

"You're not sorry," I retort, focusing on the syrup dripping at the edge of my plate. "And he's not my man."

"Who will you entertain now?"

Our eyes meet.

"I'll manage," I say.

"I'm sure you will," she replies. "But what will you do when these European men see the video of your *incident*?" She's doing everything she can to make me explode. I wipe all expression from my face.

"I'll be alone then, lose this competition that you wish to win so desperately, die and then haunt you in your dreams."

She gives me a pitiful look. "I know you're upset. But don't be aggressive."

"You're the one who's being aggressive."

She doesn't have time to reply because I leave the room, slamming the door behind me.

How Bella and I met. At a party, in the Golden Club. I arrived with a man, Jason maybe? I don't remember. She noticed me straight away, in a way that she hadn't before. It was because of the man, of course: he was popular and powerful. She came to me when I was ordering something at the bar and asked for a martini. Her eyes were big with golden glitter on the lashes.

"Are you new?" she asked.

"I've been here for almost two months," I said.

She smiled. "I've never seen you."

"Nor I you," I said. It was a lie. I'd seen her many times around. I'd watched her and many others around the Palace, trying to learn from them, as they lay barely clothed around men, laughing and flirting. I learnt what it meant to be seen, to get men's attention, even though I found it pathetic. And Bella was one of those I watched the most.

That night, she took my hand and told me her story as if we had always been close. And just like that, day after day went by, until I forgot there was a time when we weren't friends, when I noticed her but she wouldn't see me.

Aura and I spend the afternoon at the pool on the terrace. Despite the sun, it isn't too warm outside, but the water is kept hot during the colder seasons. I lie down on a sunbed, looking at Aura swim underwater, her contours losing shape.

I doze off for a while and when I wake up I go to stand at the edge of the swimming pool, in the blue light. The golden and white tiles are warmed by the sun, and a soft breeze makes the leaves dance. I dip my feet into the water. Aura swims towards me.

"Something's troubling you," she says.

I nod. I tell her about Bella's constant sniping, swinging my legs back and forth in the water.

"You know she's always been like that," Aura comments. "Either every politician likes her more than the other Lovers or she gets frustrated. The only thing that makes her feel liked is to get the attention of politicians who're already being entertained."

"I know."

Aura swims backwards, her hair dancing around her. "You still feel sorry for her, don't you?"

I stare into the pale sun. "Maybe I do."

"You shouldn't. From the way she behaves you'd think the only special thing about Lovers is the *sexual interest* men have in us." She says "sexual interest" like Lara would, mimicking the way she savors each word.

"But maybe she's right. That's how life is for us."

Aura looks at me with a sad expression that makes me feel wrong.

"I don't like you because of your sex appeal, you know," she says.

I laugh. She swims away again, a blurred shape in the light blue water, and I think of my mother, when she used to complain about the billboards with women crowding around politicians. "As if women were only made to be sexy and caring..." She always repeated to Lily and me that we should be selfish and assertive. "Generosity destroys women," she used to say, "they keep giving and giving, and men take everything and leave them empty." I always imagined these women as painted wooden dolls set in rows, all carved out inside. "We must look out for one another. We must be ready to fight to defend ourselves, or else the world will break us," mother also said. She always knew what was right, even though no one taught her anything.

No one taught Bella anything either. That's why I feel sorry for her. Because I had a mother who, despite everything that's around us, made me see things for what they were, while Bella didn't.

"Do you think Sebastián will still want me?" I ask Aura.

"Go and see him today," she says, walking out of the pool. "You'll be okay."

I go to Sebastián's room with lacy underwear and vanilla perfume. My stomach feels like a piece of garbage and I wish I could grab it from the inside and throw it away. I take a deep breath and knock on Sebastián's door. There's nothing for a while. Then I hear a whispering, followed by the sound of footsteps coming. Sebastián opens the door and looks over my shoulder, as if to make sure no one else is there. He has an angry, tired look on his face. I don't like it.

"Can I come in?" I ask.

Bella's voice comes from inside the room, "Who is it?" As if she doesn't know.

I raise my eyes to the ceiling.

"What do you want Iris?" Sebastián asks me, angrily. "Go away," he adds.

I open my mouth to reply, but he shouts, "Leave!"

She must have shown him the video. Bitch.

I walk all the way to the kitchens of the Palace. No one seems to notice me; the maids in gray uniforms are emptying the dishwashers, their heads bowed down, the president smiling at them from the faded posters on the walls. The kitchen is probably the only spot in the Palace that reminds me of home: grayish, colorless, women washing and cleaning, a mismatched cacophony of sounds echoing off the walls.

I stand in one corner, staring at the frozen fish lying on a counter, ready to be dressed and flavored. They look hideous.

I can't go back. The other Lovers are entertaining now and the man I have to entertain is taken. Worse, he despises me. This makes me useless. If I can't entertain Sebastián or find someone else, I will lose every single vote and be thrown out of the Palace. And then I will finally discover what really happens to all the unlucky girls who have been forced to leave the competition. My mind travels far away, and images of guards dragging me to prison, of my mother and sister screaming for help pop up incessantly, like raindrops hammering on a roof.

After what feels like hours, Mia finds me with my forehead against the glass counter. She takes my arms and shakes me softly. I look into her eyes.

"Go upstairs," she orders in a low voice.

I nod, recomposing myself. I hurry back, running past the Guests' Rooms and slipping into the Lovers' Area as silently as I can. I look around for a heating pad. I can't find any so I fill a mug with hot water, hide in the bathroom and press it to my forehead until it's warm. Then I go to the Chatting Room and curl up under a blanket, my forehead burning.

No one's meant to be here at this hour. I turn the TV on and look at an advert where semi-naked girls are drinking champagne, cuddling a man who's resting in an armchair. 'Power and privilege,' the man says, smiling at the camera.

I change the channel. On screen the clean face of a woman stares back at me. Her hair is cut short like a man. The news ticker says: "Women's rights defender is sentenced to 200 lashes in the East." I turn the volume up. It's the late afternoon news:

In response to defending women who refuse to cover their faces, hair and hands in public, the government charges the activist with accusations of inciting corruption and prostitution, committing a sinful act by appearing in public without her face and hands covered. The carrying out of the sentence will be live on television next week.

The woman keeps looking at me from the screen, making me uncomfortable.

My mother used to read me the news from the East, whenever she could. Apparently women used to be free there once, free to speak, vote, work. Then there was the war against the Great States and the Leaders of the Eastern countries banished every form of Western attitude. They thought it would corrupt them. They thought that semi-naked women projected on gigantic screens would incite favor towards the States. So they locked their women up, and now they own them like you would own a goat or a pig. What they didn't understand is, in the Palace we are also owned, only in a different way.

The news cuts to a young politician commenting on the sentence, calling this a "terrible human rights violation" and a "desperate call for help." He has plump lips and skin the color of dark brown sugar. I realize that he's speaking from one of the rooms of the Palace, and recognize the man who was frowning during the president's speech in the ballroom.

I turn the TV off. We can't usually watch the news. Someone has probably forgotten to shut down the channel at this hour but it won't take too long before they notice. I stand and walk into the Dining Area, agitated, the activist's face stuck in my head.

Sitting on the table, drinking from a beer bottle is Adam. He's wearing a light blue shirt that barely covers the tattoos on his arms.

"What are you doing here?" I ask. I realize my face is flushed so I touch my cheeks with my hands.

"I was meant to ask you the same question."

"I've got a fever. Who sent you?" I look at my bare feet, checking that my nails are clean.

"The production team. If you're not feeling well, you should go to Dr. Brooks or the Infirmary."

"I'll go tomorrow. Thank you for your kind advice," I say. I pour water into a glass, waiting for him to leave. He doesn't. He walks up to me and touches my forehead with the palm of his hand.

"You're boiling."

"I told you, I've got a fever."

He drops his hand and the tips of his fingers brush against my collarbone. I shudder, waiting for him to strike or kiss me. Instead, he steps back and finishes the beer in one long drink.

"I'll tell the team you're sick and need one night off."

"Thank you."

He puts the empty bottle in the sink and walks towards the door. He lingers before leaving and I watch him, curious.

"You know," he starts, "there's plenty of European men to entertain."

"I know that, thanks."

"Some better than others," he adds, giving me a meaningful look. "You know what I mean?"

"I think so."

"Good," he says. "Take a bath and think about it."

He turns and leaves without another word. I go back to my room and prepare a warm bath.

Bathrooms are a form of escape because we're allowed to turn off the cameras if we want to. In mine, there's a large tub and a red mat in front of it. Recently I've turned all the mirrors to face the walls so the room now looks like it's filled with empty paintings.

Turning the camera off is a luxury that Lovers once didn't have, as I have learnt. There was a girl called Martha who became a sensation on *The President* when I was still a child. Wavy long hair, a delicate face covered in freckles. After she was chosen for Evaluation she demanded privacy in her bathroom: she made an appeal to the producers and asked to remove the cameras "so she could pee without bothering to look pretty." The producers initially agreed but the audience started complaining: they wanted to see her all the time, they were used to it. So she gave up, or most probably the producers forced her to give up.

But one day she walked into the bathroom; she was talking to herself. I was watching the show on a screen that our district shared, an old TV hung next to the poster of the president between a dirty bar and a supermarket. My mom was working in the mall. She didn't know I stopped and watched reality TV on my way back home from school every day.

"This is what happens," Martha said looking straight into the camera, "when you pull the string too tight. It snaps."

She combed her hair in a ponytail before doing it, *that* I remember. Then she took a razor from the cabinet and cut her throat. I closed my eyes, but it was too late. I saw the blood spurting from her neck and hitting a white towel.

The bath is steaming. I step into the water; this is when Martha comes back to me. She's just a shadow made of blood, but I start thinking of doing the same. My mind is a scary place now.

I think I know what Adam meant when he said that some men are better than others. The question is, where can I find the better ones?

THE VIDEOTAPE

As Adam suggested, I go to Dr. Brooks as soon as the sun is up in the morning. Her studio is quiet and cozy, the morning light warming me like a blanket.

"I've heard you had a fever, Iris," Dr. Brooks says.

"Yes."

"Are you feeling better now?"

"I am."

"Good," she says. "Is there anything in particular you want to talk about today?"

She often asks this question. She doesn't understand I come here because I have to, not because I want to.

I shrug.

"What about your conversation with Bella yesterday morning?" she asks.

"What about it?"

Dr. Brooks looks down at her leather notebook and says, "She mentioned the video of your panic attack, didn't she?"

"Yes. She told Sebastián about it and now he doesn't want me anymore." I stare into her eyes, defiant. If she says something in Bella's defense, as she often does, I'll tear up the poster of the president.

"Can you tell me what happened that day?" she asks instead.

I frown. "I've told you many times already."

"You did. But you haven't come to terms with the emotions that the memory triggers."

"That's because that video is still online!" I shout. "No one from production has deleted it!"

Dr. Brooks shakes her head with a patience that only makes me madder. "It doesn't matter where the video is. You have to learn to control your feelings regardless of what happens around you."

"Oh, so if someone rapes me, then it's my fault if I can't control my emotions?" I blurt out.

Dr. Brooks sighs. She leans back in her chair and stares at me in silence for a while. She's waiting for me to calm down, I know it, as if my rage wasn't ever-boiling. I've got enough rage to be angry for a thousand years. But I pretend to calm down.

"Tell me what happened the day of the video one more time," Dr. Brooks says. "And I'll ask production to delete it."

I raise my eyebrows. "You will?"

"Yes."

I stare down at my hands, take a deep breath. "I was having a bad day," I say. "I wasn't feeling well because I hadn't slept in a while. Production asked me to entertain a man who hadn't treated me well in the past and who I never wanted to see again."

"This man is now Secretary of Defense?"

"Yes, that's him. I told the production team I didn't want to entertain him and they told me that I had to. They didn't give me a choice. So I waited all day and tried to feel better before going to him, but I couldn't. I was getting worse every minute,

I felt like I couldn't breathe..." I stop. I can feel the panic, the claustrophobia rising inside me.

"Where were you?" Dr. Brooks asks.

"In the Chatting Room."

"Who else was there?"

"Bella, Aura and two older Lovers."

"And what were they doing?"

"They were trying to calm me down, but everything Bella said only made it worse. She said that I had to behave otherwise the producers would kick me out, she said that my temper wasn't good, that I was "unfit to care for the Leaders" and that I had to change."

"Then you started breaking things."

"I felt trapped. I felt like no one could hear me. So I started shouting and breaking glasses while Aura tried to restrain me."

"And what did Bella do?"

I breathe out, clenching my fists. "The cameras were off, it was still early in the afternoon. So she took a tablet and started filming me. When Aura told her to call for help, Bella waited before leaving the room and said—you can hear this in the video—'Oh my God, she's out of control, it's so scary.'"

"Thanks for telling me this again, Iris. I know how difficult it is for you." I despise her feigned understanding but I nod. "How did you feel after, when Bella gave the video to the post-production team and they posted it online?" Dr. Brooks asks.

I keep focusing on my hands, on the little marks my fingernails leave in my palms. "Betrayed."

"Do you still have similar feelings towards Bella?" she asks.

"Yes," I say.

"What are these feelings?"

"I think jealousy makes her mean. And I misjudged her."

"Do you think you're usually a good judge of character?"

I nod even though I remember that my mother told me I used to trust people too much. At the time I wondered if it was her who committed that mistake, because I never trusted anyone really. Then my father left us, and no one talked about trust anymore.

"Okay. Let's try to relax a bit now," Dr. Brooks says.

She starts tapping on my open palms and asks me to think about soothing things. I struggle to find a bright memory but finally I focus on my mother's belly.

I was six and she was pregnant. I put my hand on her baby bump, it was round and tight and warm. She seemed sad and said, "We'll have to share everything, Iris." I said I didn't mind, as long as the baby was a girl because boys always get the bigger share. My mom laughed. It was raining and I stuck my little hand out of the window. In the house, laundry was hanging from the ceiling and I danced around the white and yellow sheets. My father came back to the apartment with bread and coffee, drenched. I hid behind the sofa, pretending I was invisible, and father called, pretending he couldn't see me, "Where's the most beautiful child in the Silver City?"

Dr. Brooks has stopped tapping, and the memories disappear all at once.

The afternoon is warm and quiet. Aura and I sit on the terrace together eating ice cream. I sing some song that Lily used to love about children playing on the highest roofs of the city and when I'm done, Aura says, "I think people who sing and play are very compassionate."

She's lying down, shielding her eyes against the sun. Sometimes I would like to take the things she says and put them in envelopes. I would carry them around and open them whenever I feel sad. Spoken words fly away, or worse, they fade.

Aura and I first spoke to each other at a dinner party where I found out what caviar was. She was already Price's favorite Lover at the time, and at the beginning of the evening I was holding a plate of something that looked like little black peas and found myself among Price, Aura and an old man who kept asking me about "the unspeakable issue of poverty in the Southern districts." My feet were hurting because Lara had forced me to wear shoes that were too small for me and I found the old man repulsive.

"You're so mysterious," the man said, "so detached from the world." He turned to Price, "Is she not?"

Price shrugged. He didn't care much about me.

"Is that a compliment?" I asked.

Aura looked at me then, with a curious little smile.

The man laughed. "And you're funny as well."

I thought, rather than me being funny, he was *making fun* of me but I said, "Oh yes, I'm so funny, few people can handle it."

He winked at me. Thankfully a producer called both men, and when they left I remained alone with Aura.

"Do you know what this is?" I asked her, pointing at the black thing on my plate.

She smiled. "It's called caviar. It's fancy food."

I laughed. I ate the caviar, which tasted salty and weird, and she said, "James was flirting with you."

"Yeah, I could tell. I'm so *mysterious*."

It was her turn to laugh then. "It's alright, he's just a Visitor. You won't have to be with him if you don't want to."

For some reason, I wanted to cry of happiness. The way she'd said it, so honest and sweet, made me believe for a moment that I was really free to entertain whoever I wanted. Since the beginning of our friendship, I've always thought there's something hopeful about the way Aura experiences the world, something luminous that reminds me of my sister and that warms me up like a ray of sun.

I find Sebastián in the late afternoon, while Bella is doing yoga in the Exercise Room. When I enter the Break Room close to his apartments he's sipping some tea by himself, reading the news on a tablet. He seems glad to see me.

"I'm sorry about yesterday," he says. "I was afraid I wouldn't see you again."

"I can't afford to lose you," I say smiling. "I need your grades."

He laughs at this. "Is that meant to make me feel better?"

"Not really, no." I pour some tea for myself and lean my back against the door.

"So, Bella showed you the video," I say.

"She did, yeah."

The tea tastes like soap.

"They told me it was removed just this morning," he adds. "Are you annoyed that Bella made me see it?"

I think about saying, "I can't afford to be annoyed either," but I don't want to sound repetitive, so I just shrug and drink my tea.

"You're an enigma, aren't you?" Sebastián says.

I put the cup down and kiss him, not because I want to but because it feels like the right moment.

At night, when he falls asleep next to me in his large bed, I look at the ceiling and think about the video. I remember collapsing on the floor into Aura's arms, two guards storming into the room. I remember Bella shouting, "She was breaking everything, I tried to stop her, I was so scared."

I want to cry but my eyes are dry. Sebastián starts snoring. I turn on the other side, facing the windows, and roll into my own empty arms.

Outside, the Silver City stretches around the Palace. Skyscrapers glisten, as bright as stars, and posters of the Great Leader illuminate the older buildings like neon lights.

Everything seems calm. Beyond the brightness of the Silver City, Chinatown glows like a cloud of fireflies, and further beyond, endless slums lie in the darkening sky of the evening, ready to fall in a dreamless sleep. People called Chinatown "the land of the in-between", where boundaries lost their meaning and people lost their way. But I used to know every corner, every smell, every sign. I'd been crossing it to steal from the Silver City since I could remember. I used to go there with my father, before he left. We would steal money from the houses and hotels at the border, then disappear into Chinatown and back to our district. On the way home, he would buy me fortune cookies, which he chose carefully with his big, firm hands. The last quote I got before he abandoned us was: "Be on the lookout for coming events; they cast their shadows beforehand." I didn't pay enough attention to the shadows.

GILDEDTOWN

It's earlier than usual when Mia wakes me today, putting handfuls of coffee in the electric grinder on the desk. The room smells of it. When I sit up on the bed, she tells me that this afternoon we will be escorted out of the Palace to visit Gildedtown, the downtown area of the Silver City.

"Are you serious?" I ask.

"Yes. Are you happy?"

I feel a weightless joy, as if a stone was suddenly lifted from my chest. I haven't been outside for three years. Sometimes, as I walk around the Palace in the early hours of the morning, when the only lights are the screens in the recesses of the painted walls, I try to convince myself that I'm walking the streets of Chinatown. I try to think about the smells of fish and fried chicken, the loud sounds of vendors shouting and horns honking, and I savor the freedom, the anonymity of it. But it doesn't last long; I'm not very good at fooling myself.

In the past, Lovers chosen for Evaluation used to go around Gildedtown to sign autographs and visit the schools and hospitals of the rich, but five years ago the event was cancelled. Some Lover must have tried to escape during these outings, otherwise why would they call off such a perfect propaganda event? So a new rule was added: *we must not leave the Golden Palace*. Well, I guess today we can.

"This is great news," I say, jumping out of bed. I take the coffee Mia is handing me, then hug her. She looks up at me, surprised, while a large smile warms up her face.

When I let her go, she starts making the bed, still smiling. I look at the way she folds the sheets and think that, for the first time in a while, I can't wait to get ready for the day.

In the Beauty Center Lara talks about the importance of looking "natural" yet "glamorous." Her eyes are surrounded by a thick layer of glittering eye shadow and her lips are too big for her face.

"You can sign autographs, take pictures, praise the Leaders, but don't answer any questions about your lives in here," she says as she goes through some clothes hanging on a rack. She stops to examine an extravagant yellow dress and turns to look at us.

"And smile! You must look happy!"

She gives each of us a new dress and a pin with the president's face on it. I look from the badge to the dark red leather dress Lara has chosen for me and, without saying a word, I put it back on the hanger and pin the badge to a simple black turtleneck instead.

Lara sighs. "You always do what you want, Iris." She looks at me as if I were a failure of hers, a child that didn't turn out too well.

I say sorry, even though I'm not sure for what I'm apologizing exactly.

We get into the elevator all together. The screens wake up with a start-up noise. When a moving image of Sebastián appears, Bella kisses it and Victoria laughs, looking at me with a pitying expression. I wish she'd realize how pathetic she looks.

Down in the parking lot, the producers split us into pairs, each assigned to a security guard: Victoria and Bella, Margaret and Caroline, Aura and me. They explain that each pair will take a different route, to make sure that we cover the main spots of Gildedtown. A tall man with small eyes and a black beard leads Aura and me to his limousine. As soon as the others have also hopped into their cars, the guard puts some pop music on and starts the engine.

We pass silver skyscrapers and large houses with elegant facades and freshly mowed lawns. You can see them through the tall fences, and, if you look up, barbed wire loops loom against the sky like spiderwebs.

"Can you open the window?" I ask the guard. He presses a button and the window goes down. The cold wind cuts my cheek but I stick my head out and look at the pine needles on the sidewalk.

"Careful," the guards says. "Someone might recognize you."

"It smells," Aura says, smiling with her eyes closed. Her cheeks are red from the cold. I move my head back into the car and lie down against her shoulder.

I know what she's talking about. The air smells of freedom.

We reach Gildedtown when the sun is high in the sky and the air has grown warmer. The main street is flooded with cars, and on the sidewalk, spaced at regular intervals, are large elm trees with posters of the president on them. Armed sentries on guard duty stand beside each tree, quietly staring around. Motorbikes zoom in and out next to us, while crowds of workers whistle for an empty taxi. The smells are overwhelming: baked bread and melting cheese, cinnamon and pastries. We pass a hotel called THE HEART OF THE STATES with a guard holding a Great Dane on a leash; lounge bars thrumming with life; a beauty center with the sign: "buttock augmentation" next to an image of a young woman wearing a bikini that shows off her perfectly round butt. Women on the streets have elaborate necklaces and very blonde hair. Some men stand in front of a wall covered in graffiti, smoking cigarettes in their business suits. They look at us as we pass, smoke blowing out of their mouths.

"That's us."

I turn to Aura. She is pointing at a uniformed worker sweeping debris in front of a club. Behind him, on the wall next to the club entrance, someone has drawn a portrait of Aura and me with spray paint. We both look serious, detached somehow, as if the artist didn't really know whether to draw us happy or sad. Other people have since written on it, because the portrait's covered in graffiti, including the words "power and privilege" next to Aura's face.

I smile and stick my head outside the window, absorbing every smell and color, feeling the chaos of the city throbbing inside me.

Our first stop is Golden Square, one of the busiest historical sites of Gildedtown. The first president was elected by the people here, before anyone can remember. It was a long time ago, before *The President*, before the war against the East. A time of freedom, or so my mother used to say, even though she never lived in it.

My mother was what Price might have called "a subversive individual" if he'd ever met her. She and my father had that in common. They complained a lot about the Leaders together and spoke of the past as a time when the president was nothing more than "an elected populist," like European politicians might be now. As a child, I listened with interest, because in school we never read about the time before the first president. Our history started with that election.

In Golden Square, people are streaming around us: schoolboys in uniform, laughing and pushing each other; heavily made-up women towing their children by the wrist; tourists with expensive-looking coats and cameras.

The guard takes us to a noodle bar crowded with customers, half-hidden in one corner of the square. Around us, buildings are wallpapered with posters of the president, Nelson Price and other high-profile politicians. The skyscrapers are so tall that the sky among them is just a small square of blue, like the half-shut bright eye of a battered face. At the noodle bar, customers are slurping big bowls of rice, vegetables and fish, sitting on high stools. The counterman, a young woman with shiny black hair, recognizes us with a gasp. She lets us pass through the crowd and asks if she can take a picture with Aura. The guard takes the picture as I stand aside, feeling awkward.

"*The President*'s Lovers!" the woman shouts, and suddenly more and more people are gathering around us: a woman dressed in leather, a group of young men with tattoos on their faces, two businessmen in suits. They compliment us as we take pictures with them,

"You're such an inspiration,"

"You're so intense,"

"You look even prettier in person."

One of the young men whispers to Aura, "I think about you every night before going to bed."

"You should get yourself a girlfriend," I say, and Aura bursts out laughing.

We leave the square giggling, the flashes of people's cameras shining all around us.

We pass a reality TV theatre whose screens advertise *The President* and *Authentic*, a show where rich people have to perform manual tasks such as cleaning rooms and waiting tables. People slip past us, some unaware of our presence, others taking pictures of us, shrieking with excitement.

We reach a square dominated by a huge gray building. I stare at the leaves on the sidewalk, frail and orange under my polished shoes, before the guard leads the way inside. A large sign by the entrance says: Gildedtown Medical Center.

Inside, the rooms are all white, with no paintings or pictures hanging anywhere. The sharp smells of antiseptic and coconut air freshener sting my nostrils. It feels like walking into a weird dream. The guard leads us to the waiting room, where a small group of people is sitting, reading on their tablets. As soon as we step inside, there's a rustling. A pregnant woman about my age stands. She's holding the hand of a toddler who looks around, bored. Her swollen belly scares me. She stares at Aura and me in bewilderment and squeals, "Oh God! It's you! I can't believe it!"

Others look up too and, before we know it, we're taking pictures with everyone in the room. Then a middle-aged nurse takes us to the Resting Rooms, where patients are sitting in their beds with trays of fresh food and water next to them. They ask us about the Great Leaders and we ask them about their health.

As we are walking out, passing what feels like endless white corridors, the pregnant woman catches up with us again. "You're gorgeous!" She squats down and whispers in the boy's ear, "Aren't they gorgeous?" Is she about to cry? Her eyes are wet. I attempt a fake smile and wave at the boy, who seems quite unconcerned with his mother's enthusiasm.

When we're sure we have left her behind, Aura grabs my wrist and whispers, "Some women should never have children."

Right outside the hospital, we bump into an excited troupe of journalists. They surround us like bees around honey, turning the cameras on before we can even fix our hair. I almost laugh thinking about what Lara will say when she sees this. *You're hopeless, Iris.* And then she will pull her disappointed face, which makes her lips look like deflated balloons.

One of the journalists, a silver-haired man wearing a hideous tie, shoves the microphone into my hand and asks me what it's like to be famous. I look around, helpless. Some people are stopping by, looking at us with curiosity. A mother is dragging her little girl away from us, holding her in her arms; I can see her hair in the crowd, an auburn spot among a sea of nameless faces.

"Iris, what's it like?" the journalist asks again.

"It isn't easy." I smile, repeating some of the things Lara always says. "We have a lot of responsibility; girls often look up to us. We must set a good example."

"How was your first day in the Palace? Three years ago, was it not? Can you believe it? Are you grateful?"

"I'm sorry, I can't talk about that," I say.

Wide-eyed and eager for more, the journalist barks into the microphone. I'm trying to step back from him when horns start honking and passers-by shouting in the street.

The journalist turns and his troupe redirects their attention. I stand on my tiptoes to have a better view.

There's a group of women on the other side of the street, different from the ones we've seen in the Gildedtown so far. They're wearing flats and men's suits and hold leaflets and banners. At first I think that the shouts come from them, but then I realize it's the crowd around them that's yelling, "Bitches!" and "Go back where you came from!"

I make my way through the people grouped on the sidewalk to get closer. The women are silent, staring back defiantly at the crowd who keeps shouting insults. Their banners say: GIVE YOUNG GIRLS A CHANCE and NO MORE LOVERS. My eyes linger on a young girl in a faded blue shirt and overalls. She looks too skinny and her hair is tucked under a cap. I can't see her face because of the crowd. The banner she's holding says: WOMEN ARE PEOPLE. A heavy-set woman in front of me shouts,

"Whores! Take care of your Leaders!" I step on her foot with all my strength. The woman pushes me and I stumble back. The girl's face comes into full view. I gasp.

It's Lily.

For a moment it's as if someone's trying to drown me. I breathe in, unable to move any further. I try to meet her gaze but she hasn't seen me. *Go home. Leave.*

I push people aside, trying not to lose sight of Lily. But the closer I am to her, the more crowded the street becomes. Two young men push me back trying to take a picture of the banners and I fall onto the cemented ground. I stand back up. Lily is holding her banner tight, an angry look on her face. *Turn around and leave.* But all she does is stare back at the crowd.

Then all of a sudden there's a gunshot and people in the crowd start shouting. Guards are making their way through. They're holding flash grenades and pepper spray. I try to move forward but there's barely space to move my arms; the people are crushing me. Guards shove them as they reach the protesters, and I see one man firing tear gas.

"GO AWAY!" I shout in Lily's direction. "RUN HOME! RUN—"

Someone grabs my arm. I turn and see Aura. Then the black-bearded guard appears and starts dragging me through the crowd. I try to fight him but his grip on my arm is too strong.

"We need to leave," the guard orders.

"Let me go," I say. "LET ME GO!"

I try to anchor myself to the people around me, sinking my nails into their arms, but the guard pulls me out of the crowd and into an emptier side street. He takes a pill from his pocket. *No, no, no, no.* I keep my lips sealed but he forces my mouth open and pushes my head back. I swallow the pill. Aura's giving me a worried look. I try to walk back towards the protesters but my limbs are already feeling heavier, domesticated and I have to lean against the wall.

The guard leads us back into the car, the yelling crowd behind us. Aura grips my hand and I keep turning back, desperate for one last glimpse of Lily, but my sister has vanished in the sea of angry faces.

WHY IS IT NEVER ENOUGH?

When Lily was twelve, she asked me if the Lovers we saw on TV wanted to have sex with all those men. In two years she would finish school and start working in the mall, cleaning like mother, or serving hamburgers in one of the fast food companies.

"Why do you ask?" I said. We were out on the stairs of the tenement building to enjoy the breeze of the late evening.

"Boys in school say that they do."

"Well, boys are not girls so how would they know what's going on in those girls' heads?"

She seemed satisfied with my answer for a while, and just sat there, playing with little stones she used to carry around all the time. Men and women walked up and down the stairs, carrying bags of food and clothes fresh from the laundry.

"But do they enjoy it or not?" Lily asked after a long pause.

"It's complicated. Sometimes they do, sometimes they don't. But you don't have to listen to the boys, or anyone else. When you're grown up, you will do only what you want to do with a man."

I wish this had been my answer. Truth is, I don't remember what I said, no matter how hard I try.

The pill's effect hits me hard as soon as we're back in the car. It's the same one Dr. Brooks used to give me after my panic attacks. I lean my head against the window, feeling weak and exhausted.

"What was that? What's happening?" I whisper. My mouth is dry and my palms are sweaty. I feel like I can't breathe properly. I can't believe my sister is out there in the streets, among a crowd of protesters. *Where is mother? Why is she letting her*?

Aura grabs my wrist, feeling my pulse. "Are you alright?" she asks. Then to the guard, "What have you given her? She's afraid to take downers!"

I can't hear his response. I'm trying to open the door but it's locked. Aura is talking to me but I feel myself sinking down into the seat. My hand slips down the door handle. My eyes are open just a crack.

Lily is out there. Aura and the guard are raising their voices, fighting about something.

Lily is in danger. I see Aura's face coming into focus then I slip away into the darkness.

I open my eyes at the sound of the car door opening. My tongue is thick and heavy, as if I swallowed dirt, but apart from that the pill's effect is washing away. When I try to stand, my legs don't fail me.

"Go on," I hear the guard say. "I'll be right here."

I push myself upright, leaning against the car. I lift my head slowly, ready for the Golden Palace to appear, but instead find myself in front of a bright pink building. Next to it, a street sign that says Serenity Lane. Aura is counting some pills in her palm, standing by the sign. When she sees me, she swallows one and puts the rest back in her pocket.

"Good, you're awake."

My vision blurs then goes back into focus. The facades of the street are colorful with large windows on each floor and sets of stairs that lead to the front doors. At the base of the stairs are stinky garbage bags and cigarette butts. An old woman from the balcony stares at us, motionless, wrapped in her black shiny shawl, her hair up in curlers.

"You know a woman called Jo Winters?" Aura asks her. The name sounds familiar. The woman frowns, then walks back into the house.

"That wasn't polite," Aura comments.

"Maybe she doesn't want any trouble," I say.

"We're not bringing trouble." She turns to me. "Are you feeling any better?"

I ignore her question. "Isn't Jo Winters the Lover who accused Price of abusing her years after her win?"

"That's her." I wait for more explanations, but Aura doesn't give me any. I remember reading about Winters in the newspaper. She had been depicted by the press as a crazy, jealous woman and had disappeared from the spotlight after that.

"We shouldn't be here," I say.

"Don't worry. The guard won't talk," Aura comments, looking back over her shoulder quickly, at the man waiting for us in the car.

"You don't know that."

"I've told him Price allowed us to make a little detour before going back."

"That's not true." My mouth still feels a bit slow. I bite the inside of my cheek.

"Of course not. But he doesn't know that. And even if he suspects something, he won't speak with all the money I've given him."

I look at her. Her face is expressionless. "Where did you get the money?"

Aura breaks into a laugh as if I made a joke.

"Aura…" I start.

"Don't," she cuts me off. "Whatever you saw back there, you keep your mouth shut about it."

I've never heard Aura talk like that and I'm about to point it out to her when a girl appears at the window. She's smoking a cigarette and looks no older than fourteen. Her arms and belly are covered in tattoos. She looks at the car with curiosity, then blows smoke out of the nostrils.

"You famous?"

"We're looking for Jo Winters," Aura says. "Does she live here?"

"First floor," she says, then turns and shouts, "Mom, visitors!"

We climb the stairs and ring the bell. No one answers so I open the door, quietly. In front of us there's a heavy-set woman with a baby on her hip and a mayonnaise-stained spoon in her hand. Her sweatpants are fluorescent pink and her socks mismatched.

"Are you Jo?" Aura asks. She has a confused look on her face, as if she can't believe what she's seeing. I have to admit I didn't expect this either.

"That's me. What do you want?" Behind her I hear the TV on. The girl we saw at the window joins her mother. She smells of smoke and cheap deodorant.

"We just wanted to see you. Are you the Jo Winters that was on *The President* fifteen years ago?"

"I'm busy right now," Jo replies and walks back into the kitchen.

"Well, come in," the girl says and closes the door behind us. She sits on a plastic chair, staring at us. I keep standing, looking around.

A little child comes into the living room and curls up on the girl's lap. She has ash-blonde hair and scraped knees. I'm not used to seeing kids around in the Palace so I stare at the child, quite shamelessly. She hides her head under the girl's arm and I remember that Lily used to do the same thing whenever other people tried to talk to her. I feel a sudden urge to leave the room so I join Jo Winters in the kitchen. She's making something that doesn't smell too good. Sliced peppers, onions and tomatoes are mixed on the cutting board. While checking the oven, she keeps shifting her baby from one hip to the other.

"Do you need help?" I ask.

She speaks without looking at me. "Look, I've done nothing wrong okay. I'm fine here with my kids and I want nothing to do with that show anymore."

"We're not here for that."

"Well then, what are you here for?" She turns to me as she says this and I can see the wrinkles around her eyes and on her fat neck.

"I don't really know."

"Maybe you want to know what life is like when that fucking thing is over?" She raises her voice, as Aura joins us in the kitchen. I'm about to say no, but Aura whispers, "Do they send you money?"

Jo looks around the room angrily. "How stupid are you exactly? Does it look like they're sending me money?"

Aura shakes her head.

Jo continues. "They used to send me money. I got job offers for women's lingerie companies and other shit like that. Then I testified against Price and guess what? No one wanted to hire me anymore." She takes the cutlery from a drawer and starts setting the table. I notice there aren't enough chairs.

"What happened with him?" Aura asks.

Jo looks straight at her for a moment. "You should know. Aren't you one of his favorites?"

Aura blushes. Jo places two dirty-looking glasses on the table.

"Anyway, I'm not the only one to complain. They sell you this reality show thing as a dream that will last for the rest of your life, but for them your life ends when you get older. No one wants to hire a former Lover when we're fatter, pregnant or already with a kid. Men are all the same you know. They can fuck whoever they want but when it's you doing it, well that's not right." She gives a hysterical laugh. "Funny thing is, I didn't even want to fuck them. They made me do it."

Whatever's in the oven smells burnt. The girl has joined us in the kitchen. She is frowning and caressing her little sister's head. She turns to us and says quietly, "You should leave."

Jo gives the baby to her daughter and steadies her hands against the sink.

"I saw you on TV," she says. She isn't looking at either of us so we don't know who she's referring to. "You look like one of those who can think for themselves. But it doesn't end once you're out of there. They never leave you alone if you don't keep your mouth shut."

The girl holds the baby's head in a protective way, while the other child grabs on to her shorts. "You really should leave now," she repeats.

Aura grabs my wrist and drags me out of the kitchen. I hurry to keep her pace. Jo comes after us, sweat trickling down her forehead.

"But you should be glad you're alive!" She shouts, a fork in her hand. I can tell her daughter wants to help but she has the baby in her arms and doesn't want to drop it. "Cause that's something else that happens; they just wipe us out. Not pretty enough, not funny enough…"

Aura takes me out of the house, slamming the door behind her as Jo shouts, "Why is it never enough?"

We run down the stairs and get in the car. It's started to rain and the air smells of it. When I look up, I see the girl staring at us from the window and, above her, the old woman on the balcony, calling out, "Yeah, leave, go back where you came from."

We drive back to the Palace, raindrops ticking against the car windows, each of us with her own dangerous thoughts.

Extract from *The Silver Times*

"Our Generous Leaders Take Care of Violent Protests Once More"

by Peter Corbett

Yesterday afternoon a group of government dissenters marched in Gildedtown to protest against our Great Country, smashing shop windows and setting fires in Golden Square. Guards intervened, protecting scared passers-by, taking some protesters into custody for interrogation. The rest of the group was escorted back to the districts. Once again, they have to thank the generosity of our Leaders.

"These demonstrators are a threat to the Great States," the president claimed this morning. "New Town is shaken by such an outbreak of violence. All I can say is that the generosity of the Leaders can't last much longer. The people in custody will be taken to Control and Management Prisons. In the meantime, if you have any information on other protesters, I encourage you to come forward and protect your Great Country."

FACES LIKE THAT DON'T LAST

It's the last day of the first week of Evaluation, and, for breakfast, we join the politicians and producers in the gardens, under a large white tent. A little stage is set in one corner: soon some of the Europeans will make short speeches for the press, and for once we are allowed to listen.

I'm sitting with Margaret and Caroline, waiting for the first politician to step onstage. It's Sebastián. He's holding a tablet and reads a piece about elections in his country. I see Bella smiling encouragingly from a table close to the stage. Pathetic.

"When you give something," Sebastián reads, "You want something in return." He talks about fundraising for campaigns and how important it is for citizens to donate, mentioning things like "benefits for the people" and "donate to the country." Next to me, Caroline takes a pastry with cream and says, loud enough for me to hear, "He's not talking about the people, he doesn't even know who the people are."

I don't know what she means but, as Sebastián sits back at his table and photographers take pictures of him, I hear the two men opposite me muttering.

"Corporations are called 'people' now. Smart," says a middle-aged man I once entertained, chuckling. The one next to him, with a hideous red moustache, lights his cigarette.

"Billions and billions of dollars in return for tax cuts. Forget about the benefits, the people are fucked, that's what they are."

They laugh together, while smoke drifts in my direction. Caroline wipes some cream from her mouth, looking bored. Margaret, on the other hand, seems very interested in the speeches, like a curious child eager to learn all at once. I understand her. We don't have elections in the Great States. The people used to vote for their leaders once, but, after the first president was elected, only the politicians from the Palace and members of the most influential families can vote and decide for each Leader's successor.

The following politicians talk about their own elections, relations with the States and "the dangers" of the East. They mention private investments in the best hospitals of the Great Cities and the policies of the Wall. The last man to speak is a delegate called Theo Droit. I immediately recognize him as the man I saw on TV, commenting on the Eastern activist's sentence. He has clever dark eyes and broad shoulders.

He clears his throat and says he will talk about the women's rights to vote in Europe. Some men laugh. Nelson Price, from his table close to the stage, rolls his eyes. I look around. Except for two brown-skinned maids and Aura, Theo is the only black person in here.

"Though women can vote everywhere in Europe," Theo says, "they have, throughout the past thirty years or so, progressively stopped exercising their right."

"And what about the women in the East?" he asks. "They are whipped and shipped and covered from head to toe as if it were shameful for them to be seen. They are sold, still children, to men much older than them."

He has a calm, yet passionate way of speaking, and I notice

that he's careful to never mention the condition of women in the Great States. He speaks about his organization, one that pushes women to vote and work, and protects the ones who do so. When he's done, only a few photographers take his picture, but he seems unbothered by it and sits back at the table next to us.

"He's someone worth entertaining," Caroline says.

"Why don't you?" I ask.

"'Cause I'm already entertaining his boss."

When breakfast is over, Caroline takes my hand and says, "Come on, I'll introduce you. It's not like you have someone else to entertain anyway." She drags me toward Theo and another delegate, who are chatting with some journalists.

"Iris, can I introduce you to Julian and Theo?" Caroline says.

Julian looks older with hair that's turning gray and a serious face. He tells the journalists to leave us alone. Caroline goes on, "Theo's so smart they made a documentary about him in Europe."

Theo smiles, shaking his head. "They didn't do it because I was smart," he says. "They did it because I caused a lot of trouble."

"Are you already entertaining someone, Iris?" Julian asks.

"Kind of." I look over my shoulder at Sebastián, who's having his picture taken by the press.

"I see," Julian says. "Already tired of Sebastián?"

"It's not really like that." Theo and I are standing close; I can smell the scent of his shower-gel. It's something like toothpaste or mint.

"What's the name of your organization?" I ask him.

He gives me a curious look. "Equality Now."

Caroline asks Julian something I don't listen to. No one seems to be caring about Theo and me.

"Why do you think women don't vote anymore in your country?" I ask him.

"That's a good question. It could be because of lack of representation. They only see men running in the elections and think voting is pointless."

"But how could a woman do politics in a world like this?"

He opens his mouth to answer but I stop him because Price is coming in our direction.

"It doesn't matter. Let's speak no more." I force myself to smile, and leave Theo alone, feeling his eyes burning the back of my head.

In the afternoon, Sebastián watches the news in his suite. I pour some tea and milk in a cup and hand it to him. On TV, some of his colleagues from home are arguing about the elections. One blonde man with a double chin is insulting his opponent, calling him corrupt. I sit on the armrest of his leather chair.

"You don't have to be here if you don't want to," Sebastián says coldly.

"I want to," I lie. The blinds are pulled down and light comes through the cracks falling on the floor in stripes. Carelessly, he traces the bones on my spine with his fingers.

"How will your people benefit from donating to the country?" I ask.

"What?" His eyes are still locked on the debate.

"When you spoke to the press before, you said that people should donate to your campaign so that they can get benefits."

Sebastián takes the remote control and lowers the volume. He looks at me, frowning.

"Some people will get benefits."

"Who?"

"The ones who pay."

"And what about the ones who can't afford to pay?"

He looks at me as if I were an idiot. "Why do you have to put it that way?"

"It's the simplest way—"

"How do you even think the world works?" He's raised his voice.

"There's a difference between how the world works and how it should work," I say calmly.

He looks away and turns up the TV volume. I try again, "I don't understand how you can—"

He slaps me hard across the face. My cheek burns and my eyes water.

"Don't you dare question my job. You're not here for that. Now get out."

I take a last look at the screen, where the two opponents keep interrupting each other, their faces grotesque with anger.

"Leave, Iris," Sebastián repeats, without looking at me.

I leave without another word.

Lara has told us that Price is in a mood, so we hurry to arrive in the ballroom early for dinner. When we open the double doors however, it seems that we aren't early enough: the president, Price and the European leaders are already waiting for us. Behind me, Margaret swears under her breath.

"Why so early?" Bella asks.

"I think Price just wants a reason to get mad at us," says Aura matter-of-factly.

"It's the revolts in the city," Caroline whispers. "They're driving him crazy."

"How do you—" I start, but Caroline walks away from me. I can't help but think she looks very attractive in her pink sheath dress with flowers.

I take my seat with the others, careful not to draw too much attention or make any unwanted sound. Seats are numbered and there are little tags with our names. I'm between Theo and Sebastián. The president makes no speech or announcement, so maids start bringing food straight away: oysters, bread and butter, Price's favorite. I try to eat slowly to be polite but I'm hungry and a bit tired. Bella is already talking to Sebastián and I have no intention of joining in, so I turn to Theo, Julian and Caroline. Julian is saying that *The President* has a lot of success in their country and his daughters are obsessed with it, even though his mother hates it.

"Why?" Caroline asks, gulping down a large piece of bread.

"Too much nudity. Europeans can be prudes," Julian says with a weird smile.

"And your daughters are fine with the nudity?" I ask.

"They don't mind watching it. It's not their body after all," Julian says with a laugh. I focus on the bread, aware of Theo's eyes on my face. It seems like he is x-raying me, waiting for a reaction on my part. He doesn't know I've long schooled my face to dullness.

All things considered, the dinner seems to be going well. Price doesn't make any bad jokes—he's exceptionally silent—and the president keeps laughing out loud with some older European ambassador. Then, dessert arrives. The president takes a bit of his mousse and speaks over the chatter, "I have to say you enchanted everyone a week ago, Aura. When did you learn to play the piano?"

I turn to his direction and, with a pang of panic, realize that he's speaking to me. There is a moment of awkward silence. Then Aura identifies herself, adding that there was an old piano in the foster home she grew up in, and that the women there taught her.

The president smiles. "Of course it's you, I'm sorry. You both have beautiful faces."

Suddenly, Price laughs very hard. I see Aura looking down and I know we're thinking the same thing: Price is annoyed by the fact that the president got us mixed up. He thinks it's our fault, that we haven't made ourselves noteworthy enough.

"Faces like that don't last, that is the problem," Price says. "I've been with women of every sort and even the most beautiful become old. That's just a fact."

I bite my tongue. The president downs his brandy, coughs then speaks, "Don't be mean, Nelson. I'm absolutely sure that they don't have just good looks." He says *absolutely* as if he's savoring the word. Because neither the president nor Price have acknowledged our capability to speak, I say nothing.

"Iris likes to write," Bella says. I turn to her and she looks at me as though she's doing me a favor, an annoying smirk on her face. Two years ago, I told her that I enjoyed keeping a journal back home, where I recorded the memories of my father, the changes in Lily as she grew up, the things my mother told us. Silence falls again like a curtain. A Lover who enjoys writing sounds like something subversive.

"What do you write?" Theo asks. He sounds actually interested, unaware of the tension that's filling up the room, suffocating me.

I don't look at him when I say, "I used to. I don't anymore."

Aura intervenes, "Now she sings."

"I remember that," the president says, relaxing his fat neck against the backrest. "You have a lovely voice."

But Price doesn't forget, and neither does he forgive. "Now women write?"

A few politicians laugh, including Sebastián. I attempt a fake smile, thinking hard about kicking Sebastián in the face.

Price claps his hands. "Cultivate the mind, well done. What for?" I don't have an answer to that and hope someone else will speak. But he keeps talking: "Girls who think too much do silly things… incidents, let's call them that."

I think about Martha, slicing her throat with a razor, and want to throw up.

"Incidents like what?" I ask. Suddenly everyone looks at me.

"Women can't handle too much emotion. They let themselves get overwhelmed," Price says.

"And then they kill themselves," I say. The president clears his throat but I ignore him. I'm too busy staring into Price's cold eyes.

"And then they speak too much, that's another problem," Price says.

"Fill Nelson's glass, he needs to get drunker," laughs the president. A trembling maid hurries to follow his order but Price sends her away.

He turns back to me. "Iris, sing for us, will you?"

"Now?"

"Yes, now."

I realize my hands are shaking. I wish I could shatter all these pretty glasses on the floor, right in front of Price's eyes.

"No one's playing," Caroline points out.

"If Iris is so good, I'm sure she doesn't need a base," Price says coldly.

I pick up my drink and swallow it all the way down. Then I stand and sing from my stomach, like my mother taught me, hoping that the audience feels the punch that I'm feeling in my chest and throat, the emotion coming out in flashes. The room grows quiet, and I catch sight of some maids standing in the doorway, looking at me with their mouths open.

When I'm done, my legs are shaking. Price looks into his glass, his face still red with anger. The president claps his hands, the way he does when they bring magicians or trained exotic animals to the Palace and he's enchanted by their performance. I feel like a circus act. I excuse myself and say I need to go to the restroom.

"I'll go with her," Aura says quickly.

Everyone watches us as we stumble out of the ballroom. I walk down the corridor and open a door that leads to a balcony. Outside, the city is glittering in the darkening sky.

"That was intense," Aura says. She fumbles with the sleeve of her dress until she finds a little pillbox. She opens it and swallows one blue pill.

"I hate everyone," I say.

She sighs, hiding the pillbox again so that it doesn't show.

"You're always so angry," she says, turning away from me. Her dress leaves her back naked and I look at the ridges on her spine.

"How can you *not* be angry?"

"Anger traps you. And we're already in a prison." She turns back to me. For a second, it looks like she will reach out and touch me, but then she doesn't. "Come on, let's go back."

In the ballroom, everyone is drunker than before. The president asks Aura to sit next to him and tells her he would like to spend some time with her. With a calm smile on her face, Aura says, "Thank you for this opportunity."

When Sebastián leaves with Bella, I entertain Theo and Julian. They make me laugh and drink a lot, until I forget about the scene I made before. When we leave, it's late night. Theo gives me a sad smile but doesn't ask me to join him in his room.

On my way back to the Lovers' Area, I find Margaret smoking a joint on the terrace. She has taken her heels off and is staring into the distance.

"No entertaining for you tonight?" she asks, without turning.

I step closer, feeling the chilly wind on my bare shoulders. "It seems I'm not that popular," I say.

She laughs, blowing smoke out of her mouth. "You're still slum trash."

"You're no different."

She turns to me quickly. Her cheeks are covered with a thick layer of foundation. For a moment, she looks like the blonde woman who'd come to the school in my district, scouting for pretty girls.

"You're right," Margaret says, finally. "We're all the same." She takes another puff of her joint then says, "Want some?" It's the first time she offers me something of hers.

"No thanks."

"Of course," Margaret says. "You're too good to do drugs, aren't you?"

I don't know what she means so I simply say, "Goodnight."

"Goodnight," she replies.

As I walk back to my room, I think about the time when I saw Margaret fighting with one of the Leaders. I had walked into the men's toilet at the club by mistake and there she was standing, applying some mascara in the mirror. A man was kneeling on the floor, fully dressed, whispering to her in a way that sounded like a wailing.

"You're pathetic," she was telling him, "fucking pathetic." She saw me as I slammed the door shut but didn't say anything.

Later, when the episode aired and we watched the scene in the Chatting Room, she told everyone that he wanted to leave his wife and that she had to remind him how stupid that was. I found this incident extremely significant, as if Margaret were telling us that if she wanted, she could easily break the rules, but at the same time she could pretend she was loyal to the show. It was like a form of revenge, a subtle way of disturbing the hierarchies of the Palace, where every man has a precise role and subsequent privilege, and Margaret has none of both.

Back in my room, I almost expect to find Aura curled up under the sheets. But my bed is empty and the president's face is smirking at me from the wall.

AURA

2nd week of Evaluation

We're all sitting on the sofa, Caroline smoking a cigarette, me sipping coffee. Our scores are about to be announced. The morning is beautiful, with sunlight that diffuses everywhere like golden dust. We must look good on camera, wrapped in the shining light, like those angels with halos around their heads that are painted on the ballroom's ceiling.

I couldn't sleep last night and I'm afraid I might doze off at any moment. I kept thinking about Lily with that banner. I should have told her, I should have explained how dangerous that is when I had a chance.

If I close my eyes, I can see her walking around the main square of our district, her slender figure against the backdrop of the dark brick buildings. She was chewing a mouthful of noodles out of a paper box and she was mad at me because I'd been out all night stealing.

"Lily, I need to take care of you. If I stay home, we won't have enough," I was telling her, following her around as she walked.

"But why?" she asked, frowning.

"Because we're poor."

"Why are we poor? Why can't you work in that bar like Amelia?" Amelia was our neighbor. She'd had a kid when she was sixteen and worked in a fancy bar in Chinatown, where the owner paid the girls a lot more if they did striptease at night.

"Because men in those bars aren't nice to girls."

"Why?"

"Stop Lily."

"Why can't we be rich like those girls on TV?"

"Shut up!" I shouted as I slapped her in the face. I'd never done that before.

She stuck her little nose in the air, said, "I hate you" and ran away.

"Iris, wake up." Aura is shaking my arm.

I open my eyes and lift my head slowly off the arm of the sofa. The scores have already been announced. Aura earned a ten, Bella and Victoria a nine, but everyone else got a five. The number shines next to my face onscreen as if it were a star, not a death sentence.

"Fuck me," Caroline says shaking her head. She puts out her cigarette as if trying to pierce the ashtray. My head feels heavy, but I force myself to think. Aura got the best grade because the president chose her at dinner, but what about Bella? It was Sebastián. He punished me because I asked him about the elections. Because I "overstepped his boundaries," as Price told us never to do.

Margaret downs some anxiolytics with her coffee. Caroline turns the TV off.

I want to shoot someone. I can't lose this game.

I go to sit on the terrace because it's one of the few places where cameras don't work. Aura soon joins me. She has a tired look on her face but manages to give me a sad smile.

"I'm sorry about the grades," she says. As if she had to apologize.

I shrug. "I should've kept my mouth shut with Sebastián."

"You'll find someone else to entertain."

"Will I?"

She ignores me. "The audience likes people who say what they think. Look at Caroline. She has a big mouth and yet she's popular."

Not now she isn't. "I'm not like Caroline. I don't say what I think."

"No, you're better." Clearly the audience doesn't seem to agree with her, but I keep my mouth shut. Aura doesn't deserve my anger.

"How was last night?" I ask. "The president?" I heard her go back to her bedroom early in the morning. I heard the door open and close, the water running and then silence. I could almost picture her taking her pills and dropping dead on the bed.

She glances around to see if anyone's listening.

"It was okay. We didn't have sex."

"That's good."

"I've heard he doesn't like it too much. He's more into *other things*." Other things could be anything really. Strangling girls. Watching the news with them. Asking for blowjobs.

"Like?"

"He wanted to talk so we talked and then I played the piano for a while."

"What else?"

"He made me try a few dresses on, and looked at me while I did it. Though I may have hallucinated this part because he made me drink and I had taken a couple of downers before."

"You shouldn't mix."

"I know. Dr. Brooks warned me about 'having visions' and dreams that feel like they're real. But I wasn't dreaming."

"She once tried to give me a pill to 'wipe out my existential pessimism' saying that the effects could result in long, vivid nightmares."

"I've tried that actually. It does give you nightmares." She rests her head against the wall. "It was the thing that they gave us in the foster home."

I'm feeling really exhausted but I keep my head up and still. She rarely speaks of her foster home, and whenever she does, I must listen. It's not as if she has anyone else to talk to. She stares at her feet, her mouth curved in a sad smile.

"Pills are like men. The closer you get to them, the more they take from you. It's like living in the world in someone else's shadow and praying all day that that person's merciful."

The maids have started cleaning the Chatting Room. I can hear the vacuum behind us. Aura caresses the sapphire ring on her finger. One of Price's gifts.

"At least men are easier to control," she sighs.

"They are, to you."

I take her hand. It's cold and dry. She tightens her grip and suddenly comes closer, a scared look on her face.

"I have to tell you…" she whispers. "I've seen something in his room. Something about a secret organization they're trying to track down."

"What organization?"

"I don't know, something about women's rights. I think it has to do with the protests in the city." Her voice is so low that I'm reading her lips. "They're suspicious of everyone in here, they think some members are *inside* the Palace."

"Could it be?"

She shakes her head and draws away from me. "I don't know. I'll go now." She stands quickly, and her face goes back to normal: sweet, confident.

"Don't speak to anyone about this," she adds before hurrying away.

"Of course not," I say, but my words are barely audible even to myself. My heart hammers my chest. I look up. The sky is a perfect turquoise blue. I wonder what it would feel like to touch and shatter it.

I go to the photo studio to update my profile. I've avoided this place for a while because it's cold and stinks of fake—the smells of sweetened air freshener, deodorant and perfume are all mixed up together. The photographer, a man in his thirties with tattoos on his arms and a ponytail, is taking pictures of a Lover with shiny curls and big, round breasts called Amy. When he sees me standing by the door, he says, "Finally giving in on that profile update, uh?" Then he turns and shouts, "Get Iris ready!"

Before Evaluation, I refused to take pictures in my underwear for what the producers referred to as "the calendar." Victoria's photos are hanging on the walls of the studio. She's lying on the floor in high heels and lingerie, water pouring over her, soaking her hair and bra. Next to her, there's a picture of Bella eating spaghetti in a skimpy apron while tomato sauce drips all over her. "Such a natural shoot,"

Aura commented with a grim expression when the photos were framed.

A couple of Lara's assistants, young women with heavy makeup and long claw-like nails, take me to the changing rooms to do my hair. Through the open door I see Jared, a producer with gray hair and bushy eyebrows, come in to talk to the photographer.

"Is he going to stay here during the shoot?" I ask, my voice low, as the assistants tie my hair back. They nod. I step into lacy blue underwear and walk into the light of the studio. Jared frowns when he sees me. He has never really liked me. Once I heard him say that I'm too "challenging." It was around the time I tried to refuse the pills Dr. Brooks was giving me. "She'll stop being challenging, eventually," Price replied. "They all do."

"What about heels?" Jared asks. His voice is unpleasant, scratchy.

"I'm not wearing them."

"That's alright," the photographer intervenes, winking at me. "We'll do a more natural shoot."

For what feels like hours, he takes pictures of me sitting on stools, touching and re-touching my hair, dancing around, drinking champagne. When we're done, I wear the robe the assistant hands me while Jared looks at the photos. Because no one tells me what to do, I keep standing next to him, feeling useless.

"What's wrong with your thighs?" Jared asks me.

"Nothing's wrong with them."

His ears become red. He's aware of the cameras filming us and can't accept being contradicted by a Lover. I pity him for that.

"When I ask you what's wrong with something," he says, his voice rising, "you don't say 'nothing's wrong.' You say: 'maybe this is what's wrong? Or this? What can I do to improve?'"

I keep still. "I don't see what's wrong with my body. But if you do, feel free to photo shop it as much as you want."

"Yeah, we'll take some of this flesh out," the photographer says, removing a slice of my upper thighs with a click. Jared shakes his head.

"Go change," he orders me.

When I walk back to the Lovers' Area, a thick fog is rolling over the city. There seems to be no one around and, for a moment, I linger by the windows to watch the skyscrapers rise from the mist, lighthouses in the endless expanse of gray.

Back in my corridor, I hear the familiar sounds of soft laughter, toilets flushing, drunken snorting. I can't wait to clean myself, wash away the body makeup that clings to my legs like glue. I open the door of my room and slip out of my shoes. Then, I walk into the bathroom.

I fall onto my knees.

The water in the bathtub is red and is dripping on the floor.

There's a body in the water.

Her eyes are open but empty,

her arms like broken wings,

cuts run deep in her forearms.

It's Aura.

A PRETTY GIRL IN PRISON

The day of my capture, I was unconscious for hours. When I came to, I was in a silver van, handcuffed, the man with the tattoo of a snake around his neck sitting next to me. He was counting some cash, the paper crumpled in his hairy hands. Next to the driver was the short man, looking at me over his shoulder. When I looked back at him, he licked his lips vulgarly, and I thought of how it would feel to choke him. My hands on his large throat, his face purple, his mouth open, gasping for air.

We were driving towards the outskirts of the city as rain beat against the windowpanes, and I started praying. There are many different prisons in the Great States. "Detention centers" are for minor offences like children stealing at the market or old men begging on the street, "reform centers" for thieves, smugglers and killers. "Border homes" are prison camps where immigrants from beyond the Wall stay for months before being released, while "control and managements prisons" are labor camps where political prisoners are held, far away from the city. Anyone who insults or conspires against the Great Leader is sent to a control prison under the charge of "anti-state crimes." No one really knows what goes on in there, because once you're in a camp you never get out. Sentences for the CMP are for life.

I knew I hadn't offended the Great Leader by stealing but still, I prayed that I wasn't going to a control prison. I looked outside the window and made out a block cement building barely visible in the rain. I caught a glimpse of a sign on the side of the road: REFORM CENTER 101 FOR OUR GREAT LEADER, next to a faded and soaked poster of the president.

When I was brought in, everyone stared at me as if they had never seen a woman in their lives. There was a family waiting to visit an inmate, a black kid playing with little toy guards on the floor. In the corridor of cells, some women were lying wrapped up in dirty blankets, motionless. Others were staring through the bars.

"You afraid, pretty girl?" laughed the guard that was dragging me through the corridors. I shook my head. I felt hopeless. How could I escape such a heavily guarded place and go back to my family? Before leading me to my cell, the guard brought me to the common room of one of the prison units. He told me to get rid of everything except for my underwear, my socks and my T-shirt. He made me turn around and cough, then he searched my socks.

The room I was dragged into was small and had only a tiny window high up. My cellmate was a woman whose husband used to beat her. She had killed him, stabbing him with a kitchen knife when he had come home drunk one night and cracked her rib. She had big, muscular arms and a thick neck, but I wasn't really afraid of her.

One day, she went mad and started sobbing and undressing. I tried to calm her down before the guards could come for her, but she was eager to get rid of her striped uniform. Her eyes were closed and she was laughing while tears streamed down her face. She took the uniform off and I saw a big scar on her belly: brown, swollen, long. I felt something inside, splitting my own body open. I crammed my hands over my mouth; my stomach twisted inside me, making me sick. I kept imagining the wound open and raw, bloody and infectious. I slapped her across the face until she opened her eyes.

"Don't do that again," I said, then put her on the bunk bed. She fell asleep crying.

That's when I started having my stomachaches.

I steady myself, my hands on the sink. The stabbing pain in my stomach prevents me from breathing properly, as if someone's twisting a knife inside me.

"Aura," I say.

"Aura, it's okay."

"Aura?"

She doesn't reply, just lies in the water, her fingertips wrinkled. On the floor next to her, a sharp kitchen knife smeared with blood. I try to reach the bathtub but I feel too weak and I'm afraid I might faint. I crouch down next to the toilet and stare at Aura's hands then at my own. I'd slap her to wake her up, just as I did with my cellmate in prison, but Aura's body is too fragile. Crawling, I manage to turn on the camera stuck next to the sink.

"Help," I croak. "Aura isn't feeling too well."

I wait on the ground curved into a ball, my hands sunk into my abdomen. Someone knocks on the door and enters. I hear Mia shout then other steps, fast. Other shouts. I drag myself closer to the tub, to protect Aura's soaked body from them. I take her hand into mine, holding the rim of the bath with the other. I see Caroline, Margaret, Adam and two guards moving too quickly for my eyes to follow.

"Oh God, she's dead. SHE'S DEAD!" someone shouts.

"Iris, let her go!"

I wish they would shut up. I wish they would do something. A guard walks closer and moves Aura's arm so that the long, bloody cuts on her skin are more visible under the light.

"Don't touch her! Don't fucking touch her!" I shout but they're trying to drag me away.

Adam kneels in front of me. "What happened?" His hand is on my arm; the snake tattoos that stretch on his fingers wrap around my wrist, paralyzing me.

"Get her a doctor, she's not feeling well," I say.

Caroline gives me a pitiful look. "Iris—" she starts.

"No! Get her a doctor!"

I shout until my voice cracks and my stomach hurts so much that I faint.

It's the pain in my stomach that wakes me up. I'm in the Infirmary, where the doctor does monthly checks to see if anything's wrong with our health. I've never liked this room. There are no windows and the light is cold. I try to stand but my arms are hooked up to a drip. Dr. Brooks is sitting on a chair next to the bed, typing on her tablet. To my right, a girl with a swollen lip is staring into the middle distance. I blink a couple of times before I realize it is Mia. Her cheeks are streaked with tears.

"Mia..." I start.

A nurse appears and hastily draws a curtain between Mia's bed and mine. Dr. Brooks raises her eyes. Her hair is tied back and she has more wrinkles than usual, or maybe it's just the light.

"How are you feeling?" she asks me.

"Aura..." I start, but Dr. Brooks shakes her head. My

mouth is dry. I feel like I'm sweating so I wipe my forehead with my sleeve.

"I'm so sorry." I almost choke on my own words.

"It's not your fault." Her tone is calm and patient as usual, the tone of someone speaking to a retarded child. "I have already talked to the doctor. You need to lie down and rest. You have a stress-induced ulcer."

"My medicines?" I manage to croak.

"The nurse will give them to you. Now rest, you will be fine soon."

I wonder how I will be fine now that Aura's gone but I close my eyes and try to do as Dr. Brooks says.

I didn't stay long in prison. Apparently, a pretty girl like me didn't belong in such an ugly place. I spent a couple of months taking out trash to the prison yard and working in the laundry, the tasks that were assigned to me.

Then one day two guards came for me and told me it was time to go. My cellmate had told me that prisoners were often uprooted without any warning. But with me it was different. They brought me to the visiting area, where a man with very white teeth was smiling. It was Nelson Price.

"Hello Iris, do you want to sit down?" he asked. As if I had a choice. I sat down. I had my striped uniform on and hadn't washed my hair in a while. He was wearing a bright coral suit, which looked completely out of place among the grayness of the prison. From the way he looked at me, he made me feel aware of my own filth.

"You don't need to be afraid of me," he said, his smile unfaltering. "I'm here to get you out of this mess."

That's how I ended up in the Golden Palace.

Price's smile hasn't changed a bit since that day in prison. He's sitting opposite me in his apartment, in a large magenta armchair, giving me his dashing grin as though it were the most charming thing in the world. Next to him, on a yellow sofa, are Jared the producer, smoking a cherry-flavored electronic cigarette, and Dr. Brooks. I notice that there are no posters of the president in here, only a large, framed picture of Price and Michael hung above the armchair, looking down at me. I sit up. I still feel weak because of all the painkillers they put into my body but I try not to collapse on the floor.

"Do you know why you're here, Iris?" Price asks.

"No."

He scoffs. "I thought you were chosen for this show because you were smart."

You chose me because you thought I was pretty.

"So?" His smile has dropped; he's getting impatient.

"I'm here because Aura died," I say staring at a spot right next to Price's face.

No one speaks. Jared keeps smoking his cigarette, the disgusting smell of cherry filling the room like gas. I look outside the window: the sky is clear blue, and there are some stars in it. It's already late evening. I've lost track of time. Price starts tapping his fingers on the arms of his chair.

"Yes, that's why you're here," he says. "And how are you feeling?"

"Better."

He stops tapping. "You know that we can't afford to have a sick Lover in here." He looks suddenly dangerous. I'm amazed at the speed with which his features can shift from fake smiles to homicidal looks.

"Of course. I'm not sick."

"You're aware that Aura killed herself because she was sick?"

"She didn't look sick to me, sir," I say. Wrong answer. Price sits back, staring at me like a killer does before slicing his victim into two.

"She didn't look sick to *you*," he repeats slowly.

Dr. Brooks intervenes with her soothing voice, "She was sick, Iris. That's why she killed herself. You can do nothing about that."

I look in her direction but in my mind I'm still watching the sky. It seems so thin and delicate; I could just put my hand through it. And what would there be on the other side? Just darkness, emptiness.

It's Jared's voice that speaks this time. "Soon you will have to go to *The Late Night Show* and you'll be asked about Aura." He puts the stinking cigarette aside and raises his voice, "Are you listening to us, Iris?"

"She's taken many painkillers," Dr. Brooks says. "She is tired."

"She can be dying for all I care. When the producers speak, she will listen."

"I'm listening," I say.

"Good," Jared says. "When you're on the show and they ask you about Aura, what will you say?"

"That she killed herself," I recite. I avoid saying that, if Aura really wanted to kill herself, she would have overdosed, as she did many times in the past.

"That's right. Because she did." I suppose he keeps repeating it until I believe it too.

"Can I go now?" I ask.

No one replies. Jared starts smoking again. Price stands up calmly and turns on the TV on the wall. There's a video on pause; Price presses play. On screen, I see myself in the ballroom, glitter shining on my cheekbones, my dark eyebrows making me look strong and resolute. When Price claims that "girls who think too much do silly things, incidents," I hear myself say: "Incidents like what?" and then, with a challenging expression: "And then they kill themselves." I notice that they didn't select any close-up of Price's face, but only of the president, who seems very amused with the little scene I was making. I look down, my head hurting.

"Did you know that Aura wanted to kill herself?" Price asks.

"No."

"I thought you'd say so. Then tell me, when was the last time you saw her before she died?"

I think of the two of us on the terrace, Aura whispering that she had seen something in the president's apartments.

"On the terrace," I say. "After the grades were announced."

"You know cameras don't work there," Jared says. "What did you talk about?"

"The grades. Her past. She told me about the foster home she grew up in."

"And why would she do that?" Dr. Brooks asks. "Aura had a troubled childhood but didn't like to talk about it." *As if you knew. As if she told you one damned thing about her past.*

"I think she said she had a bad dream about it and wanted to talk."

"I see," Dr. Brooks says. She turns to Price, who nods slightly. "Go, Iris, get some rest and go back to work when you feel better."

Jared stands and opens the door for me. I'm dismissed. I look back at Price's face one more time before leaving. It has turned a mottled purple; his ears are red. Yet, he's still smiling. It is frightening to look at.

Extract from *The Silver Times*

"Lover Found Dead in the Golden Palace. What Happened on The President?"

by Nicholas Cole

Aura Johnson, renowned in the States for her role in *The President* show, has died at the age of 24. Last night the popular Lover was discovered lying in a bathtub, her wrists slit, a knife on the bathroom floor. She was already dead when fellow Lover Iris found her and called for help. The cameras had been turned off so there is no footage available from the Surveillance Room. This has led to a debate on whether cameras in the Lovers' bathrooms should be compulsory again, as they were before Lover Martha made her appeal years ago—before killing herself with a razor.

The Great Leader's forensic team concluded that, "Aura's death was most certainly caused by bleeding and that the mode of death is suicide." Vice president and producer Nelson Price released a statement on the tragic event: "Fame is hard to handle, especially if you're on reality TV. That is why we have a trusted therapist in the Palace, Dr. Jane Brooks, who supports and checks on Lovers. But some women can't handle fame, it's an inherent weakness."

"Aura was wonderful," Brooks added, "but her mental health was already fragile before she joined the show. She had a troubled past, many ghosts she could not face. We did everything in our power, but eventually we couldn't help her."

"Protests Spread in New Town. Our Great Leaders Request Military Intervention."

by Peter Corbett

Protests against our Great Country have quickly spread in other areas of New Town in the past few days. The demonstrators have become more and more violent and have now been officially labeled as "a threat to the city and the Great Leaders." Sixty more people have been taken to the CMPs. More guards have been stationed in every district and are currently rounding up suspects for interrogations. A list of names of wanted agitators has been printed on signs in the main streets of the city. In the meantime, the Leaders ask everyone, especially in Gildedtown, to avoid leaving their homes late at night.

MURDERERS

Aura and I tried to run away once. We planned everything in the shower, whispering to each other while our hair was plastered to our faces. Actually, I planned everything. Aura tried to change my mind many times—"they'll catch us, they have hidden cameras everywhere"—but when she realized I would do it with or without her, she promised she would come with me. There wasn't much for her outside the Palace, but I'd told her that we could leave New Town and go west, past the Great Cities and into the unknown plains. We would open a diner in some small godforsaken town where it would be impossible for the guards to find us, where posters of the Great Leader would be scarce and faded. My mother and sister would join us, help with the cooking and cleaning, while Aura and I would also sing and play for the customers. We rejoiced in our silly little plan, thought about it before we went to bed.

We knew of a Lover who'd escaped. She came from prison like me, and knew how to beat people up. The story we heard goes that she initiated sex with a guard in the club's toilets in the early hours of the morning, when the cameras had just stopped working. When he started losing control she tied him up, stuffed his mouth with her underwear and took his clothes. The underwear thing is a detail Lovers enjoyed talking about, as if it was very amusing. The guard was found just one hour later, but the Lover had already stolen a van and driven away. We were sure she couldn't make it, that she would be found and punished at any moment. But no one's found her, not yet. I like to think she's safe, somewhere far from here.

Aura and I couldn't do the same thing because guards weren't easily fooled after that incident. We chose one rainy afternoon when Price and the producers were busy and we went to the basement to look for Aura's maid. Her name is Gabriela. *Was.* We found her in the empty dormitory of the maids, a place with a low ceiling and many grayish bunk beds. And no cameras.

"That Visitor is following me again, it's exhausting," Aura told Gabriela. "Can we hide in here for a while, Gabi?"

Gabi wasn't stupid and must have suspected something, but she nodded. As soon as she left, mumbling about vacuuming the Lovers' Area, we took two gray shabby uniforms from a wardrobe and changed into them. We knew there was an exit somewhere in the basement because Aura had seen a map of the Palace in Price's room. We just had to find it. We looked around the bathrooms and kitchen, checked each emergency exit in the corridors. Finally, we found the way out. It was a small door close to the corridors that lead to the Club. We looked for cameras but didn't see any: no one bothered to check what the maids were doing in here.

We opened the door and glimpsed at the big parking lot behind the Palace for a second. The air was cold and there was the smell of gasoline, our promise of freedom.

Then someone grabbed us and pulled us back. The door slipped through our fingers. I felt Aura struggling next to me and I kicked the man who was holding us. There was a groan and Aura freed herself. She sprinted towards the door without realizing I was still held back.

The guard shouted, "Leave and she dies." His voice was cold like glass shards. Aura turned. *Go, go*, I wanted to say, but I could feel a gun to my head. The guard pushed me to the ground. I could see Aura's feet, still on the floor. *Leave, run now*. But she didn't move.

"I'll stay," she said quietly. "Leave her be." Her voice wasn't shaking.

We were brought to Price's office. I could already picture myself going back to prison or worse, given to the guards. But Aura asked Price to be alone with him. I was quickly dismissed and waited outside the door, my heart in my hands. I heard Aura crying loudly but I couldn't hear what she was saying. When she joined me outside, she gave me a sad, little smile.

"We're alright," she said.

Turns out the guard was sacrificed and so was Gabriela. Gabi had betrayed us but Aura had managed to turn the whole story around. The exit near the club was walled up the day after and no one talked about our attempted escape.

I don't know what Aura told Price. I don't know how she managed to get us out of that mess. All I know is she could've left, but she stayed, because of me.

Mia shakes me until I wake up.

"Iris?"

"Yes?" I mumble. The morning light is white and blinding. I'm shivering.

"Are you okay?" She has a troubled expression on her face; her lip's still a bit swollen, purple. "You were shouting: leave, run."

I wipe my forehead. "Just a nightmare."

"Maybe you should take your medicines," she says handing me a couple of pills. I put them on my tongue and, as soon as she's gone, spit them out in my hand. There's one for the stomach and one that's meant to knock me out. I swallow the first one and flush the other one down the toilet.

Then I go back to sleep.

I stay in bed and look at journalists talking about suicide prevention onscreen. They interview some people about PTSD and recovery from attempted suicide. They list things that people should be careful about. They say that if you experience anxiety, depression, addiction, eating disorders or self-harm, you should see a therapist.

I look at the president saying that Aura was one of the best Lovers on the show. He calls her "a gentle young woman, beautiful and inspiring." He's reading from a tablet, in case he forgets her name again.

I look at Bella crying to the cameras and saying, "No one expected it. It's so sad." She chooses the word *sad*. She doesn't say tragic, dreadful, awful.

I stand, wobble to the bathroom and put two fingers down my throat. The vomit is yellow and sickly. I wipe my face and brush my teeth until my gums get sore.

Back in bed, I watch a group of women with banners on screen, screaming and marching in the streets. There's a girl with a leather jacket and a shaven head. A woman with gray hair, shouting. A mother with a baby in her arms and a shawl around her head. They're raising their fists in the air, rebellious. The camera focuses on the banners briefly: MURDERERS. MONSTERS. SUICIDE CAN'T BE USED AS A COVER UP. AURA WAS KILLED.

Smart of Price to show these banners. A Great Leader doesn't crush revolts. A Great Leader must be loved and supported. So what does he do? He turns the protesters into liars. And where do liars go? Lies are a serious anti-state crime, an unforgivable political offense worthy of a life spent in a control and management prison.

Soon Price (and every newspaper and news channel with him) will say: "Why do these women spread lies about our Great Leader? This is the proof that women are too emotional, they must be kept at bay. Leaders are merciful but only up to a point. Let me give these people some advice: go home, be safe, take care of your children."

What he won't say: *Be safe before someone hurts you. Before we stop tolerating your insolent, useless uprisings. Before we root you out, like weeds, and feed you to the pigs.*

I try to empty my mind and relax my body as if I was taking a downer. Clouds gather in the sky, drifting like crumpled sheets of paper. Outside, the air must be sticky and wet. Aura's face is already fading; her hands aren't. They were little hands, like petals, smooth and delicate. They cupped perfectly around my cheeks. They were warm. I wonder why, when we lose someone, some things die away with them and others don't. The face always dissolves first, but the body lives on and so do voices, words.

"I can still hear dad talking, but I can't remember what his face looked like." My sister's voice pops up in my head. "Do you think I can't remember because I didn't love him enough?" *No, it's his fault. It's because he left us too soon.*

My father disappeared one winter morning when I'd just turned twelve. Men leave nothing behind when they walk away, except for broken hearts and angry tears. And unfounded feelings of guilt. I woke, washed my face in the sink and noticed that all his things were gone. I ran outside in the cold, shouting his name, as if he could still come back. I spent the day wandering around Chinatown, asking people if they had seen him: old men with blackened teeth, tattooed women outside nightclubs, busy waiters at every stall from the Food Centers, as the smell of chicken noodle and salted fish filled my nostrils. Rain was pouring over the streets and stalls, flooding the pipes, soaking the dirty curtains of the shops. When I finally got home, my feet were cold and wet, my face burning. My mother was back from work, making some tea to warm Lily. My sister was very little, and too skinny. She used to follow me everywhere, and as soon as I sat on the bed, drenched, she curled up next to me. My clothes dampened her face.

"Where have you been?" my mother asked angrily, even though I could tell she knew. She had been crying too, her eyes were puffy.

"Looking for dad."

"You won't find him. And even if you did, he's not coming back." She poured some tea in a cup for Lily, then wrapped me in a blanket and scrubbed my feet until they got warmer. "Sometimes you lose something and you never get it back."

Why is it always so hard to understand that?

It's late in the evening when someone knocks on my door. Slivers of a cold, gray light stripe the floor. I stand, stepping on each stripe, and make my way to the door. When I open it, the bright light of the corridor creeps inside, unwelcome. Silhouetted against it is Theo Droit.

"Hello, Iris," he says. He's still wearing his business clothes, which look somehow cheaper than the other politicians'. "I was wondering if you wanted to take a walk around. I'm in need of some fresh air." He's referring to the terrace. Does he know there are no cameras there?

"Alright," I say. I take a warm jacket, fling it around my shoulders and step out of the room with him. He walks slowly, which is unnerving. I struggle to slow down my pace to be next to him.

"I heard what happened," he says. "It's everywhere on the news. I'm sorry."

"I know."

"How's your stomach?"

"It's fine now. It's happened before and I'm still alive."

"Is it related to stress?" He eyes me with a curious look that I don't like. What does he care?

"Could be," I shrug. He doesn't insist. We reach the terrace that leads back into the Chatting Room, the very same where Aura and I talked for the last time before she was killed. I sip in the view of the city, shining skyscrapers against a dark blue sky.

"I want to ask you a question," he starts, "but I need to know that you're going to be discreet first."

"I'm very discreet."

"Good."

He stays silent for a while and I'm wondering whether I should kiss him, or entertain him in any way, when he speaks again. "How long have you been here?"

"Three years. Is this the question?"

He ignores me. "Three years is a lot. In all this time has any other Lover died, apart from your friend?"

Yes. "Not that I remember."

"You'd remember if something like that happened. Do you feel safe in the Palace?"

I look at him. His question could be a trap but it's impossible to tell because his expression is impenetrable.

"Why would you ask that?"

"A Lover just died." He doesn't say *committed suicide*. "And before coming to the Palace, I met with a young woman who'd left the show two years ago, maybe you remember her?" I raise my eyebrows. "Her name is Sophie. She had been diagnosed with bipolar disorder. I went to see her with a journalist from *The Silver Times*, and she said some pretty scary stuff about how things run here."

I remain silent. Of course I remember Sophie. She was chosen for Evaluation during my first year in the Palace, but left the competition after the first week under unclear circumstances. I remember Bella saying that Sophie was "too unhinged."

"Do you know where Sophie is now?" he asks.

"No." And that is the truth.

"Neither do I. She disappeared. She gave the interview and two days later her apartment was found empty."

"What are you trying to say?"

"I think you know what I'm saying. Do you know anything about why Aura died?"

"She wasn't happy I guess," I say.

Theo raises his eyebrows. "You don't believe she killed herself."

"I believe what the producers tell me to believe."

"Did she know anything she wasn't supposed to? Anything that could be labeled as state secrets?" Is he really asking me this?

"I wouldn't know."

"Do you know about the WLL?"

"What?"

"The Women's Lives Liberation movement? Protests have spread all around the city in the past few days, you must have seen it on TV."

"Ah, yes."

"They think Aura was murdered because she knew something. They also talk about how Lovers are abused in here. They mention Sophie and other girls who disappeared and also a video of you having a panic attack in the Palace."

"That video was removed from the Internet."

"It was, yes, but that's not the point. I know you have seen things and I want you to tell me about it."

"Or?"

For a moment, he seems confused. "What do you mean?"

"Or what will you do?"

"I'm not threatening you, I hope you realize that."

"It doesn't sound like it."

He takes a deep breath. "I see you around the Palace, Iris. There's something about you… you try to hide it but you can't. And whatever it is, if you could tell me, I might be able to help."

I look at him. He's not joking. What does he know about fear? What does he know about consequences? Men like him are children, they're free to do as they please. They live in a bubble and outside the bubble there's me and many other girls like me, who not only clean up their mess, but also can't commit mistakes of our own. Because when we do, we can't take them back.

"It's better if you leave," I say coldly.

He seems surprised, hurt. "What are you going to do if I leave? I can protect you if you speak to me."

"Leave," I repeat.

He gives me one last frustrated look, then walks away, leaving me alone on the terrace.

I take a deep breath.

I don't need anyone's protection.

FISH TANK

The president has announced that there's a party by the pool tonight, "to distract the people who watch the show at home from the horrible protests that terrorized New Town in the past few days." "Exotic costumes are expected," he added with a wink.

The last time Lovers had to wear exotic costumes my face was covered in sticky glitter and my boobs were practically out. "It's an *Eastern* design," Lara had said excitedly, touching the purple cups for breasts covered in pearls and sequins. "I thought women in the East weren't even allowed to show their faces?" Aura had asked.

I push the memory away. I'm drinking wine in the Chatting Room even though it's only five o'clock, and my head feels placid like a domesticated pet. Outside, the sky is a featureless expanse of steel blue like the sea in the summer evening. Cameras are on, the green light blinking at us next to the poster of the president. Caroline is reading a book, huddled in one corner of the sofa. I wonder whether she just steals them or someone gives them to her. Whatever the case, production doesn't seem to complain that she reads books while cameras are working. Or maybe they do, but Caroline just doesn't care. Victoria is having a heated discussion with Margaret, as one of Lara's assistants takes her measurements for her costume. When the assistant wraps the meter around Victoria's waist she sucks her belly in, barely breathing. I see her ribs, stark against the pale skin.

"You heard what Price said," Victoria breathes out. "Some people just can't handle it." The assistant kneels, holding the meter next to Victoria's legs.

"Do you really think she killed herself like that?" Margaret asks, her voice sharp. "She didn't seem to me like someone who'd do it."

Bella, who has been brushing her hair by the window, puts the brush down, her body suddenly stiff.

"There was a knife next to the tub," she says.

"You give her too much credit," Victoria hisses, ignoring Bella. "She's dead because she was weak." She never liked Aura too much. Victoria is one of those women who can't stand being second and needs to be the center of attention all the time. Aura took that from her. She also believes that people who kill themselves insult their Great Country. Because they didn't CARE FOR THEIR GREAT LEADERS enough, they only cared about their own suffering.

"Don't talk like that about someone who's never done you wrong," Bella says, her voice sounding cautious. "Anyways, we all need to move on, forget about this."

"I thought you'd be happy she's gone, Bella," Caroline comments without raising her eyes from her book. "Now there's only five people instead of six."

"Wow. You're so mean," Bella says. She tries to look outraged but the result is pitiful. I wish she could see herself in a mirror.

"Didn't you say, just the other day, how hard it would be to win with Aura around?" Caroline says, turning a page.

"Oh shut up, Caroline, you should really learn to shut up," Victoria says angrily, almost stepping on the assistant's fingers. "You always have an opinion on everything but guess what, we don't want to hear it. You're so..." she frowns, looking for the right word to express her deep disapproval, "unladylike."

Caroline raises her eyes with a sly smile. "And you're fucking useless."

"What about Iris then?" Bella intervenes again. "For all we know, she might have killed Aura herself. Do you know that she was in prison before coming to the Palace? And what about the video?"

I put my empty glass aside. "You do realize I'm here, right?"

Bella looks at me and there's so much loathing in her eyes that it hurts. The worst part is that to her, her hatred is self-righteous. She's competitive and works hard to gain her place on this stupid show, while what on earth have I ever done to deserve my position?

"Aura was weak," Victoria repeats, pouring herself a glass of wine. "And she did what weak people do."

I stand quickly, catch hold of her wrist and slap the glass out of her hand. Wine spills everywhere and the glass shatters. Everyone drops silent. Victoria yanks her arm free and shouts, "What's your problem? Calm down, take some pills."

"You should watch your mouth when you talk about Aura," I say calmly.

The assistant takes a step back and winces: there's a shard stuck under her shoe. I kneel quickly and try to help but she runs away, mumbling something that sounds like "Lara will know about this."

"I told you she's out of control," Bella says out loud, walking out of the room. The others follow. Before shutting the door behind her, Victoria turns and gives me one of those looks you give to madmen harassing people on the street.

I huddle down and start collecting the shards on the carpet. They're cold and sharp against my palms. I wish I could just squeeze them until blood comes out. I wish I could show my bloody hands to Bella and Victoria, and tell them, "See what you did." There's a meanness somewhere inside me, shouting, asking me to do the wrong thing.

But I'd rather die than give Victoria the satisfaction of calling me "weak," so I throw the shards in the dustbin without cutting myself. When I look up, the president is staring at me from the poster, smiling.

Fuck you.

I knock on Caroline's bedroom door but there's no reply. I open it anyway: the blinds are pulled down so it's dark inside, with streaks of light poking through the slats. It feels very hot, stuffy, as if the air hasn't been cleared in some time. Caroline is lying on her stomach, her elbows propped on the pillow, a cigarette between her lips glowing in the semi-darkness. Without turning, she must know it's me because she kicks her feet against the mattress and says, "What is it?"

"I need a favor."

She sits up, looks at me with sudden curiosity.

"Go on."

"I need to speak to Adam, the guy from the propaganda department."

She frowns and turns the light on. I see the freckles on her arms and shoulders.

"He's probably in post-production now. Why do you want to see him?"

"Just take me to him, will you?"

The post-production studio isn't too far from the Lovers' Area. To get inside, we have to ring the bell next to a security door. It takes a minute before the door opens. When it finally does, Michael is waiting for us on the other side. I automatically take a step back.

"Aren't you supposed to be entertaining some old man?" he asks, grinning.

"Very funny," says Caroline. She doesn't care about him, about his arrogance; I envy her for that. "Can we see Adam?"

Michael rolls his eyes, as if Caroline has asked him the same question many times in the past. "And who else…"

He leads us inside. The studio has many rows of desks where men are working, sitting on black leather chairs. We walk past them, following the line of potted plants that leads to a big room at the end of the studio.

Michael opens the door and says, "Your bitch's here, man. And she brought company." Caroline ignores him. Adam is lying on the sofa, looking at some Lover's profile on a huge television set. He stands when he sees us. Someone calls Michael from the editing room and he disappears again.

"We already talked about this," Adam says as soon as Michael is gone. He's looking at Caroline, quietly, as though I wasn't here. Caroline's face shrinks into an apologetic expression that looks wrong on her.

"I know, but Iris wanted to talk to you."

"What are you doing with Julian?" Adam asks her.

I step back and clear my throat.

"Stay," Caroline orders me before I can say anything.

Adam takes the remote control on the sofa. The screen turns white and then Caroline appears, fighting with Julian. Her hair is wet, her eyes puffy. Julian tells her she's fractious; she tells him she doesn't really care about him.

"What's this about?" Adam asks.

"You know I don't like him."

"You *have to* like him," he says, pausing the video. "It's your job."

Caroline's nostrils flare wide. I feel out of place.

"Ask him what you need, Iris," Caroline says grabbing my arm. Her grip is tight and her palm sweaty against my elbow. Adam looks at me as if he just noticed I was there. I look back. I wish Caroline would leave, but after witnessing her little moment of intimacy I can't tell her *I* want some privacy.

"I want to see the footage from the night Aura died," I say. I keep my voice calm and firm, to remind him that this is not a request, but a right of mine. Adam's expression remains blank.

"You heard her, give her what she wants." Caroline's voice is harsh now, resentful.

Adam ignores her. He sits back on the sofa, slowly. "There's no footage from that night."

My heart is pounding but I speak with indifference, "Why is that?"

"The cameras weren't working."

"Isn't it a bit suspicious?" I ask.

Adam shrugs. "I don't have it. I can't help you. If you don't believe me, ask someone else."

"Let's go," Caroline says to me. I linger but she takes my arm and drags me outside. We walk away from the studio, the editors watching us as we pass, touching our bodies with their burning stares.

I arrive at the party alone after an hour with Lara and Mia at the Beauty Center. Mia's lip wasn't swollen anymore but she had dark circles under her eyes and seemed skinnier than ever. I tried to ask her some questions but she wouldn't talk.

A black steel gazebo with glass walls has been built on the terrace to protect the party from the rainstorm that's drenching the city. Maids have set tables and potted plants around the pool. Posters of the president, Price and a couple of other politicians have been glued to the glass walls. POWER AND PRIVILEGE. CARE FOR YOUR GREAT LEADERS. I walk past the tables, looking around, trying to breathe properly in my *exotic* red-feathered mini dress. Most of the Lovers are here, drinks in hand, wearing weird costumes with feathers and sparkles, breasts and cheekbones glistening, nails sparkling with colored gems. Scattered among them like bees in a flower garden are the European politicians and some of the producers. Bella and Sebastián are huddled together near the pool. She's wearing a waist-hugging nude dress with drops of glass hanging from her sleeves. Sebastián looks proud of his conquest, smiling around and showing her off as if she were a dog.

I take a large martini from a passing maid, listening to the sound of rain against the glass walls. A soft music is playing in the background, the type of music that makes small talk easier and safer. I'm about to find someone to talk to, when Adam joins me.

"I was looking for you," he says. He's clean-shaven, the tattoos on his arms covered under the sleeves of his white shirt.

I finger my necklace, feeling each gem. "Why?"

"I didn't say this before, but I'm sorry about Aura."

"As if you care."

Unexpectedly, he takes my arm and leads me closer to the speakers. Even if the music's louder here, he keeps his voice low.

"Listen, about what happened before in post-production… the things me and Caroline said…"

"I won't tell anyone, if that's what you're worried about. Go on with your dangerous secret romance," I whisper through gritted teeth. I finish my martini then take the drink from his hands and finish that too. I hand both glasses to him.

"I'm not a waiter," Adam says.

"Right, you're an assistant."

I place the glasses on a table myself and step away from him but he grabs my arm. His face is close to mine; he looks older than he is from up close.

"They're saying that you're losing control. That Aura's death has hurt you and that production has to keep an eye on you."

"So that's what you're doing, isn't it? Keeping an eye on me."

He lets me go. "You want that footage so badly?"

I look back at him, surprised. "I thought you said you didn't have it."

"I can find it for you but you have to work with Theo Droit. Entertain him and do the things he asks you to."

"Why should I trust you?" I ask sarcastically. "You say you have the footage and then go to Price and tell him I asked for it."

"Your sister's part of the WLL protests, did you know that?"

I wince. "How do you—"

"I'm not threatening you. She's at home with your mother now, she hasn't been caught yet."

"She's safe," I whisper.

"For now. I'll try to keep an eye on her. But you go to Theo, talk to him."

"Why Theo?"

"Smile now," Adam says cutting me off. "The Great Leader's here."

Out of the corner of my eye I become aware of Price and Michael entering the gazebo. I do as Adam says, even though the smile feels fake on my face, like a piece of puzzle that doesn't quite fit.

"Enjoy your night," Adam says, winking before leaving. I remain alone, rooted in my spot gaping like a dead fish. When Michael's eyes find me from afar, I hurry away from the speakers, my heart pounding in my chest. *Lily is safe.*

Theo is sitting with Julian and Caroline, eating from trays with silvery fish, oysters and tartare. Caroline seems annoyed when I take the empty seat next to her but doesn't say anything. She fumbles to find a cigarette and lights it. Julian's arm is on her shoulder and I'm afraid she might butt out her cigarette on his hand in a sudden fit of rage.

"Look who decided to join us," Julian says. His smile is unfriendly. I can't help but look at the fish's blank eyes in his plate. They're round, shiny and silvery.

"Let's walk around the pool," I tell Theo. He looks perplexed but stands and follows me, leaving Caroline and

Julian behind. In the watery world of the gazebo, our bodies, with their bright costumes, look like fish in a tank.

"Adam came to talk to me," I say.

"Have you changed your mind?" Theo asks. It's unnerving the way he asks questions, without being specific, without waiting for an actual answer. Because he doesn't get to be the only mysterious one, I stand on the tips of my toes and brush my lips against his. He takes my shoulders in his hands and kisses me back, while the music grows quieter, and the chatter around us unthreatening.

It's very cold on the empty terrace and the air smells like the sea. Everyone's gone inside, except for Theo and me. Most of the clouds are gone now, and a pale, frail moon is visible. It seems close enough to touch.

How funny the stories we tell ourselves are. As everyone left and I stayed behind with Theo, I almost felt happy. How romantic, I thought, as the rain kept hammering against the glass walls of the gazebo, blurring everything.

But the truth is, I don't want to be touched tonight, and I'm afraid that my treacherous heart, beating too loud, will give me away. The thin line that runs between what people see and what they can't see, what unfolds outside and what breaks inside. Tomorrow on the show I will look glamorous and lucky and maybe even I will convince myself that the night was blissful. But now I want to run away, to shout that I'm free. I want to go back to my room and sleep by myself, but it's impossible.

When I go back to the Lovers' Area, it's early morning and the camera lights have turned red. Caroline is standing in the semi-darkness, rummaging through the kitchen drawers.

Except for her, the area feels empty and quiet. The feeble glow of dawn casts long outlines on the floor; Caroline's shadow is clear on the carpet, black and sharp-edged.

"Oh, it's you," she says when I shut the door behind me. She's wearing a white, sleeveless cotton onesie that makes her look like a child.

"Can't sleep?" I ask.

"I never sleep." The onesie is unbuttoned at the top, and I see her small, white breasts. She must be searching for a cigarette.

"I was thinking before… why did Bella say you were in prison?" She speaks as if it wasn't five in the morning and we were just resuming a conversation from a minute ago.

"Because I was," I say. "She probably thinks I killed someone. Like murder's the only reason why people are locked up in a reform center."

"Right. Though Bella doesn't strike me as someone with little imagination."

"She's not. She just hates me."

Caroline laughs. She finds a cigarette in the silverware drawer and sits on the floor. She is barefoot, the golden polish on her nails shining. I'm waiting for her to ask me why me and Bella aren't friends anymore, but she says, "How was prison then?"

"Bad," I say sitting beside her. "I stayed only a couple of months, then Price came to bring me here."

"Price?" she asks. "So you didn't audition or anything?"

"Do people really audition? I've never met anyone who did."

"Some do."

"Did you?"

She rests her head against the wall. "Not exactly." I stay silent, waiting for her to go on, but she smokes, looking at the ceiling.

"Do you know what the Safe Centers are?" Caroline asks after a while.

"Where volunteers take care of homeless people in the Great Cities. Is that where you're from?"

She nods. "When I was young my mom worked for a man. His name was Mike." She inhales from her cigarette for too long and coughs.

"Mike," I repeat.

"Yes. We lived in Chinatown. During the day, my mom worked in a coffee shop. But during the night, I don't know what she did. I mean, now I can imagine, but I didn't know at the time. Mike always came to pick her up and brought her back in the morning. After a while, we needed more money and we moved into his apartment."

"How old were you?"

"Twelve." She puts out her cigarette in an empty cup before going on.

"Soon Mike was broke too. My mom loved him and kept giving him everything. Then one day he said he needed more girls and suggested I started working too. I guess he was also working with some reality TV scouts. He was desperate to make money in any way at that point. My mother cried and begged and humiliated herself in every way possible." Caroline frowns, as though thinking of her mother like that bothered her more than anything. "So I told her we had to leave. She couldn't. Mike had promised that he would find someone else and she believed him. So I said to her that if she didn't want to come I would leave by myself. She said okay because she didn't really believe it. She believed Mike but didn't believe me."

"But you left."

"Yes. The next morning I took a bus to the other side of town and found a Safe Center. Mike had mentioned it in the past so I thought I might check it out. It was huge, completely built underground, and volunteers took care of people in need. There were refugees who needed to hide after the building of the Wall, women running away from their husbands, young men in trouble, orphans. I was happy there, I was useful."

"And your mom?" I ask.

"She found me after a while. She was so sick, I'd never seen her like that. She'd started taking Mike's drugs. She was never strong. She came to the Center for help and died there."

"I'm sorry."

"It's okay. I was safe in the Center, safer than I'd ever been with her."

"That's sad."

"It's just a fact. Then one day the guards came into the Center and destroyed everything. They thought we were harboring some rioters. When our leaders convinced them that there was no harm in what we were doing, the guards said the Center could remain, only if checked every month and if it provided Lovers for *The President*."

"I grew up watching our show, but I never wondered how Lovers were chosen. The guards started picking girls from the crowd. Most of them were underage. I mean, I was too, but those girls were not volunteers, they were just helpless. No one noticed me. I was in a corner, trying to calm this baby down; it wouldn't stop crying. Then another volunteer pointed at me, this stupid asshole who hated me just because

I wouldn't sleep with him. 'She's pretty,' he shouted. He said it like being pretty was a crime."

"I had this shitty apron on that was stained with fat and hadn't been washed in a long time, I still remember that. A guard asked me if the baby was mine and I said no because it wasn't. Maybe I should've said yes but I couldn't understand much of what was happening. The guard told the others to take me instead of the girl they were holding. They took us to the office of some TV producer. Some girls were crying and complaining but I kept my mouth shut. The producer liked me and said I would do for *The President*. He sent all the others back to the Center. And that was the end of it."

"That's a pretty sad story to tell before going to bed," I say.

She laughs bitterly, takes my hand and looks straight into my eyes. A week ago, I would've felt intimidated.

"You know, I really envied what you and Aura had," she says. "Female friendship is never easy, especially in this place."

Opening up to me seems normal to her, easy.

"If I think about her," I say, "I feel guilty. Like I should've done more."

"It's normal to feel that way when somebody you care about dies. But it doesn't mean it's true."

"One time we tried to run away. We were almost there and she could've left, but she stayed." I don't know why I'm telling her this.

"You would have done the same."

Would I? I never thought about it.

"It's not your fault Aura died," Caroline says. "You know that right?"

There's a light in her face, but also toughness, resilience. Now I see that, though different, she reminds me of Aura in a sense. She's like one of those stones I once stole from a villa in Gildedtown. They looked gray and ordinary in the shadows, but when put under the light they sparkled. When you hold something so precious in your hands you feel like it's never safe, because others will soon realize that it's a gem, and they will try to take it.

"Right, Iris?" she repeats.

I shake my head because I don't believe it. I know it is my fault.

THE LATE NIGHT SHOW

I wake up after lunch and see that Mia has left a plastic container with fried chicken and salad outside my door. I don't want to eat by myself so I take the container and go to Caroline's room. She's sleeping with the curtains wide open, her head under the pillow, the colorful image of the president staring at her from the wall. There's a filled ashtray on the nightstand and the room smells disgusting. I tiptoe to the windows, careful not to step on any of the dirty clothes left on the floor, and fling them open. Caroline twists into the sheets like a fish in a net.

"What the hell," she mutters.

"Good morning," I say.

She looks up at me, her eyes red, her voice hoarse. "I'm exhausted."

"So am I. But it's *The Late Night Show* day," I say. "We have a whole afternoon of prepping ahead of us."

"Fuck that. I'm hungry," Caroline complains.

"Which is why," I say, "I brought you this." I hand her the fried chicken.

Her face brightens up. "Where did you get this? My maid only brings carrots and other cow food."

I laugh at "cow food" while she rolls out of bed and gobbles up the chicken, licking the fat from her fingers and leaving the salad on the side. When she's done, she lights a cigarette. I pick the salad and eat it slowly.

"You smoke too much," I say.

"What do you care?"

"I don't. I'm just saying."

"You know Helen?" she asks.

"No."

"She used to be on the show. She didn't make it though; I think she's now with some guy from the production team. *Anyway*, Helen was a dancer in a club in Gildedtown but she didn't get paid enough. She kept running out of money for drugs. So when Lara offered her a job in here, she accepted."

"That's pretty desperate."

Caroline laughs. "It is."

"What's that have to do with you smoking too much?"

"I'm just saying. There's a lot worse than me."

"I never doubted it. You're quite great actually. Fun to be around."

She smiles and her eyes shine like glitter.

"Come on!" she drags me to the bathroom by the arm. "Let's get all cleaned up for Lara."

We're called to the Chatting Room and ordered to sit on the sofa. Adam, Michael and Jared are standing in front of us with grave expressions, like parents ready to scold their naughty children. Dr. Brooks sits in the armchair, staring at us quietly. She can be patronizing even without speaking.

"This piece of legislation just passed," Jared starts, "and

you might be asked about it on *The Late Night Show* tonight."
This is unusual. Production never talks politics with us.

"The Trafficking Women's Protection Act was signed by the president last night. So a question you will most probably be asked is, do you think that Lovers can be defined as 'trafficked women'?"

"Why?" Victoria asks, shifting uncomfortably next to me.

"Can we?" Margaret says.

"You're not prostitutes," Dr. Brooks says with her patient tone. "We don't do non-consensual sex trafficking here."

"What do we do then?" I ask.

Michael scoffs as if the sound of my voice was an affront to him.

"You engage in occasional voluntary sex," Adam says.

Caroline laughs. Everyone falls silent and turns in her direction.

"What's so funny?" Victoria asks.

"Be civil, Caroline," Dr. Brooks says patiently.

She shrugs. "As you want. What's non-consensual sex trafficking then?"

"It has to involve some form of force and coercion," Dr. Brooks explains.

I snort. "Wait, isn't it exactly what's happening here?"

Caroline laughs again.

"Why don't you shut the fuck up?" Michael lashes out.

I stare back at him, defiant. Dr. Brooks stands and touches his arm, gently, as though she were his mother. Then she turns to me, "You shouldn't joke about these things, Iris."

Adam takes the remote control and turns the TV on. "This is the reason why they might ask you." On screen, there's a debate titled "TWPA: A hypocritical move on the president's part?"

"I don't think showing this does any good," Jared says.

"They're gonna find out anyway. Better from us than on the show tonight," Adam points out. I stare at the TV. A reporter is saying that a recent law signed by the Great Leader defines anyone who engages in a commercial sex act while under the age of 18 as a trafficking victim, regardless of consent. I was nineteen when I joined *The President*. Caroline is nineteen now and has been on the show for one year at least. If only this law had passed last year, she would be a *trafficking victim*. Dr. Brooks takes the remote from Adam's hands.

"Jared's right," she says." This only brings harm."

"I'd like to hear," Margaret says. "How can we prepare for the interview if we don't know what they're talking about out there?"

"You listen to us," Michael says. Margaret doesn't look very reassured. On TV, the president talks to the reporter, saying that the show is about "solidarity and love" and that Lovers are protected rather than exposed. Dr. Brooks turns the TV off.

"Let's make this simple," Jared says. "If they ask you, just say that you're lucky to be here and that no one forces you to do anything."

"Just say the truth," Michael adds. Adam looks at his feet. Is he embarrassed?

"As long as you stick to what we just said, you'll be fine," Dr. Brooks says. "Now rest a bit more. Lara will be waiting for you at the Beauty Center in less than an hour." She gives me a look before leaving, as though warning me to keep quiet, to remember my place.

When Adam comes back to the Chatting Room, everyone has left except for Caroline and me. Caroline rolls her eyes dramatically when she sees him.

"Occasional voluntary sex?" she says.

"Lower your voice, Caroline."

"You know what the problem about these laws is?" Caroline continues, her voice as loud as before. "That they're laws about exploited women written by men who don't know shit about exploitation, coercion, manipulation. Anyways, what do you want?"

Adam rolls his sleeves and I see the tattooed snakes, blue and green, their narrow bodies creeping around his arm. I think about the tattoo of the man who caught me on that snowy day three years ago. The man who ruined my life forever.

"You have to be careful," he says in a whisper. "Things are changing out there."

"What's changing?" I ask.

"They passed the law only because of all the pressure from the WLL. They thought that something like this would calm the protests down. But it had the opposite effect. These laws are making people angry. The protests have spread to other Great Cities now. And the Leaders won't tolerate it much longer."

Caroline asks, "What's this have to do with us?"

I raise my voice above hers, "Have any protesters been arrested?"

Adam grabs my arm. "Lower your voice, I said. The mics are off but you never know who's listening." He moves closer to us both, and I can see his fingernails chewed down to the nub. "Last night, after the TWPA passed, some radicals went to the red-light district in Gildedtown and destroyed everything. They shattered shop windows and beat up men in the clubs."

"Who are these radicals?" Caroline asks.

"The same people who organize protests against the show. They're part of the WLL, the Women's Lives Liberation movement. Price suggested we deal with them differently from now on. Which is why it's crucial you don't say anything subversive. You could encourage them and Price might punish you."

"Differently?" I ask.

"He wants to criminalize them. And now he can do that officially. If they were harmless before, no matter what the press was saying, they're not anymore. They can be arrested. Anti-state crimes, you know."

"Wait—" I try but Adam interrupts me.

"Lily's alright. But there are guards in every district now, and they'll catch more and more people. Just don't say anything against the show, not even as a joke," he says, then slowly to Caroline, "please." She nods, touching his hand for a moment only. "I should leave now," he adds.

When he's disappeared out of the room, Caroline starts biting her nails.

"Who's Lily?" she asks.

"My sister."

In the long pause that follows, I expect her to comment on this but when she finally stops chewing her nails she says, "Adam asked you to speak to Theo, didn't he? To help him?"

"How do you know?"

"He wanted me to do the same." Is she a spy? Aura

mentioned someone was passing information to the WLL from inside the Palace. It could be Caroline, or Adam, or both.

"And? Are you doing it?"

She gives me a genuinely surprised look. "Of course not. And you shouldn't do it either, not even if he promises to check on your sister. It's dangerous."

"Fucking him is dangerous."

She shakes her head. She doesn't even seem surprised I know about this. "That's different," she says.

"How?"

"It's different because I love him."

Poor Caroline, I think. *She's fucked.*

Later in my room I search for "red-light district" on a tablet even though we can't access most websites from inside the Palace. Thankfully, the information hasn't been blocked yet. The pictures that pop up show a street with girls in their underwear and pigtails behind the shop windows, and posters of the Great Leader next to bright signs that advertise "wild entertainment" and "peep shows." I tap on the picture of a destroyed shop and quickly take a look at all the other images from last night. Protesters were holding metal bars and rods. They tore down the posters and sprayed red paint on the walls: FUCK THE LEADERS. There's a picture of a woman smashing a window, the shards flying all around her. I zoom in on every face, every half-hidden body. Then I clear the tablet's history and put it away.

I breathe in and out, in and out. Adam was right. Lily wasn't among them.

We spend the rest of the day in the Beauty Center, fixing our looks, prepping our lines.

"Never look down," Lara keeps repeating like a litany, while her assistants trim our hair and do our manicures. "Never look too serious. Smile but not too much, laugh but not too hard. Don't rush, take your time walking on stage. Don't sweat or I'll Botox you next time."

When we're ready we gather on the roof, where a helicopter is waiting for us. Victoria keeps adjusting her leather corset, which seems too tight across her chest. Caroline looks unconcerned by how short her dress is; her ass might be out in a moment and she wouldn't care. Thankfully my dress is slightly longer than hers, with puffy shoulders. Lara has stuck little green gems under my eyes; they sparkle, tickling my skin, and I have to clench my fists to avoid scratching my face.

We fly over the city, so high that I can see the harbor and the sea. The lit-up skyscrapers are reflected in the water, swaying with the ripples. They're like dancing torches, guiding us in the darkness. *The Late Night Show*'s headquarters are in a glass dome that sometimes, on clear nights, can be seen from the Palace. We land next to the dome. Outside, a huge crowd is gathered, shouting our names, waving flags with our faces. I try to smile while the camera flashes blind me. On my right, Bella waves and giggles, as excited as I've ever seen her. Being on *The Late Night Show* has always been a dream of hers.

We are accompanied inside and then backstage, where a blue-haired assistant and a blonde producer in high heels are waiting for us.

"Drink some coffee, water, whatever you need," the producer says, constantly looking at her phone with a nervous twitch of her head. "We start in ten minutes, let's get you miked."

The assistant hands us cups of coffee and water. Then he points at some small orange cartons on a makeup table. The cartons look like anxiolytics—they have a pharmaceutical feel.

"In case any of you need some mood stabilizers," the assistant says.

The producer looks up from her phone. "They make sure you won't throw up onstage," she adds matter-of-factly.

We hear the applause and roaring of the audience as the host and runner of *The Late Night Show*, Stephen, steps on stage. I watch him on a small screen in the corner of the suite, though I've seen him many times on TV already, interviewing politicians and celebrities. He's in his fifties and asks inappropriate questions, laughing as if they're jokes. He wears golden rings with large precious stones. He looks a bit like Nelson Price: rich, powerful, entitled.

"Every screen in New Town is turned on tonight!" Stephen says and his voice echoes everywhere, "No one would miss this for the world." His face becomes larger when he speaks, slightly intimidating.

Next to me, Margaret grabs a carton. Bella fixes her lipstick, her hands shaking a little. Caroline lights a cigarette. The assistant tells her she can't smoke inside.

"Oh really? You just offered us drugs and now I can't smoke?"

The producer nods quickly to Caroline then goes back to her phone, typing frantically. Victoria is the first to be called. I follow her and spy from backstage. The stage is an elevated platform, so that she has to walk a small staircase to get to it, with the neon *The Late Night Show* logo digitally projected at the back, next to the poster of the Great Leader. Around it, the seats of the audience are arranged like an arena.

Victoria sounds confident in her interview. She doesn't talk much, but flashes her gorgeous supermodel smile, her legs pressed together to one side like a true professional. Stephen touches her arm a lot as if they were intimate and not strangers, while Victoria talks about her own "love for the Leaders" and "the importance of upholding their traditions." I feel the pain in my stomach quietly creeping in, unwelcome. Caroline joins me.

"I'm sweating; it's disgusting," she says. "I should have let Lara Botox me." She lifts her arms, looks at her armpits. "Can you see it?"

I shake my head. I can't think properly. "Did Adam have anything to do with Aura's death?" I ask. The moving lights onstage illuminate Caroline's face for a second. She looks at me, incredulous.

"I don't think this is appropriate right now."

"Just answer me. Is that why Aura was killed? Because she saw something he wanted her to see?"

She shakes her head. "I don't know about Aura."

"But Adam would, wouldn't he? Didn't he tell you?"

"We don't talk about that."

"What do you talk about then? Did you know him before coming here?"

She looks me straight in the eye. "Why do you ask that?"

"I heard you the night of the club. You said 'ever since I've come here, you've behaved like nothing happened before.'"

She opens her mouth and for a moment I think she'll insult me, but then she says, "He was a volunteer at the Safe Center with me. We were together."

"And he came here to help you when you were chosen?"

"He left me before that. I didn't know where he'd gone until I found him in the Palace."

"You know you can't be with him, right?"

She lowers her voice to a whisper and her face becomes angry, defiant.

"Listen, I don't care about this stupid competition. I won't win anyway. I'll go home and he'll leave the Palace too."

I can't believe she's actually saying this. "Is that what you hope for? To lose so you can be with him? You do realize how stupid that is, right?"

"WHAT DO YOU THINK YOU'RE DOING?"

We jump. The blonde producer appears behind us, her face sweaty and panicked. She grabs Caroline by the arm and shrieks, "It's your turn! Turn the mic on!"

We have only a second to exchange a scared look before Stephen's voice comes loud and clear from the stage.

"Next is our youngest Lover… CAROLINE!"

The producer pushes me back and Caroline steps onstage.

I watch her on the small screen in the suite. The dress is too short; a glimpse of her underwear is visible, but Caroline doesn't seem to notice. She sits with her legs slightly open, a cheeky smile on her face, and chats with Stephen about Julian, "the man of her dreams."

I press my hands into my stomach. The pain is getting worse. Mia has left some pills for me in a little container. I open it and down two tablets. I try to breathe. My hands are shaking; my heart feels like a stone in my chest. If I walk onstage now, I'll just throw up. *That's what's peaceful about the downers*, Aura told me. *You just take them and your body relaxes like a puppet.*

I pick one orange carton and sip. It tastes bitter, like cranberry but I drink the whole thing. Bella and Margaret are staring at me. I try to lean on a chair, but my name is being called. The blue haired assistant shakes my shoulders, hysterical, "Come on! Go, go!" He drags me back through the corridor, then pushes me forward. I stumble into the light. On my left, Caroline goes back into the darkness.

"Remember what Adam told us," she mouths in my direction. "Don't say anything against the show."

Walking seems suddenly harder than ever. I try to do it while smiling and waving, though my hand feels like it doesn't belong to my body. The audience is clapping and cheering. I reach for the plastic chair set for me in front of Stephen and sit without ruining my dress. Up close, he looks like a wax figure, the pale foundation thick on his face. I keep my legs closed, perfectly aligned, and twist my ankles a little bit, just like Lara has told me.

"Welcome, Iris," Stephen says. His rings twinkle under the lights.

"Thank you, Stephen. It's a pleasure to be here, with all these amazing people watching." I hear myself talk but it's as if I was listening to someone else. My mouth is dry. Maybe the orange carton was a mistake. The crowd cheers louder. I see someone holding a sign with my face on it, next to the writing "power and privilege." It reminds me of the graffiti me and Aura saw in Gildedtown. I point at it.

"Look at that sign, Stephen!"

"Which one?"

"The power and privilege one. That's crazy, to see my face next to those words like that. I don't think there's ever been a female Leader, has there?"

Stephen looks at me, shocked. "There hasn't."

I laugh, then I shout towards the sign. "Thank you! That's so flattering!" Fucking carton. Words come out of my mouth before I can stop them. The audience sways and I need to hold onto the chair.

"I'm just joking, Stephen!" I say. His face only grows more rigid. Someone in the crowd yells my name. I laugh, sending a kiss in his direction. Stephen crosses his legs, recomposing his face into a pleasant expression. He's wearing dark blue socks. His ankles are big.

"So, Iris," he says, "let's start by talking about what everyone wants to hear. Let's talk about Aura."

I nod, feigning understanding. "Of course."

"We all cried when we saw that scene…" He doesn't look like someone capable of shedding a tear but I keep nodding. "You looked so desperate. She was your closest friend on the show, wasn't she?"

"She was." There's one awkward moment of suspenseful silence when the audience waits for me to say something. I feel like I can't breathe and hope the dress won't tear; it's squeezing my waist. I blurt out, "Out there, there's a lot of ordinary people and a few special ones. Aura was one of them."

Stephen nods, a little bit too impatiently. "And she killed herself, is that what happened?"

I look at him, then straight into the camera behind him. "Yes."

"Why do think she did it?"

"I don't know."

"Will we ever see this in an episode?"

"That wouldn't really be right. Watching someone die like that. We have to remember that we're people." I smile and touch his arm gently, just like I saw Victoria do before, "We're people just like you." This makes the audience feel special; they clap and whistle like mad. Stephen attempts to pacify them.

"Now… calm down. We still have questions to ask. I want to talk to you about the Trafficking Women's Protection Act." I can almost feel the other Lovers relaxing backstage. If he's asking *her*, then he won't ask *us*. And Stephen's asking me because of the panic attack video, I know it.

I smile. "Always asking uncomfortable questions, aren't you, Stephen?"

He smiles back. "They are only uncomfortable if you have something to hide."

"I'm as transparent as a glass of water."

"Then you can give us an insight on what's *actually* happening inside the Palace? Do you think the criticism against the show is fair?"

My tongue is heavy inside my mouth. "Well, Stephen, you might say I'm biased…"

"Just give us your thoughts."

"… But all I can say is that on the show we never do things we don't want to do."

Stephen raises his eyebrows. "So explain this tweet by the vice president's son, Michael Price. This is from a couple of days ago. Michael writes: *Iris is a tight bitch who doesn't like rules.*" Why did no one warn me about this? I try not to look too surprised.

"That's a man who's used to getting what he wants. He was angry just because I wouldn't sleep with him." I fake a little laugh.

Stephen seems amused. "Is that so? Poor Michael."

"Poor him," I echo, smiling. *He's a son of a bitch and he's not to be pitied.*

Stephen doesn't speak for a moment and I think that he'll finally change the topic, but then he says, "You say that on the show you never do things you don't want to do. But then, Iris—and I hope you don't mind me asking—what about the video of your …" he struggles to find a word, "*incident* that caused a lot of criticism and was recently removed from the Internet?"

I arrange my features into a sad expression. "I'm glad you asked that actually, Stephen, because I struggled a lot with anxiety before joining *The President* and that scene was the result of it. But now, thanks to the help of our wonderful therapist in the Palace, I feel much better and I'm glad I can say it here, on your show, in front of all these people." The audience cheers. Stephen seems annoyed by my response. Maybe he was hoping for a brand-new panic attack on my part. That would have given his show a lot of views.

"Thank you for clearing that up, Iris. Before I let you go, I'm just going to ask you to sing for us, will you?"

"Of course."

"You remember the song you sang during the first night of Evaluation?" Stephen asks.

"That's exactly what I was thinking about."

The audience claps excitedly. I open my mouth but he stops me, "Oh no, please, don't sing seated like that. Stand, let everyone see what wonderful work they did on you!" He's doing it on purpose. He wants me to feel watched, to feel vulnerable. I stand, a bit awkwardly. I smile, because I'm well trained, and start singing.

I used to embrace the night
Stars were candles in the dark
I had a friend, a spark
who flashed in the fading light

Midday is midnight
Dreams are hollow
I wish I'd remember
a path to follow

Candles in the wind
Our lives are so thin
My friend is gone
but the world carries on

I sing looking at the audience's faces, so covered in makeup that they look as if about to collapse, skin uselessly falling under the bright lights of the stage. It's a type of brightness there's no hiding from.

When the interview is over, I find the restrooms and lock myself in. Everything is an unpleasant pink shade, even the toilet paper. I sit on the floor and put two fingers down my throat. My stomach hurts and spasms and I throw up everything. The vomit smells of cranberry. I flush and struggle to my feet. The cold water of the sink down my throat is a relief.

When I walk out, Adam's in the corridor, his hands in his pockets.

"What are you doing here?" I ask, more angrily than I want to.

"I flew in with a couple of other producers." When I try to walk past him, he blocks the way.

"You shouldn't have said those things about Michael," he says. "He'll be angry."

"Then you should have told me about his stupid tweet."

"Are you high?" he asks, trying to look into my eyes.

I push him. "Let me through."

"You shouldn't drink those cartons."

"*You shouldn't do this, you shouldn't do that.* Shut up!"

He takes my arms and makes me stand straight. "Stop acting like this. I came here to check on you."

"I'm fine."

"Let's go now," he says in a patient tone, as if he were talking to his dog.

I push him again, erratic. "You're disgusting, having an affair with Caroline." He tries to put a hand on my mouth but I step back. "You of all people should know. Every day you watch footage of us with other men, men we despise and then you take advantage of a nineteen-year-old girl who believes every bullshit you tell her! She wants to lose so she can be with you, you know that?"

"You know nothing about me," he starts but I look past him and freeze, because Caroline is walking towards us. Adam turns and shuts up too.

"What's wrong? Is Iris okay?" Caroline asks. She is frowning, her platinum bob messier than before.

"I'm fine."

"She's fine," Adam repeats.

Caroline shrugs and walks back. I follow her. The other Lovers are waiting for Bella, who is still on stage. Jared, his pulled silver hair held with hairspray, is speaking to Victoria, complimenting her on the interview. He stops talking when he sees me and takes out his electronic cigarette. I sit as far from him as possible but he keeps staring, quietly smoking.

"Nice interview, Iris," he says.

"Thanks."

"What's that thing you said? About female Leaders?" He comes closer, exhaling a cloud of tobacco into my face.

"I don't remember."

"Leave her," Adam says. "They gave her the mood stabilizer."

Jared smiles at me like a torturer does with his captive. I leave the room with the excuse of watching Bella. Her interview is brilliant obviously, because she's an expert liar. She convinces Stephen and the audience that Aura and her were close friends, and gets so emotional telling some anecdotes about Aura that she actually starts crying. I hate her. I think about walking back onstage and slapping her, first with the back of my hand, then with the palm. The gems I'm wearing would make her nose bleed. Then I remind myself that cameras might be filming us backstage as well, so I look at Bella and imagine someone good and kind, someone capable of loving without ulterior motives. I smile.

Back in the helicopter, I look out of the window, at the water that laps the Silver City. It's calm and infinite and reflected in it, each building seems made of shards of light. For a moment, I think of letting myself fall, my body a wasted thing that collapses into the glowing water. I'm tired of being a thing that others can use as they like, a monkey trained to say what they think. Aura once said that sometimes in order to survive you have to create a character that other people will like. At the time, I thought that wise, but I guess that didn't work out too well for her. I shouldn't have listened. The more I try to be what others want me to be, the more people dislike me and take advantage of me. Maybe I should be the one taking advantage; maybe that's the only way to turn things around.

I close my eyes and think with the hum of the helicopter.

HUNGRY DOGS

In the morning I take my coffee outside to the courtyard, trying to enjoy the breeze and fresh air. My face still itches after last night's makeup. The sun in the sky seems closer to us today, throbbing like a wounded heart. Bella's reading a magazine on a sunbed: **"The hottest women in the Great States and the men of their dreams."** I walk past her, take my shoes off and feel the grass under my feet. It's soft and unreal, like everything else in this courtyard. The place is peaceful and gives you a sense of freedom, but you mustn't be fooled. You have to remember that even the animals at the zoo might look happy behind the glass.

"Do you think there's a God that watches over us?" I turn and Bella is right behind me. She is wearing a large t-shirt and leggings with a tiny hole on her knee. I think of Jo Winters, with her fluorescent sweatpants and mayonnaise-stained spoon.

"I'm not sure," I say. "I hope there is."

"Sebastián believes there is. Last night I woke up and he was praying."

"Did you hear what he was saying?"

Bella frowns. "He said: 'Please God, let me do the right thing.' Or something like that."

"That makes no sense."

She watches me. "Why?"

"If you want to do the right thing, you just do it. You don't pray for someone else to help you out."

Bella considers what I just said. "Well, I thought about it and I guess praying can help. God or no God."

"How would you know?"

"I tried last night, after Sebastián went back to bed. I knelt just like he did, and asked God for forgiveness."

"What do you need forgiveness for?"

"Well, I won't tell you that. I've already told God."

I look away, sipping my coffee.

"I'm sorry about Aura and the things I said the other day," Bella says. She has a genuine, hurt expression on her face and her light eyes are watery.

"It's okay," I say.

"No, I'm really sorry," she insists. "Do you forgive me?" For a second, I see flashes of the time we were friends, moments of joy during days like this, when the sunlight is warm and the breeze a caress on the face.

"I forgive you," I lie.

For one month after the video of my panic attack was shared on the Internet, I was given pills by Dr. Brooks. I would read the names on the glass containers and wonder how on earth anyone could come up with such words: Solfoton, Benadryl, Nembutal, Zyprexa. I felt constantly dizzy, and I would stay seated by myself for hours before entertaining, panicking about my helplessness. I hated being tired, debilitated, and under the pills' effect my muscles were slow, my brain catatonic. Aura would try to console me, telling me it was "like smoking a joint after all." Even when I started feeling better, Dr. Brooks would give me a pill whenever I raised my voice or cried in front of her. She was trying to tame me, I knew that, and I wasn't strong enough to fight back.

One of those mornings, when the pill's effect was washing away, I went to talk to Bella. She had avoided me after sharing the video, as if I'd wronged her somehow, and not the other way around. I found her in the Exercise Room as usual. She smiled when she saw me. She was holding a water bottle and her thin hair was tied back.

"Welcome back," she said. Her tone was sweet, not the voice of someone who'd publicly humiliated me.

"Thanks."

"How's the treatment?" She knew about my pills, of course. I shrugged. She took her towel and folded it, then went to leave the room. I closed the door, blocking the way. I knew cameras were working, but I didn't care.

"Why did you give the video to production?" I asked. Even though my heart was hammering my voice was calm.

Bella frowned. The answer was obvious to her. "To help you."

"To help me."

She sighed and I felt a wave of anger rushing through me. "You really need to learn to control your emotions, to care for others better. Sometimes, it looks like you only care for yourself."

"I was having a panic attack, Bella. You realize that's not the same as being selfish."

She ignored me. "When the Leaders choose you to entertain them, they have the right to know what you are. It's better this way." I didn't have a reply for that. She walked past me and left the room.

I went to Dr. Brooks's office after that. It was lunchtime and I knew she wouldn't be there. The door was open. I sneaked inside and went through the files on her desk until I found the one labeled BELLA. I read it all, checking the door every other second, my hands shaking.

Dr. Brooks's notes focused on what she referred to as "Bella's trauma," the abandonment she suffered at the hands of her father. According to her, that event had shaped most of Bella's behavior, making her "an envious psychopath." Dr. Brooks wrote that Bella was drawn to good, well-loved people because she wished to be like them, but also to harm them in order to relieve her painful feelings of envy. That's why she chose to attach herself to popular subjects, befriending them to then devalue them in every way possible. On the paper, I followed a side note that said: "wishes to insult or physically harm them." The trauma of her father leaving her made Bella believe that 1. If she isn't the best among all she'll be left behind. 2. She was abandoned because she wasn't good enough, and thus needs to show that no one is *really* good. The direct consequence of this, Dr. Brooks wrote, is that "anyone around her who is liked and loved is considered as a threat to her." On the final page of the file, written in a small type, was the comment: "Vice president and other producers confirm that Bella's characteristics make her the perfect subject to create complex dynamics for the show."

I put the file away, leaving Counseling behind as quickly as I could. For weeks after that, I couldn't stop thinking about Dr. Brooks's side note. To what extent, I wondered, can Bella physically harm others before the producers complain?

Theo has called me to his room, which I have noticed is smaller than Sebastián's, and now he's asking me what I want to do. It's an interesting question, which no one has asked me in a while. What do I want to do?

Theo waits patiently, seated by the window. He is wearing a light blue shirt and jeans. He looks handsome. There are two posters, one of the president and the other of Price, but I notice that Theo has moved the desk so that it faces the opposite wall—surely it would have been the other way around before?

"I want to read something," I say, thinking of Caroline and her books and newspapers.

"Sure. What do you want to read?"

"Whatever you are reading."

Theo looks amused. I frown.

"You think it'd be too hard for me?"

"I never said that." He stands and gives me two books from the top of the pile on his desk. "This is what I'm reading." The books are called *Invisible Women* and *The Struggles of Democracies*. I take them carefully.

"What are they about?" I ask.

"Read and you'll find out."

I look at the books. I look at him. He smiles then sits back at his desk, his tablet in hand. When he seems focused enough on his work to forget about me, I start reading, flipping the pages quickly, taking everything in. *Invisible women* is a collection of laws from some countries in the East. Chapter twelve is entirely dedicated to little girls and their compulsory dress code.

> **The impulses of men are a horrible thing, ungodly, obscene. There is a monster inside each man, ready to stir and attack at the slightest provocation. Therefore,**

children must be warned, and do all in their power to keep men harmless. Arms covered, hands covered. Long sleeves and gloves are to be distributed to every girl older than five. Skirts down to the ankle, pants are for boys only. Hair must always be kept covered. Hair is sexual, erotic. Hair wakes the monster.

I put the book away, disgusted. Theo's still pretending to work, giving me time. I open *The Struggles of Democracies.* The book is long and quite complicated, with sentences and words that I struggle to understand. I flip through it, trying to make sense of names and dates, when a sentence about dogs catches my attention. It says that if you have two dogs, both hungry and wanting to be fed, and one dog is patient and the other is not, you tend to feed the impatient one first. The same happens in politics: the people who make noise are the ones who are listened to the most, while the patient ones are eventually drowned in the clamor.

I look up at Theo. He is staring at me with a quizzical look. "So?"

"This one is complicated. I don't know any of these names."

"I didn't think you would. No one reads this stuff anywhere. It's not… *advised* to do so."

"Why do you read it then?"

"I tend to be fascinated by the inadvisable." He leans back in his chair. His shirt is slightly unbuttoned at the top. I set the books aside and walk closer to him. He also stands, automatically, and his body meets mine.

"You're brave," I say. The sentence sounds weird on my lips, maybe because, for once, I'm speaking my mind on camera. It feels scary to say such a simple honest thing but also liberating somehow and for a second dizziness takes hold of me. I close my eyes and Theo touches my neck with his warm hand before kissing me, as though he knew I would feel faint. As though he were telling me he would catch me if I fell.

We stand in the bathtub with our clothes on. When I ask him about the cameras, he says he has already "taken care of it." He turns the water on; it sprays my back and his face. My clothes cling to my body and he peels them off one by one, tossing them onto the floor. He runs his hands across my body and I shiver, even though the water's warm.

"Sorry," he says. "Now I know you're not wearing a wire."

"What about you?" I ask. "How do I know you're not wired?"

He starts undressing. He takes off his soaked shirt, then his trousers and underwear. His body is dark and warm like Aura's was. He moves closer and speaks in my ear, his mouth near the jet of water.

"When you leave this room, you need to go to Adam. He will meet you on the terrace where you last spoke to Aura."

"Why?"

"Because he's got something to show you."

"And if they catch me?"

He moves a strand of hair out of my face, as water trickles between my breasts.

"They won't. But you have to be careful. I've been told Price isn't merciful to spies."

"Price isn't merciful to anyone," I say.

This new danger, this sense of purpose is thrilling. Feelings are a weird thing. While I undressed moments before I felt anxious and scared. I didn't want to be touched because I felt like I had no other choice. Now that Theo is giving me one, I want him. I suddenly want him like I haven't wanted anything or anyone in a while.

I move forward, cup my hands around his face. He doesn't say anything and I wonder why. Maybe he doesn't want me? Our bodies touch and Theo's expression shifts. He opens his mouth to speak, and I hope he won't say things like, "You don't have to do this" or "You are very beautiful."

"You sing well," is what he says. "I remember you singing the first night of Evaluation."

"My mother taught me," I reply, as water drops trace paths on his face.

"What else did she teach you?" He seems genuinely interested. Maybe this is all women want from a man, that he pretends to listen to us and care about what we have to say. But the weird thing is, I think Theo really cares.

"All the things a woman should never learn to do."

"Like what?"

"Like singing. Or dancing." I avoid saying that she's also taught me all the things a woman *should* learn, because I'm not sure how Theo would react. He laughs for a second, then looks at me straight in the eye, his face as serious as before.

"Are you afraid?" No one has ever asked me that, but then Theo always asks weird questions. I'm afraid, but does it matter? I can't say "yes" and I can't even say "no" because it would be a lie, and I don't feel like lying to this man. He lifts his hand and caresses my collarbones. In the feeble light of the bathroom he is made of shadows, and I'm shameless. He embraces me, and I think that maybe, with this man in the darkness, I don't have to fake. His body on mine is warm, his touch is gentle. And our shadows on the walls are making love, silently.

I meet Adam on the terrace at the appointed time, wearing a large sweater borrowed from Theo. He's already waiting for me, staring at the view with a tablet in hand. He doesn't turn when I join him.

"I'm sorry about the things I said last night," I say. "I was angry."

"Don't be. You drank the carton. You were drugged." His blonde curls are kept in place by a headband and he looks nice.

"If anyone asks you why we met tonight," he adds, "tell them I'm trying to keep an eye on you after Aura died."

"Was Aura helping you as well?" I ask. "Is that why she died?"

Adam looks up at me, sad. "She wasn't. Now I want you to swear that you will never tell anybody what I'm about to show you."

"I promise." I think of a game Lily and I always played back home: *Swear or promise*? If she swore I knew she was saying the truth, if she promised I had to figure out what the lie was.

Adam turns the tablet on. He glances quickly behind his shoulder but the Chatting Room is empty, the lights turned off. He takes a flash drive from his pocket and plugs it in. I walk closer. He looks around once more, then he presses play. A clip appears on the screen. I see a room, golden wallpaper on the walls, tall windows, white curtains. Nelson Price is sitting at his desk tapping his fingers impatiently.

"Where did you find this?" I ask Adam.

"In the deleted files," he says. "Now watch." With his finger he points at one corner of the screen, where the date is written. It was the first week of Evaluation. The file hasn't been edited, so the whole scene is shot from the same perspective. The camera must have been on some piece of furniture in front of the desk. There's a girl standing in front of Price. She's wearing heels, blue straps wrapped around her ankles. Even though her back is to the camera, I know it's Bella from her white pearly skin, the curves of her hips.

"I swear, she's dangerous," she is telling Price in a hushed voice.

"I have so many fucking things to deal with right now, Bella," Price says, visibly annoyed. "Why do you keep bothering me with Aura?"

Bella tortures her fingernails. "She keeps saying stuff like that and she will ruin everyone's reputation, even yours, if no one does anything about it."

At the words "even yours" Price's gray eyes get cold.

"What did she say about me?"

"That you are old and disgusting," Bella says without hesitation. "That she wishes you were dead so that she didn't have to entertain you anymore."

I stare at the screen, my mouth open. She's fucking evil.

Price slams his hand on the table. "I'll throw her out. I'll make sure she gets the worst grades ever seen in this fucking show and then I'll dump her in the streets."

"She's too popular," Bella insists. "She'll win anyway, no matter what you do."

Price stands, his fists tightened into grips, "After everything I've done for her..."

"She could kill herself," Bella says.

Adam looks at me when Bella says this, but I keep staring

at the screen. I keep staring at her devious face. I should have seen this coming, but I kept hoping there was something good in her because I cared about her once. That's what we do when we love someone, we keep hoping for the best and denying the worst. Now I have no other choice but to see Bella for what she is: a vicious psychopath.

"Will you take care of it?" Price asks. Bella's head isn't in the frame but I can picture her nodding, a little smile of satisfaction curling her lips.

"Good girl," Price says. "What do you want in return?" Bella moves forward and the back of her head appears. I imagine crushing her skull.

"I want to win," she says.

The clip ends as if the camera had suddenly been switched off. Adam unplugs the flash drive. He looks into the screen with empty eyes.

"Bella killed Aura," he says. "Michael told me when I asked him why there was no footage from that night. He was not confessing, just bragging. He had to make sure that Aura went back to her room early but she didn't want to. She wanted to sleep in your room. So Michael left her there and called Bella. He wanted to test her, to see if she was loyal enough to do it herself. Bella gave Aura the pills that killed her and then called a guard who staged the scene. But this clip is all we have. I couldn't find anything else; I don't think the murder was recorded at all."

So Aura did die of an overdose. Her own pills killed her.

"How long did it take her to die?" My voice sounds cold, devoid of any color.

"I don't know. She was sleeping though, so I'm sure there was no pain."

The lights in the Chatting Room behind us are suddenly on. I jump.

"Iris?" It's Mia's voice, calling me from the inside.

"I'm right here," I call back.

She runs outside and joins us on the terrace. "I was looking for you," she pants. "They just told me… Mr. Theo? He wants to see you."

I frown. "I was in his room just half an hour ago."

"Who told you, Mia?" Adam asks.

"The guards in his corridor."

"I'll walk you," Adam says.

I shake my head. "No. You go back to production. I'll go by myself."

As I walk past them, away from the Lovers' Area, I hear Adam tell Mia, "Remember to check on her. And next time, take your orders directly from the man in question, not from his guards."

I walk along the corridors back to where I just came from, my fists clenched, my breathing ragged. I remember the time me and Bella were friends. On the better days she seemed good and understanding, but other times she was as cold as a blade.

"I'm so happy I've found you," she told me once. In the club, drinking, before we had to entertain. *Me too, me too*, my heart cried out. When you're alone and hear words like that, you forget everything that comes after; you cling to them until your hands are chapped and your feelings limp. But then the day after she wouldn't talk to me, and I would wonder what I'd done wrong. Trying to see her for what she is was like catching hold of a fish before it wriggles and races away.

But now I've finally caught the fish, and the hook is too deep inside her flesh for Bella to swim away. *I will drag her out of the water and I will make her drown.*

A sudden sound behind me makes me jump. I look around but the corridor is dark and its shadows still and quiet. In front of me there's the spiral staircase that connects every floor of the Palace. I take a few more steps towards it. Then I turn again. Michael Price is standing at the opposite end of the corridor, lit by a chandelier above.

"Here's the little bitch," he says with a horrible grin. Something's wrong. Out of the corner of my eye I see that the cameras are off, which shouldn't be at this hour of the evening. Without thinking, I turn and run to the staircase.

"Take her!" I hear Michael shout and there are other hurried steps, heavy, which tell me he isn't alone. *Fuck.* I jump down the stairs, missing step after step, almost breaking my ankle. The sound that my heels make is shrill and horrible, why was I even wearing them? I hold on to the white banister and fling myself over it, falling one floor below and hurting my leg. I tear my shoes away and then I'm running again, holding my heels tight in my hands. One, two, five, seven floors and I open a door on my right. I'm in the underground maze of the Palace, close to the club and the maids' dormitory. I drop one heel and the sound echoes all around, loud and shrill.

"Stop running or I'll kill you!" Michael shouts. His voice sounds still far above, maybe a couple of floors, but what about the guards? I keep running even though the lights are off. I need to get to the club. Someone turns the lights on. Everything is bright and clear but I manage to throw myself beyond the club's door just in time. I close it behind me and drag a table in front of it. Then I hurry in the darkness, until I find the small staircase that takes me to the balconies all around.

Loud bangs on the club's door. The guards are kicking it, trying to open it. It doesn't take them long. With a loud crack the table is pushed away from the door and two men step inside, Michael behind them. I lie low on the floor of one balcony, my shoe in my hand. I need to get to the other exit, the one at the end of the balcony railing, which leads back upstairs. I know there is an exit there because I entertained a man in that corridor once, when the club was half-empty in the early morning and everyone was looking for a private spot.

"Iris, come out," Michael says, faking the childish tone of someone playing hide-and-seek. His voice echoes in the silence of the club. "Come out now. Let's have a chat."

The guards start overturning things as they look around, smash glasses and bottles. I catch my breath and crawl back, my palms sweaty, my ankle throbbing.

"What was it that you said on *The Late Night Show*?" Michael shouts. "*Michael was angry just because I wouldn't sleep with him.*" He speaks in a childish voice again, mimicking me. "*Poor Michael.* Didn't anyone teach you to shut up? Didn't anyone tell you that you're a tight bitch? Why do you even think I wrote that tweet?" His voice breaks with anger.

Suddenly, silence. The guards whisper something to him and the next thing I hear is their footsteps up the stairs. I move quickly into the darkness. I feel the walls with my hands until I find the emergency exit door. I open it as silently as I can and close it behind me. I breathe in. Then I start running back to the Lovers' Area.

When I finally get back, sweat rolling down my back, my bare feet swollen and bruised, everything is quiet. I lock the door of my room and drag an armchair in front of it. I look at the poster of the president, breathing in and out.

I feel buried. I feel like I could shout and yet no one would hear me.

People are trying to erase me. Michael, his father, Bella, the audience, they all want me to be silent.

Fuck that. I'm tired. I'm done being the person others want me to be. I'm going to change, and I won't care whether they like me or not.

MADWOMAN

I wake up sweating, with a cold sense of purpose I haven't had in years. I shower, dry my hair and cover my damaged feet in plasters. My ankle is swollen from last night but I don't really care. I look outside the window before dressing. The sky is empty, no clouds or light, nothing. Just an endless expanse of gray, like smoke. Somewhere out there, my mother and sister are waiting for me, but I can't go back, not yet. I wear a leather skirt and a red sweater, lipstick and mascara.

In the Chatting Room Victoria is watching TV, alone. On the little glass table next to her, there is a cup filled with pear juice. I pour some coffee for myself and sip quietly, staring at her. She turns.

"What do you look so nice for?" she frowns. "Your man?"

I shrug.

"He's so *black*. I personally find black men scary." She scoffs and turns back to the TV. When I keep staring at her in silence, she turns again. "Are you offended? Is it because Aura was black too?"

I give her a cold smile. "Your ignorance doesn't offend me."

Victoria sits up. "You know what? Maybe you like black scum because they stink like that dirty place you came from." She waits for some reaction on my part but I keep my smile wide. Victoria shakes her head as though I was some kind of nutcase and turns back to the TV. Silently, without her noticing, I take her glass of juice from the table and spit into it. Then I move it closer to her, smiling to the cameras. I leave the room only after she has picked it up and drunk.

Unfortunately, I have to go to Dr. Brooks today. I arrive at my Counseling meeting a bit early and accept the cup of tea she offers me. Dr. Brooks seems in a good mood; she smiles placidly as I take a sip. I can't wait to ruin it for her.

"I have to show you something," she says. She takes her tablet from a shelf, and places it in front of me. I admire her clean fingernails, elegant hands. With a pang of sadness I remember my mother's hands, rough and dry, the nails always broken for all the cleaning.

Dr. Brooks selects a clip and presses play. It takes a moment to upload before Bella's face appears on screen. She looks a bit deranged. In front of her are Theo and Julian.

"I hope I'm not intruding or anything," Bella says, "but I thought you should know… I thought I should warn you…" Theo frowns, visibly annoyed by Bella's presence. "I know it's none of my business or anything…"

"Then maybe you should mind your business," Theo interrupts. His voice sounds meaner than I've ever heard it. Bella blushes.

Julian pats her on the back. "Go on, tell us."

Bella wrings her hands, her lower lip trembling. "Maybe you haven't seen this, but there's a video of Iris… it's not flattering… she can be very dangerous, she's a bit mad, aggressive… She was also in prison before coming here, so you know…"

Is the bitch trying to get rid of me too? Bella raises her eyes to see Theo's reaction but his face is expressionless.

"Thank you for being so thoughtful," he says. "I'll do anything I can to tame the madwoman." The sarcasm in his voice makes me laugh out loud.

Dr. Brooks looks up at me, studying my reaction. She probably agrees with Bella about the "mad" bit. She presses the pause button and puts the tablet aside.

"What do you think Bella was doing here?" she asks.

"Trying to take out the competition, as she always does because she's cruel and insecure and thinks she can't have anyone's attention unless she's the only woman worth fucking."

"Vile language, Iris."

"Oh, I'm sorry. Still, she's a psychopath and you should know it better than me."

"You don't think maybe Bella did that because she is scared of you? Maybe you should try to reach out to her?"

I do everything in my power to keep calm. All I want is to remind her of her own notes on Bella, on how she diagnosed her as "an envious psychopath."

"I remember one time when a politician Bella was entertaining found me in a corridor alone. He tried to kiss me so I bit him, hard. I didn't do it because he was gross; I did it because I knew Bella would care. And of course, what did she do in return? When she saw the clip on the show she told me to go fuck myself. But I guess I can't complain. We both know that Bella can do much worse, can't she?"

Dr. Brooks leans back in her chair. "I feel a lot of anger coming from you, Iris. What's the first thought that came to mind when you saw Bella and Theo together in the video?"

"I just thought of slitting my wrists, but don't worry, it's fine." I really hope she won't say that I'm exaggerating.

She says, "What triggered this reaction?"

"That's a stupid question."

She sighs. "You're being very dramatic, Iris."

"I guess that's how I express my feelings. Lucky for you that I express them because otherwise I'd just kill myself and then you'd have too many suicidal Lovers on your conscience."

"You remind me of my daughter," she says. "So angry all the time." This is the first personal thing she ever said to me. I didn't know she had a daughter. There aren't pictures of her anywhere.

"Why don't we do some meditation?" she asks. "It will help you deal with your bad emotions."

"As you wish."

I close my eyes, eager to escape from my thoughts for a while, safe, undisturbed. This is the only thing I enjoy about Counseling, these little moments of peace when I can go back to what I have lost.

"Focus on something that makes you happy," she says softly, "a good memory. Try to go back to the moment, to remember what it felt like." I hold out my hands and she starts tapping on them gently.

What should I think about?

The summer when I was eight or nine and my father was still with us. The weather was humid and flies were all around my district. At night, the apartment was too hot. I couldn't sleep, my hair stuck to my forehead because of the sweat. At dawn, I got up and opened the shutters; the air outside was fresh and pleasant. There was an orange glow like a halo around the tenement buildings. The night before, I'd seen people watching *The President* on the screen of my district but I didn't know exactly what it was yet. I was thinking about it when my father woke up. He wore his jeans and gave me my summer dress to put on. I didn't know where he wanted us to go, but my father never liked it when I asked too many questions, so I kept silent. We left the house quietly. He took me all the way to Chinatown while my stomach kept rumbling because I'd had nothing to eat. The streets were empty; it was Sunday and everyone was sleeping. I remember my little feet, moving quickly to catch up with my dad's pace, and the garbage on the streets: rope, irons, pins. As the sun flew up in the sky, the sidewalk became hotter. We got to a stall that sold doughnuts and smelled delicious. My father bought two, one for me and one for him, then he made me eat it very quickly. He looked at the building behind the stall, holding my hand tight. The sign on the shop said "acupuncture." Inside, the place was full of weird looking women and tattooed beauticians. My father whispered in my ear: "There's a room at the back with the ladies' bags. Go there and take one. I'll wait for you outside." He gave me a little push and I went in. No one seemed to notice me. I looked at the white, long fingers of a middle-aged woman who was reading a magazine. I walked to the back of the shop. A beautician with the tattoo of a dragon on his temple smiled at me. I entered the cloakroom, where colorful bags were aligned on the shelves. I didn't know how I was meant to take one outside without people noticing so I picked a bright pink clutch and emptied the content in my underwear. There was a lipstick and a lot of crumpled banknotes. I put the bag back and met my father outside. He patted my head and told me I was a good daughter.

Maybe this is not a good memory after all.

By the time I'm back to the Lovers' Area, it's almost five in the afternoon. Lovers are entertaining all around the Palace and the Dining Hall sounds empty from the outside. I'm about to open the door and walk in when I hear a cracking noise, like a pile of dishes breaking. I stop, barely breathing. Has Michael come back for me? I flatten against the wall. My room isn't far; I could run and lock myself inside. But what if he kicks the door down? Then another noise follows, like a soft, suffocated sob. I catch my breath and open the door.

Inside there is only Mia, kneeling down. She is trying to collect the broken dishes scattered around with her right hand, while keeping her left to cover her face. The curtains are drawn and dust is swirling in the faded light. I move closer, slowly. There's blood on Mia's hand. When she sees me, she jumps up with her mouth open but keeps her hand on her nose, her eyes big and frightened. Tears are streaming down her face.

"It's okay," I say. I open the big refrigerator and find a package of frozen corn. "Here." I press it to her nose to stop the bleeding.

"What happened?" I ask but she just shakes her head. I take a cloth from the sink, wet it and clean the blood from her face and hands, very carefully. Her big eyes look at me as I wipe her cheek and I try to read into them but I only see fear and pleading. I look around the room, looking for something sharp, to defend myself in case anyone comes.

"I'll bring you to the Infirmary," I say but Mia shakes her head. "I will if the bleeding doesn't stop."

"Please, no," she begs me. Her voice sounds clouded. "Cameras will be on soon."

"I don't care about the cameras."

I make her sit on a chair, her hands wrapped in the cloth holding the frozen corn against her nose. I quickly pick up all the broken dishes and throw them into the garbage. They clatter and I keep looking around nervously but no one comes. No one hears, or they pretend not to. Mia is shivering now, tears twinkling on her cheeks. The bleeding seems to have stopped. Her nose is swollen and dark red, like frozen meat.

I take her hand and tell her to follow me.

I lead her down, stairs after stairs, until we get to that deserted room where I would always go before I was chosen for Evaluation. We pass the president's portraits and the last set of stairs, the one with the white bannister. Mia's hand in mine is little and rough. Down the stairs, there are no lights. I walk more slowly, carefully setting my feet down. The floor creaks. I reach the table and turn off the camera stuck under the lampshade. I turn the light on.

"No one can hear us here," I say. She settles down in the armchair in an uncomfortable way, as if she was ready to jump back up at any moment.

"Mia, I need you to tell me what happened."

"I tripped," she whispers, looking up at me. The white of her eyes sparkles in the faint light of the lamp.

"I need the truth," I say.

She shakes her head. "I can't."

"Then help me figure it out."

Mia starts sobbing, a desperate sob. She turns her face to one side so I can't see her properly.

"This isn't the first time it's happened, is it? I saw you in the Infirmary after Aura died. Your lip was swollen."

She shakes her head, then speaks indistinctly while crying.

"What?"

"Ask Margaret," she says without looking me in the eye.

"I will." I stare back at her. "I'll take care of this."

She doesn't stop crying so I hug her. Her body is little, wounded, shaking.

I wash Mia's blood from my fingers, streaks of red water flowing down the drain. Then I prepare to meet with Theo for dinner. I arrive at his guest room almost running, scared to bump into Michael's guards, my face flushed. Theo opens the door straight away, smiling. When he sees me, his smile drops.

"What happened? Were you running?"

"Nothing. I'm fine."

He's laid out a table on the balcony for me. I take my place and fill my glass of wine to the brim. We eat under the clear sky, bright stars winking in and out of view, in silence. When we're done, I kiss him on the lips, take him to the bathroom and turn the cameras off.

"What is it?" he asks.

"Something bad happened. I need your help."

I hope he doesn't think I'm messing with him. But he just looks at me, waiting.

"I need you to get someone out of here."

Back in my room with the door locked and the sound of some Lover's music in the background, I can't sleep. I walk up and down, breathing in and out with every step. I look out the windows. I reorganize my clothes. Nothing works.

I lie down on the carpet with my eyes closed and think. Thoughts crowd in my mind, pushing one another for space. I focus on one memory, the most vivid I can find.

I was choosing bread in a crowded market, holding Lily's hand tight. She was little, but already a beautiful child with big, expressive eyes. She wanted to look at the fish, she liked staring at the fins and tails. She kept begging me with her tiny voice, "Let me go, please, please." I let her go. I chose the bread, and when I turned around, there was no one in front of the fish stall. My blood ran cold.

"Excuse me, have you seen a child, brown hair, she looks like me?" I asked around, in panic. No one had seen her.

Then someone said, "The tall man took her. Her father." I turned around and saw a bony, old man who was cutting a piece of chicken with a knife. He didn't know we had no father anymore. Before he could do anything, I tore the knife from his hand and started running. People screamed around me. I pushed an elderly woman away, while children scattered, letting me through. There must have been guards around but the market was loud, overcrowded, animals crying and birds singing in cages, vendors shouting prices.

I saw him, tall, bald, holding Lily in his arms. He was walking quickly while Lily tried to wriggle out of his arms. To the eyes of passers-by, he could have been a father scolding his disobedient child. But he had a silver earring, and I knew what that meant: that there was a market for Lovers, men who looked for children in the poorest districts of the city to sell them to the reality TV scouts.

I grabbed him by the shoulder and held the knife to his throat. Lily was crying in his arms.

"Let her go," I said. His eyes were green, his face snake-like.

"You don't have the balls, girl," he said.

I stuck the knife in his thigh. He fell on his knees, gasping, and I took Lily from his arms before she could be hurt. We ran away, disappearing among the stalls and back into our district before anyone could find us.

I would do anything to protect the ones I love.

Extracts from *The Silver Times*

"Public Execution of the Leader Behind the Protests Raging in New Town"

by Nicholas Cole

Last night the president announced the upcoming public execution of the woman behind the riots that spread around New Town. Many protesters under interrogation in the Control and Management Prisons referred to this woman as the organizer and agitator of the protests that vandalized the red-light district in Gildedtown. The Leaders charged her with accusations of inciting riots and committing numerous anti-state crimes. The sentence will be carried out in Golden Square next week.

"Escape from The Golden Palace: Missing Maid Wanted"

by George Graham

The president offers a $1,000 reward to anyone who has information on Mia Pérez. Mia was born and raised in the Palace by her mother Lia Pérez, who recently died in the vice president's villa, where she was working as a housekeeper after being moved out of the Palace. Mia was the vice president's personal maid. She disappeared from the Palace last night after stealing a large amount of cash and is now believed to be hiding in the city.

MARGARET'S SECRET

3rd week of Evaluation

I wonder where Mia's going to go. Is she going to be better off outside the Palace? She must be, she is young and full of resources. And she has Theo's "friends" helping her. At least, this is what I was told.

Yesterday morning, after I told him about Mia the night before, he called for me during his coffee break and told me to bring Mia to his room to tidy it. I obliged. Mia didn't ask questions and I left her there making Theo's bed. I didn't see her for the entire day. I was nervous but thought better of looking for her. In the evening, when Theo called me to his room to entertain him, Mia wasn't there.

"She's safe now, she must be out of the Palace this very moment," he whispered in my ear as we lay in the bathtub together, my body fitted in his arms.

I turned to face him. "She's gone?" He shushed me.

"But I didn't even get to say goodbye," I said.

He frowned. "What did you expect? I couldn't risk you being involved in any way. I need you here." I lied down again, my back against his chest. "I hope you will trust me now," he added, caressing my wet hair, brushing a strand from my face. That was why he did it, to make sure he had my trust. I wondered what I had to do in return then.

"I don't trust anyone," I said.

I look for any news of Mia in the newspaper that Caroline gives me. I read it in the Chatting Room in the morning, before the cameras start working. There's only one short article in the local news, but apart from that no one seems to care. Most of the paper is about the upcoming execution of a WLL agitator, which will take place in Golden Square in a few days. The articles depict the ferocity of the protesters, who have terrorized the people of New Town roaming around "like rabid dogs," and the final "victory" of the Leaders.

"You know this woman's innocent, right?" Caroline asks when she sees me reading.

"What?"

"They just need the people to think that they're doing something. That they've found the culprit."

I look back at the paper, my hands shaking slightly. I think of Mia, lost somewhere in the city at this very moment, a team of guards ready to punish her on Price's orders.

"They won't find her," Theo assured me last night. He said his "friends" are not as powerful as Price's but they're everywhere in the city. They will wait for Mia in a safe place and take her away.

"Where?" I asked.

Theo looked at me warily. "I can't tell you that."

So I have to trust him but he doesn't trust me.

The grades are announced today. I don't really know what to expect. In the Chatting Room I take the empty seat next to Caroline, who seems nervous and keeps fumbling with a cigarette. Margaret sits on the floor, chewing some bubble gum. On the other couch, Bella and Victoria drink green shakes, whispering to each other, casting glances in our direction. I wish they would just raise their voice; they look like twelve-year-olds gossiping about someone's dress.

The President's opening theme plays on screen and I sit up, alert. Our profiles appear with our new grades, added to the ones from the past weeks.

	Week 1	**Week 2**	**Week 3**
Iris 21	**7**	**5**	**9**
Margaret 20	**7**	**5**	**8**
Caroline 20	**8**	**5**	**7**
Bella 21	**6**	**9**	**6**
Victoria 21	**6**	**9**	**6**

Nine! Victoria snorts loudly; her expression is a weird combination of disbelief and outrage. I turn to Margaret to watch her reaction but she's staring into her lap, shoulders hunched, as though trying to disappear. Caroline claps me on the back.

"I guess they liked your temper on *The Late Night Show*," she says.

"I was drugged," I say, laughing.

"It's not fair," Victoria moans staring at the screen. "All Iris did was entertain that black guy and whine about Aura." I hate when she talks about me in third person.

"Maybe the audience liked it when I spat in your juice and watched you drink it."

Caroline bursts out laughing, looking at me with a mix of shock and admiration.

"What did you just say?" Victoria shouts.

"You heard me."

"You're a fucking nutcase! You don't need a therapist... you need a fucking brain operation!"

Caroline cuts her off. "Should I spit in your drink too? I might get better grades."

"I'll tell Price about it," Victoria says, her lips a thin line.

Margaret hurries out of the room, ignoring us. Caroline pours some coffee for herself, still giggling. "About what, people spitting in your glass? A bit too late now, isn't it? Anyway, I'm going to go get a wax." She disappears with her cup of coffee in hand.

"You should be ashamed of yourself, Iris," Bella says caressing Victoria's hair, trying to soothe her. Her voice is like ice.

I bite my tongue and hurry to follow Margaret before Victoria or Bella can find any way to insult me again. They would regret it.

Margaret walks quickly, her steps muffled by the carpeted floor. She hurries past the spiral staircase, then the Guests' Area, and I follow her thinking of a way to talk without cameras filming us. But then she opens the double doors that lead to the terrace. I look at her as she takes a joint from her pocket and fumbles for a lighter. There seems to be no one else around. I step onto the terrace too and close the doors behind me. Margaret turns, suddenly aware of my presence.

She stares at me, uncertain. "I thought you were still with the others."

"I had to leave before the impulse of strangling Victoria was too strong."

She doesn't laugh. "Happy with your grade?"

"Sure. You?"

She nods, scratching her cheek. I'm trying to find a way to ask her about Mia when she says, "That maid of yours ran away."

"Yes."

"Did you do it?"

"Did I do what?"

"Send her away."

I try to look surprised. "Why would I do that?"

"I remember you and Aura tried to escape once. Price told me. He said you used the exit door underground, near the club." She watches me, waiting for confirmation.

"Do you want to know so that you can leave too? That exit's been walled up."

"Where would I go? There's nothing for me outside."

She looks up at me, I look down at her. The moment stretches out between us, long and quiet.

"I found Mia in the Dining Hall with her nose broken," I finally say, "two days ago. When I asked her what happened to her, she said I should ask you."

"Why would she say that?"

"You tell me. Did you hurt her? Do you know anyone who did?"

"It doesn't matter."

"Of course it does."

She looks around before answering. When she does, her voice is thin and sharp as a blade, "Do you really want to know?"

"Yes."

"It's Price." She looks at me with a defiant stare, daring me to do something about it, to offer my help now.

"And you know this because…?"

"What do you think?" she snaps. "I go to his room every other night. He does the same to everyone." She rearranges her features in an attempt to look unbothered, and I can tell that she's been practicing this expression.

"Now leave."

I stay where I am.

"We need to do something," I say.

She scoffs. "Suit yourself. Who are you going to tell? Dr. Brooks? She knows anyway. The producers? Everyone reports to Price. Unless you want to speak to the president… No, you're not going to tell anyone."

"How can you stand it?"

She shrugs. "My dad used to beat my mom. My brother used to beat me. The world sucks. Some people even enjoy it. Being submissive and all that. Even though I'm sure you wouldn't understand." For a few seconds she keeps silent. I take a breath and my voice comes out flat:

"Do *you* enjoy it?"

Her face hardens but she stays silent.

"Listen to me. We will find a way—"

"What if I deserve it?"

"Don't even say that."

She stands, takes a step closer to me and I smell the joint, strong and sour.

"Sometimes I feel like my thoughts are diseased, that I'm what's wrong." I know what she's talking about. I have those days too.

"But what do you know?" she says, oblivious to my pain. "What do you care?"

She leaves, and I'm left alone on the terrace, the smell of smoke harsh on my skin.

The sun floats like a throbbing ball of heat. Under this light, every color is still, definite. No shadows, no blurred edges, just a startling clarity.

I think about the look Margaret gave me when she told me about Price. There was challenge in it, but also disgust, as if I was a piece of waste. It's the disgust you feel when confronted with the assumption that others can understand your pain, when they really can't. But despite what Margaret might think, I know that feeling very well. It's like loneliness together with a sense of being lost and knowing that no one will come to find you. No one will care.

I wish I could've told her that before she left. Instead, I couldn't stop her. I felt something cracking inside my body, like my heart breaking into pieces. And yet I keep standing here, a peaceful, quiet look on my face. It's the hardest thing to look like that when you're broken inside. It's like hanging on to the edge of a cliff with all your strength, trying not to fall, every minute, every second.

In the Dining Area, Adam and Jared are talking to Victoria. It's lunchtime, and she's eating a cucumber salad, the vegetables so shiny that they look like plastic. On the opposite end of the table, Caroline tortures the meat in her plate, glancing at Adam every once in a while. There's a book next to her, open, face down.

"Ah, the Lover of the hour," says Jared when I walk in. I attempt a smile and take a glass bowl with ice cubes floating in it. I pick one cube and pop it in my mouth. Lily used to do this in summer; she would pick the cubes one by one and roll them on her arms, on her neck. She would then eat one and speak with her mouth full of it.

"The nutcase, you mean," Victoria says.

"Don't fight now," says Jared, an amused expression on his face. "I have good and bad news for you Iris, which one do you want to hear first?"

I move the cube into one cheek with my tongue. "The good."

"The president has called for you. Tomorrow night you will entertain him."

Victoria chokes on her salad. Adam is giving me a worried look. I wish I could wipe it from his face.

"Thank you," I say. "And the bad?"

"Your sister," Adam starts, "was arrested last night. She was part of a revolt in Gildedtown." The ice cube melts, freezing my tongue. Victoria looks suddenly happier; she puts down her fork and waits for my reaction. Even Caroline has stopped playing with the food in her plate. I keep quiet.

"She's too young to be taken to a CMP," Adam adds, "so she's in a reform center. Production thought you might want to know this."

"Go to Dr. Brooks to talk about it," Jared adds coldly. "We don't want your performance with the president spoilt by this."

"Of course," I say. I keep staring down at the fork and knife in front of me, savoring the sharpness, the danger of it. I could stick them into Jared's eyes, or use them to cut his tongue. Caroline picks up her book and pretends to read. Victoria says something I don't listen to and the men answer. Out of the corner of my eye, I see Adam and Jared leaving. When the door is closed behind them Victoria turns to me, but I'm ready for her.

"The next time you call me nutcase in front of a producer I will break your nose." Victoria sits back. She is scared of me now, I can see it. *Good.* "If you think I'm joking, go and ask Dr. Brooks about the things I did in prison."

Victoria stands, overturning her chair. She leaves slamming the door behind her. I pick up a fork and finish her salad. The cucumber actually tastes like plastic.

"Are you alright?" Caroline asks me. She's still pretending to read. I turn to check the clock hanging on the wall. It's two o' clock and sure enough, the cameras are red. I reach out, take the book from Caroline's hands and put it down.

"Do you know what Price does to maids and Lovers?"

Caroline watches me. She doesn't shake her head.

"You know, don't you?"

"I've only heard rumors. And you shouldn't talk about it here."

"Who told you?" I insist. "Adam?"

"Yes," she says. "He told me to be cautious."

"Well, no one told Margaret anything."

Caroline seems surprised. "You talked to her about this."

"I asked her to do something."

She shakes her head. "She won't speak. She's loyal to Price."

"I know that now."

"Well, what did you expect?" Caroline stands and starts walking around the room, back and forth, as if pacing a prison cell. She stops in front of a poster of the president and Price. OUR GREAT LEADERS.

"Iris?" Caroline says, looking at the poster.

"What."

"I think you're getting mixed up with the wrong people. Think about your sister."

I look at Price's face on the poster, all bright colors and smiles.

"That's exactly what I have to think about. I have no other choice but to mix with these people."

In the evening I go to the club, where a small party has been organized to celebrate the third week of Evaluation. There are some producers, the European politicians and us six Lovers. *Five Lovers*. The president is nowhere to be seen. Price stands in a corner with Margaret, speaking in her ear, while the pink-haired bartender hands us all drinks. The place has been cleaned and tidied since Michael's guards destroyed everything. Still, when I walk in Theo's direction, I step on a small shard of glass, a piece of a smashed bottle. I shiver.

Theo is sipping a glass of wine, alone. I wish to talk to him, but we have to be careful here.

"They told you about your sister," he says, looking around. His white shirt is unbuttoned at the top, revealing a thin necklace with a golden pendant, a clenched fist.

"Yes."

"Come to my room tomorrow at dinner. We will talk."

I look down. "I can't tomorrow. The president has called for me."

Theo takes my chin in his hand and lifts my head until our eyes meet. "This is good. Keep your eyes open and then tell me everything." An image of the president blindfolding me, forcing me to do horrible things comes to mind. I wipe it away. The bartender is handing me a drink. I take it and sip, ignoring the sudden stomachache.

"Are you scared?" Theo asks, as if we were alone in the tub again, as if there were no cameras. The question makes me feel agitated. It's dangerous to say things like that out loud, because then they become true. If you keep them to yourself, you still have a chance of fighting them.

"No," I say. "I'm never scared."

In the night, I wake up sweating in Theo's room. My stomach hurts and everything inside my body feels like it's twisting. I stand and go to the bathroom to be sick. I throw up before I can even get to the toilet. The vomit smells like fish and makes me want to throw up again.

I lie on the bathroom floor, trying to regain some strength. I think that I haven't taken the Love Pill and hope I will remember in the morning. I stand, slowly and painfully, then take a roll of toilet paper and clean the floor. As I scrub, I feel like my body is rotting, my stomach crumbling and collapsing. I try to keep my mind focused, alert, but I panic when I think that my brain might be falling to pieces too. I take a sponge and pour soap into in until it is drenched. Then I rub my arms and neck and rinse them off in cold water, shivering.

When I go back to bed, Theo is shaking in the dark. Maybe he's having a bad dream. I stand next to his trembling body for a while, feeling a sort of weird connection that I don't think I ever had with a man. I savor the shared pain. Then I take his hand in mine and wrap myself around his arm. The shaking stops, and he breathes normally. I quickly fall back asleep.

A NIGHT WITH THE GREAT LEADER

I've been sent to Dr. Brooks to talk about my sister. I've been here for half an hour already, the sun filtering through the drawn curtains, but there's been no progress. This annoys Dr. Brooks, I know it, even though she looks calm and patient as usual. She wishes I would "open up to her," but what could I possibly tell her about Lily?

"You must be under a lot of stress right now," she says. I stare back at her, quiet. She's trying to approach the topic of my sister from every possible direction. "Your maid left the Palace. The president wants to see you. Your sister is in prison. What do you think about her activities, Iris? Do you think her arrest is fair?"

"If your son went to prison and I asked you the same question, what would you say?" I ask.

"It would depend on the reason why he was arrested."

"Wrong answer. It wouldn't matter because he wouldn't go to prison in the first place. He is a privileged man, he has nothing to complain about, nothing to fight for. My sister is poor and the only thing she cares about is her family. She doesn't have that anymore because I'm here, far from her, and every day she has to watch me *entertain* men. If you were in her place, what would you do? Would you stay at home amusing yourself when you see me on TV, or would you go out and protest? What would be *fair*?"

"That wasn't my question."

"That was what your question was implying."

"Life is made of difficult choices," she sighs. "Choosing one thing or the other doesn't make us better people."

I lie back in my chair. I find it outrageous that she could say something like that.

"Do you know what Price does to Margaret?" I ask.

She's taken aback but manages to keep her face expressionless. "I wouldn't trust everything Margaret says. She's unstable and has a tendency to lie when uncomfortable."

"*You're* lying. You do know about her, Margaret told me."

For the first time in three years, Dr. Brooks struggles to say something. She opens her mouth but no sound comes out, so she closes it again, frowning.

"How do you live with yourself?" I ask. "How dare you ask me if I think the arrest of my sister is *fair*, when you listened to a girl's cry for help, and yet you chose to keep silent?"

Our conversation doesn't last long after that. Dr. Brooks scolds me for accusing her and tells me that therapy doesn't work if there's no trust on the patient's part. I remark that it would be unproductive for me to trust her.

We're actually on the verge of a fight when Lara knocks on the door, apologizes for the interruption and tells Dr. Brooks that I have to get ready for the Great Leader.

In the Dressing Room Lara examines different pieces of colorful underwear, while a chubby assistant applies foundation on my legs. There's only the three of us, surrounded by mountains of bright clothes, sparkling shoes, makeup and glitter. There are mirrors on every wall and my image is reflected a thousand times, my every movement repeated to infinity. The foundation feels sticky. I try to complain but Lara ignores me. She makes me try different bras until my breasts look as small as possible.

"I'm sure you remember when he called that girl 'cow,'" Lara says squeezing my boobs; she's struggling to flatten my chest inside an orange lacy bra. I didn't remember that and I didn't need her reminder. "We don't want to be called cows, do we?"

"I'm not a cow," I say, looking at the ceiling, struggling to breathe.

Lara ignores me. She fastens the bra, steps back and takes a good look at me.

"Thank God you're skinny," she says. A sad expression darkens the assistant's face while she applies some gloss on my lips. Lara gives me a pink dress to put on and tells me things I don't really listen to. She always says the same things anyway.

By seven she forces me to eat a salad with eggs. One egg. As if I could get fatter in just one hour. I chew slowly to make the egg last as long as possible, while Lara mumbles something about how to fix my hair when the president speaks to me.

By eight I'm ready to entertain. Lara is making me practice my "grateful smile" one last time, when the assistant runs back into the room telling us I have to wait because the president is napping. Lara starts complaining on the phone with the producers—"what am I supposed to do? Do I send her up now? Why didn't anyone tell me he was napping?"—while the assistant checks if my teeth are clean. She offers me some mints with a sneaky smile but Lara slaps her hand quickly.

"She can't eat candies now. They'll ruin her teeth."

By nine, I'm being called. *Summoned*, as Lara says. She gives me a little push and walks out of the Dressing Room. I hurry to follow her. We take the elevator to the 39th floor of the Palace while Lara keeps looking at her tablet.

"Will I sleep there?" I ask.

"It depends," she says without raising her eyes.

On what?

The elevator stops and the doors open to reveal a white staircase. I've never been here. Lara pushes me again.

"Go on, honey. First door on the right. And remember to *smile*."

I turn to ask her whether I should knock or not, but the elevator doors close and her high-heeled figure disappears. I look around. On my right is a corridor with just one door. On my left is a painting of the president with his first wife, a European girl called something like Alyona. I can't really remember. I was never interested in the history of the Great Leaders.

For a moment I think about going back, all the way to the Lovers' Area, and locking myself into my room. Has anyone ever refused a night with the Great Leader? I doubt it. *Keep your eyes open and tell me everything*, Theo said. What if he gave me a good score only because he wanted the president to notice me and call me to his apartments? The thought angers me. That would make me expendable. *Show him that you're not expendable then.*

I knock on the door on the right. It opens straight away. A maid is waiting for me inside; she's small and thin, with big reproachful eyes.

"You're late," she says.

"I was told he was napping."

"He *was*. He woke up ten minutes ago." She speaks with a harsh, resentful voice. I've never heard any maid talk to a Lover like that.

"Am I meant to teleport?"

She shakes her head, exasperated. We take a wide staircase with a golden bannister. At the top, the double doors are folded back, and I see the president eating from a long table spread with a buffet. He's wearing an orange robe. The maid pinches my arm hard, as if telling me to greet him, but I shake her away.

"Hello Iris," the president says, "you're late."

"So I was told."

He smiles, pleasantly. "Leave us, Tanya. And close the doors."

The maid nods and I hear the double doors close behind me. Then a lock. Tanya has locked us inside. I instinctively look around. The room is big and has two other doors. There are also knives on the table even though they don't look too sharp.

"Come forward, eat something," the president says. "I'm sure Lara gave you nothing for dinner. She's never been fond of fat girls."

I smile at his generosity. *How thoughtful of him*. I survey the buffet and take some grapes, even though I'm starving. The president sits comfortably and pours some wine for himself. Behind him, a poster with his smiling face. It's unnerving to see him doubled like that. He sees me looking.

"What do you think?" he asks. "I've always thought they made me too cheerful. A good leader must be generous, but not a fool. I would have gone for a more serious expression, more authoritative." I can't tell whether he's serious or trying to test my loyalty. I decide to play safe.

"I remember walking back home from school when I was little," I say, "and looking at the poster on the walls of my district. That smile was comforting."

He grins; his face is a little flushed. I wonder how much wine he's had already. I can tell he likes the idea of me adoring his portrait, a little girl lost in a tough world, her Great Leader the only guiding light.

"Drink a glass, will you?" he says. The bottle is close to him, on the table next to the sofa. I take two steps in his direction, grab it and pour it in a glass. I can sense his presence, his proximity like fire. *Don't get too close or you'll burn.*

"Come on, drink some more. Indulge your Great Leader," he says, smiling placidly. He actually calls himself "Great Leader." I find this incredibly funny, just like people who talk about themselves in third person and, for a moment, I want to burst out laughing.

"It's very good," I say, "I've never tried anything like it." I arrange my features in an appreciative face. *Poor me, struggling until the Great Leader's generosity saved me.* His smile becomes wider. He definitely likes that. This makes things easier somehow. Men who think of themselves as benefactors are always manageable.

He stands and takes some weed from a drawer. When he leaves it open, I find myself looking. There are plastic bags filled with weed and, under them, a folder titled 'WLL.'

"Do you smoke?" the president asks. I look away from the drawer quickly.

"Not usually," I say.

He chuckles, holding the weed high. "With this, all your

worries go away." He touches the sleeve of my dress and fiddles with it for a moment. Lara has created a look that she thought the president would like the most: beautiful, delicate flower. The dress is of a light shade of pink with long sleeves and a tiny belt around my waist. My hair is loose, wavy, perfumed. My skin pale, my cheeks rosy. The president surveys the look, the plastic bag in his fat hand, and says, "What about a change of clothes? Something a bit... *sexier*. There are costumes in the other room." He nods to his right. "Go and choose. I'll wait here."

I walk to the door, open it and pull it closed behind me. I'm in some sort of entertainment room with two snooker tables, a wet bar and an open wardrobe filled with costumes. The costumes look nothing like what I'm wearing, they're more like the exotic outfits Lara gave us for the pool party, all feathers, lace and glitter. So the fragile-flower-girl outfit wasn't apt. Maybe the president wants Lara to send him girls dressed like that so he can have them change clothes in here. I survey the different costumes trying to find something decent, aware of a small camera stuck to the wall above the wet bar. The size isn't a problem. We're all the same here, after all. I find a silver silk top and a piece of glittering cloth that resembles a skirt, if only it was some inches longer. There's also a fake fur and I lift it, smell it.

I suddenly remember Aura telling me about some secret files she'd seen in the president's room. She'd said it was about the WLL and that the Leaders were suspicious of people *inside* the Palace. Those files might contain information about the protests outside, but also about us, whether they suspect any of the Lovers or not.

"Iris? Are you trying on the whole wardrobe?"

I drop the fur. I put on the top and the skirt, and find a pair of shiny heels.

"I'm ready," I shout.

"Then come out."

I open the door. The president is smoking the joint, his legs outstretched on the sofa. The orange robe is open on his chest, which is flabby and hairless.

"Those costumes are incredible," I say, flashing a smile.

"You look gorgeous," he says. *I look like a whore.* "Now come and finish your wine." He makes me sit next to him. I look towards the drawer but he's closed it. The wine tastes different, sourer. Maybe he has put some powder in it. Sex Drug, they call it in the Palace. A tranquilizer like the ones Aura used to take, only more dangerous. The person who takes it experiences a state of alienation, dissociation. In my district we called it the Rape Drug.

"You don't like it?" the president asks.

I drink the whole glass because I can't refuse such generosity. When I'm done, I turn to him. I can see every line, every pale shade of his face. He looks like a toad.

He moves forward and kisses me. The kiss is disgusting, wet and hesitant. It's the way a benefactor kisses his protégée. It makes me think of a fish. I feel sick and tired, the wine—and whatever he's put in it—are hammering my brain.

I stand feeling heavy, uncoordinated. He asks me to sing for him. I steady myself against the table; everything around me feels more and more like a hallucination. I sing while the president eats cheese and grapes and octopus. The octopus looks funny, slimy. When he's done eating, I stop singing. He makes me change into my rosy dress again and lays his head on my lap. He speaks about the many responsibilities of a Great Leader, of all the lives he has changed in the States. The room is blurred now and the president's head is soft, light. I listen, trying to make the room stop spinning.

At some point, he falls asleep. I remain still, his head on my lap, unable to think. Somewhere across the room, the clock strikes three. Three in the morning. It takes me a moment to look up at the cameras. They're red. I lift the president's head gently and put a pillow under it. I tiptoe to the drawer and open it. In the silence of the room, the sound makes me jump, but the president looks fast asleep. I take the folder carefully, moving the weed aside. Inside it, there's what look like transcripts of conversations the Leaders had about the protests.

- We have waited long enough. Rioters have to be eliminated.

- I agree, some have to die, but you can't kill them all.

- We can. We kill them all in the CMP, then take just one out and make a public execution.

- That won't be enough. The whole WLL movement is based on the fact that Lovers are prisoners, that these girls need help. Because Lovers are taken from their districts, they think it could be their daughters, their sisters. They think Lovers are people like them, so we need to show them they're people like us. If you kill just one protester, they'll keep being scared, and so they'll keep protesting.

- How do we show them that Lovers are with us?

- We double the amount of public executions. This week is this woman, the next is another man. We put the executions on TV, broadcast them live. And right after that? We show the Lovers drinking and having fun.

- We make it all about coverage.

- Exactly. One moment you show them what kind of dress Iris is going to wear, the next you broadcast an execution.

You change from Bella flirting with a Leader to fear in the streets. Shove it in their faces. Show them that Lovers are with us.

- And in the meantime we keep Lovers under control. They can't step out of line, not even one tiny disobedience, because anything can be interpreted as a protest now, as an incentive for the WLL.

The double doors burst open and the president's maid enters. I shove the folder back into the drawer so loudly that the president turns in his sleep.

"Well, what are you doing?" Tanya hisses, visibly annoyed.

"I was looking for some weed—"

"Go back to your room!"

I hurry outside, stumbling, my hand skimming the cool walls.

It's four in the morning and I don't know where I'm going. I'm wide-awake and I have no direction, no safe haven. A haven can be a person as well, but I don't have one of those either, not anymore. I find myself walking to Theo's room, my feet moving of their own accord. Pathetic. Just for tonight, I tell myself. The fear of loneliness is a disease, once it's spread in your body you can't fight it back.

When I knock gently, Theo opens the door. He's wearing some gray pajamas. He looks at me without surprise, lets me in. Am I that predictable? I wouldn't want to be.

I lie in his bed as far from him as I can. He doesn't touch me.

"Goodnight," he says.

Goodnight.

THE LION'S DEN

I wake up before lunchtime, alone in a large bed. A hideous white light filters through the curtains. The TV is on at a low volume, and I listen to a middle-aged reporter talk about the upcoming execution of the "dangerous agitator" behind the WLL protests.

It is estimated that more than a thousand people will gather to watch this woman being shot in Golden Square, under the just eyes of our Leaders. Though the agitator pleaded for mercy, the Leaders can't and won't be merciful in front of such a hideous crime …

I turn the TV off and roll out of bed. Theo has left a message on the table for me: *I will be back soon. Wait for me. PS: Feel free to read my books.*

I take a tablet and, without looking at the new clip of the president's entertainment that's appeared on my profile, I scroll down to read the comments.

Isn't Iris getting a bit too old to be on the show?

She tried to make her boobs look smaller! Pathetic!

I don't understand why he didn't fuck her. If I had Iris in my own room—

I throw the tablet away. It falls on the sofa without a sound, as if my own anger was muffled, muted.

I take a cold shower to erase the dizziness, the hung-over feeling that clings to my body, slowing me down. Theo's soap feels good on my skin; it smells like him, fresh and inviting. My body tingles with the excitement and fear of telling him what I saw in the president's apartments. This tingle is dangerous, I know. During my first years in the Palace, I lived in some state of absence, as if I was existing somewhere outside my body. That way, I managed to pretend that each painful act of entertainment was perfunctory, apathetic.

Things are different now; I'm very much present, awake, which makes me feel more reckless and exposed, like a naked actor onstage. My relations with the other Lovers have changed too. In the past year, I hated Bella for the wrong she did me. That hate was defensive: I hate you because you resent me. Now things are more complicated. I want to hurt her, to take something away from her. When Dr. Brooks said that choosing one thing or the other doesn't make us better people, she was wrong. Bella chose to kill Aura, and that makes her a monster. What am I then, for wanting to do the same to her? What does my hatred make me?

The water is running cold. I turn it off. I wrap a towel around my body and wait for Theo on the sofa, resting under the poster of the president until I fall back asleep, tired by my own incessant thoughts and the anxiety they bring.

I'm walking with my mother along the bright streets of Chinatown. It's humid and the puddles on the sidewalk are muddy. I'm sweating in my summer dress; I want to go home. After a storm that kept the city gray for an entire day, the sky is painted with pink streaks, like feathers.

Mother's blonde hair is drawn back into a tight bun. She's carrying a basket with wrapped fish and loaves of brown bread. The bakery is my favorite place, and I know it is mother's too. Though we can only afford bread, we enjoy looking at the baked buns with red bean and cream fillings. They have light, puffy textures and I've been told that they are creamy like butter cakes.

Mother stops in front of a storefront with the sign "Vanity." Behind the window several cosmetics are exposed and, on a screen inside, *The President* is broadcast live next to a poster of Nelson Price. A group of young women is watching, while trying some lipstick colors on the back of their hands. I look into mother's eyes, reflected into the glass of the window. She is lost in thought, sad.

"Let's go home," I say.

"Poor girls," she breathes out.

"Why do you care?"

Our eyes meet. She's shocked, disappointed. "Don't you ever say that. It could be me, you, any of us. Do you think they went there willingly?"

"Some do."

"If they do, it's because their lives at home are a disaster. And who knows what really goes on behind the cameras anyway?"

Her face is fading, and so is the storefront. I'm back on the sofa in Theo's room, the sound of someone laughing in the corridor waking me up.

I wish I'd listened to mother more, so I would've been prepared.

Theo is pacing the room nervously, glancing at me every once in a while. Adam is trying to talk to him in a patient tone, but he keeps snapping back, slamming his hands on the table. Anger looks wrong on him, like a shrill voice on a large man.

I sit back under the poster of the president. When I asked Adam if his presence here wasn't too dangerous, he told me he has friends in the Surveillance Room and that sometimes he can ask them to turn some cameras off. I wish he'd mentioned that before.

I have told them everything that happened in the president' room, including the folder with the WLL transcripts. This started the argument. Adam believes that the key to bringing the show down is Nelson Price, but that we need to be careful, because he's smarter than we think. Theo wants to act quickly, too recklessly if you ask me. He wants to get those transcripts from the president's apartments and send them to a newspaper. Adam believes, rightly so, that *The Silver Times* and most newspapers are controlled by Price anyway.

"If we don't act now," Theo whispers angrily, "our whole plan goes to nothing. The longer we wait, the stronger Price gets."

"The longer we wait, the more information we have."

"We already have the testimonies of fifteen past Lovers and names of more than sixty underage girls who have been to Price's villa in Gildedtown last year. What more do we need?"

"You do?" I ask, shocked.

Adam ignores me. "Do you think fifteen testimonies are enough? You want to go to court, is that it?"

"If we need to."

"No one will listen to these women! Their voices don't matter. Do you even know how many lawyers Price has? There's a team of ten defense lawyers coming here every month, names like Spencer, O'Hara, Brenner. You were a lawyer yourself, I'm sure you're familiar with these names?" Theo nods, an alarmed look on his face.

"Who are these people?" I ask.

"The best criminal defense lawyers anyone can have. And they all work for Price. These guys defend killers, pedophiles, fraudsters. How many of them went to jail? None."

"So you want to appeal to the public, is that your brilliant plan?" Theo asks.

"It's the only plan we have. People are already outraged thanks to the WLL, and these executions the Leaders have planned will only make them angrier. If we give information to the press, they bury it. If we give it to lawyers, they will never build a case strong enough to drag the Leaders down. We leak what we have at the right moment, when we have enough."

"*When* will we have enough?" Theo asks.

Adam ignores him and takes the seat in front of me. "There's more," he says. "I saw your sister."

"What? Where?"

"In a video the producers had. They were looking at some girls that might be good for the show, they were rounding them up in prison. Lily was among them."

"How did she look?" I whisper.

"She looked alright, no bruises or anything."

"Good," I say.

"How's that good?" Theo asks slowly. He's looking away from me, out of the window.

"If they like her, they will treat her better, at least for now." I'm aware of the fact that I sound as though I'm convincing myself, but I don't really care. Theo doesn't make any more comments. Adam keeps staring, as if waiting for me to compose myself before resuming the conversation. I cross my legs and tilt my head.

Go on. Speak.

"I have a job for you," he says.

"What job?"

"I know you found out about Price, Caroline told me."

"And?"

Adam casts a worried look in Theo's direction but he's standing rigidly, his hand on the windowsill.

"I want you to go to Price's room and make him angry. I don't care how you do it. I will give you a button spy camera to hide on your dress. We will turn it on before you go in, so you can record everything and get out of there with something we can use to prove he's as bad as we know he is."

I stare at him, bewildered. He basically wants me to unleash a sadist psychopath with the risk of getting caught hiding a camera.

"It's too dangerous," Theo says between gritted teeth. "She's not doing it." From the way he speaks, it seems like they have talked about it already.

"She has to do it and she will do it today," Adam says. "It's the only way. We chose her because she's tough."

"We'll find another way. What if he really hurts her?"

"Of course he'll hurt her," Adam replies coolly. "That's the point of the plan."

Theo slams his hand on the table. "Then it's a shitty plan."

It's funny to see them arguing over me in a way. Only they're not arguing over me, they're fighting about whether I should get beaten up or not.

"I will go," I say. I'm conscious of my hands lying idly in my lap, useless.

Theo's face is strained, hurt. "You can't."

"It's my decision," I say. "I'll go on two conditions."

Adam sits back.

"You said you have friends in the Surveillance Room? Then I need you to monitor Michael Price. I want him as far from me as possible. If he tries to get close to me, you find a way to warn me."

Theo frowns. "Did something happen?"

"It doesn't matter."

"You're about to go to his father. Of course it matters. Did he hurt you in any way?"

"He tried."

"For fuck's sake—"

I cut him off, staring at Adam. "The second condition is that you'll get my sister out of prison. You will find a way and make sure she goes home safely. I understand that might take a bit more time, which is why I won't give you the tape until I know my sister's safe. If you don't get her out, then you can ask some other Lover to go to Price, and something tells me you'll have a hard time finding her."

Theo sits next to Adam, his head in his hands. He looks quite desperate, as if he was the one about to go to Price.

"Deal," Adam says.

They show me the spy camera already hidden in a fake button, then wait for me while I get ready. I sneak into the Dressing Room and take some heels and a short flimsy dress with buttons. I grab a bottle of foundation and a lipstick and apply them as quickly as possible, before anyone can come in.

"No woman's ugly enough to be *really* ugly," Price once said. "With some effort, every girl can be pretty. Ugly women are just lazy, that's it." He was introducing Lara as the new fashion stylist of the Palace. Because the man before her was quite creepy during fittings, I was excited at the prospect of a woman styling us. Then Lara opened her mouth. "Wise words from our vice president. Take this girl for instance," she said smiling at a short Lover with curls, "nothing we can't fix here." She made her step forward and started styling her while speaking to the others, "These heels make the ankles more slender, this skirt hides her thighs, this bra enhances the breasts." Aura nudged me in the ribs and whispered, "It's a pity there's nothing she can do to fix her own face." That made me laugh.

When I'm all made up, I go back to Theo's room. They stick the button to my dress and turn the spy camera on and off a couple of times to check everything works properly.

"You're ready," Adam says. "Don't fail us."

"I won't."

Theo avoids any eye contact with me. Only when I'm at the door, my hand already on the knob, he says, "Be safe."

Such a stupid thing to say.

I hold on to the banister of the spiral staircase, walking towards the Leaders' apartments. Only a few days ago, I was running away from Michael Price on these very stairs; today I'm going to see his father, straight into the lion's den.

I can almost see myself in the cameras on the walls, an elongated shape passing the posters of the Great Leaders, while men on the other side grin at the sight in the Surveillance Room. *What a fool*, they must be thinking.

I hope I don't smell of betrayal, or fear. Fear is something that some animals can sense. You can hide it in the way you move, you can wipe all emotional states from your face, but a scent might still give you away.

I climb the stairs up to the 20th floor to calm myself down, then I take the elevator to the 30th. "You have one hour," Adam told me before, "then he has a meeting."

"How do you know he's in his apartments before the meeting?" I asked. "He always eats his lunch late and alone," was the reply.

I get off the elevator and turn right into a corridor with crimson curtains. I look around, but there's no one in sight. I knock on Price's door.

The door opens after no more than three seconds, as if Price was already waiting for me, which is obviously implausible. He says nothing, just looks at me, his gray eyes mean. Then, suddenly, he smiles.

"This is unexpected," he says. "Come in, Iris."

He steps aside to let me pass. I smell fruit and deodorant on him. And wine. There are a yellow sofa and a magenta armchair, where he was probably sitting given the tray with a half-eaten sandwich on the table in front of it. A large, framed picture of him and Michael is hanging above. I take the sofa. Price closes the door.

"I don't have much time," he says, sitting back in his armchair and picking up a glass of wine. "But I assume you're here to discuss that little incident with Michael?"

I stay very still. I didn't think he would know about that. But of course Price knows everything. He gulps down some wine.

"Yes, I'm aware of the scene my son made the other night," he continues. "And it won't happen again, I assure you."

"Thanks," I say.

"He's a smart boy. He just can't stand rejection and you keep rejecting him."

"Well someone has to."

Price looks at me, unsure of how to react. Then he breaks into a laugh.

"That's not why I came here though," I add.

He recoils quickly. He looks surprised, which must feel weird for him, a man who's always in control.

"What do you need then?"

I sink my nails into my palms, feel the welcomed pain. I have thought about this, and there's only one thing that can drive him mad.

"I want to talk about Aura," I say.

He scoffs and resumes eating his sandwich. I wait without moving, trying not look down to check if the spy camera's still in place. The sound he makes while chewing disgusts me. When the plate is finally empty, he takes another glass and pours some wine.

"Drink some, Iris," he says. I take the glass from him and sip. "I thought we had already talked about Aura?"

I hold the glass tightly, bracing myself. "That wasn't really a conversation. You talked, I listened."

Price's face turns purple very quickly, like a jug filled with red wine to the brim.

"I thought you talked about this with Dr. Brooks," he says, his voice cracked with anger. "Otherwise why have I been paying a therapist to make things work in here?" This lack of control is his weakness. I can read his face like an open book and see everything he's thinking. And right now, all I see is the hostility that I sense in men towards me whenever I step out of the little box they put me into. *Bitch, bitch, bitch*, he's repeating in his head.

"Yes," I say, "but I'm not so stupid to believe everything Dr. Brooks tell me. I think she keeps repeating that Aura killed herself because she was murdered."

Price stares at me, actually shocked by my words. Then he slaps my face so hard that my mouth fills with blood. I taste it, swallow. It is that easy. The wrong sentence, and he loses control. I raise my hand to my burning cheek but he grabs it and comes closer. His face is only inches from mine.

"You *are* stupid. And the next time you bother me with your stupidity, you'll pay for it." I look behind him, at the colorful poster hung above the chair. CARE FOR YOUR GENEROUS LEADERS.

"I won't keep silent only because you don't like what I say. I'm not your prisoner." I choose each word carefully. This is great content for the tape.

"You *will* keep silent as long as you're in here," he snaps back. "In the Palace, you do what I tell you to do when I tell you to do it, just like all your other whore friends." He hits me again and I feel my lip splitting. But I'm not afraid of him. He has said what I needed him to. I stand and he takes a step back, trying to contain himself, his fists clenched.

"Get out now!" he shouts. "Out of my sight!"

I swallow down my glass of wine in one gulp as he stares at

me, wild. Then I leave, tasting blood on my lip, feeling for the camera safely pinned to my dress.

I walk back to my room, my lip bleeding, the side of my head throbbing. I feel a sick satisfaction, a reckless pleasure in this pain. It's the same feeling when people don't believe you and then you suddenly have a witness who says: she's right.

It's three in the afternoon and the Chatting and Dining Areas are deserted except for a maid dressing a cake on the table. She looks up at me with a feeble smile but when she sees my face, she turns away, ashamed. I ignore her and sneak along the corridor, back to my room. I left the door ajar. I open it and take a deep breath.

"Where were you?"

I look up. Caroline is sitting on my bed, cross-legged, chewing her nails. Her bare feet are dirtying my sheets.

"Just walking around. Why are you here?" I open the curtains and light comes in.

"What happened to your face?"

I unpin the spy camera and wrap it in a pair of socks, my back to her. Better do it now while she's here than later when cameras start working again.

"I told you you're getting mixed up with the wrong people," Caroline insists, "What did they make you do?"

I close the drawer and turn to face her. There's something different about her, and I realize that her hair is shorter, cut in a bob around her ears. She must have done it by herself, because the ends are straggly. The cut makes her look older.

"It's nothing," I say. "Nothing to worry about."

My stomach is hurting badly; I feel as if someone was

cutting me open from the inside. It must have been the glass of wine. I hurry to the bathroom.

I hear Caroline's voice from the bed. "What have they done to you?"

I bend over the toilet, my head throbbing, my throat sore. Caroline comes inside. She sits on the edge of the bathtub, watching me.

"Is it the same thing you had when Aura died?" she asks.

"Yes."

"Are you going to throw up?"

I shake my head, my lips tight.

"Can I take a bath here?"

"As you wish." I rest my head against the wall, one arm on the toilet seat.

She steps into the empty bathtub and takes her clothes off, peeling them off one by one like an onion's skin. Her body is thin, almost transparent; faint blue veins are visible on her arms and neck. Naked, she looks more like a child than a woman. She sprays herself with water then waits as the tub is filled. I haven't even asked her what she was doing in my room.

"I think I have it too," she says.

"What?"

"What you have." I inspect her body in search of bruises but don't see anything out of the ordinary. She makes eye contact with me.

"Sometimes, I really want to die," she says.

"Don't say that." I can't tell what's wrong with her. She scratches the inside of her thighs, her hands merciless. When I take her arm she shakes me away.

"Do you have any medicine?" she asks.

"No," I say. I don't want her to end up like Aura.

"Go to my room," she insists. "My maid's cleaning it. She'll have something."

I force myself to stand and go to Caroline's bedroom, which is five doors after mine. A black-haired girl with pimples is making the bed.

"Caroline's not feeling well," I tell her. "Can you go and fetch some pills from the Infirmary? Antidepressants and stuff like that."

"Can I come and see first?" she asks timidly.

I take her to my room. In the bathroom, Caroline is rubbing her eyes.

"Do you need anything, Caroline?" her maid asks. She is very short, her head barely grazes my shoulder.

Unexpectedly, Caroline says, "I need the pills Iris takes. For nausea and stomach pains."

"Do you feel sick again?" the maid asks in a small voice.

"Just get those fucking pills!" Caroline shouts.

The maid hurries outside, frightened. Caroline empties a bottle of soap in the water, then sinks her head under the bubbly surface. When she rises up again, her hair is slicked back.

"That wasn't necessary. You shouldn't shout like that," I say.

"It's the third time that I'm feeling sick this week and she doesn't give me what I need."

"Still, you shouldn't shout."

Caroline sighs. "Stop being like that."

Like what? I want to ask, but I feel too weak. Her feet break the bubbly surface and I notice that one of her toenails is ingrown; the soft flesh is reddened and swollen. For a moment, the throbbing in my head gets so strong that my vision blurs completely and the light bulb over the mirror seems to explode, sending sparkles all around the room.

"It will pass," I say both to her and myself.

"It better."

Her maid comes back after what feels like ages, holding a package tight against her chest. I squint at her, my vision still blurred, and she stares at me, a serious expression on her face.

"I'll be in the kitchen if you need me," she says. She places the package on the floor next to me and leaves as silently as she came. I unwrap it. There are the pills Caroline asked for but also something else: two little elongated objects I've never seen. On the handle two words, one under the other: "pregnant" and "not pregnant."

WE MUST NOT GET PREGNANT

I haven't taken a Love Pill in a while. The thought is like a cold shower, bringing me back to my senses. I try to go back in time, to remember how on earth this could happen. It was the stomachaches; I didn't take the Pill because it always makes the pain worse. I pick up the tests; they feel cold in my hands, like blades.

"Give me one," Caroline says. She hasn't seen yet. Her eyes are closed; her short hair clings to her face in drenched locks. I remember when my mom told me that giving birth hurt like broken bones. I wish I could just break a bone right now.

"What's that?"

Caroline is staring down at the tests, bracing the rim of the bath.

"Pregnancy tests," I whisper, holding them up to her face.

She pulls back, as if burnt. "Are you pregnant?"

"I don't know."

"What do you mean, you don't know?"

"There's two tests," I point out to her. "One for me and one for you."

"Fuck my life," she says. "I can't."

"We have to." I try to hand one of the tests to Caroline. She doesn't take it.

"There's no chance that you're pregnant?" I insist.

The air feels steamy and nauseating now. Caroline rests her head against the rim of the bath. Mascara is smudged on her eyelids.

"It's not unlikely," she says after a while. "I didn't take the pill when I did it with Adam."

"Then you should take the test too," I say.

We lock ourselves each in our own bathroom. Seated on the floor with the test in my hand, I think about the word "impregnate" for a while. It means to make a woman pregnant but also to soak or fill something with a substance. It makes me think about a stuffed rabbit.

I wonder where Caroline's maid got the tests from. Mia once told me that there was a black market for maids in the Palace, where they trade stuff like I did in prison: cigarettes, clothes and toothpaste. I picture them passing pregnancy tests to each other, hiding in the basement toilets and praying for the best. The thought fills me with pity.

I drink a whole bottle of water and bring myself to read the instructions. I get rid of my clothes, stand naked on the toilet, take the cap off the test and hold the stick as still as possible under the urine stream. It's harder than I thought. I hope I have peed enough. The instructions say that I have to wait only three minutes for the results but it feels like an unbearably long time. I put the test on the sink and hug my knees.

Every bad thing I've done in my life comes back to haunt me: when I slapped Lily, when I accused my mother of sending dad away, when I hurt myself in the Palace after the panic attack. For each, I try to find excuses that make me feel better. I slapped Lily because I thought I failed her. I yelled at my mother because I couldn't understand why father had left us. I hurt myself because I wanted to feel in control.

By the end of the three minutes, I'm deeply convinced that I deserve to be pregnant. My hands are trembling and I clench my fists. I splash my face with water, gargle and spit back into the sink.

I risk a look at the test. The writing says, "not pregnant."

I wrap the test carefully in toilet paper, then hide it in my pocket. I walk to Caroline's room and knock on her door.

"Who is it?" She asks from the inside. Her voice sounds feeble.

"Iris."

"Come in."

I walk inside. The curtains are closed and the room is a bit stuffy. Light comes in like mist. Caroline is in the bathroom. She's sitting on the toilet with an angry look on her face, her underwear at her feet, her newly-cut hair still damp from the bath. She is smoking, tapping the ashes into an empty teacup. Her legs are very thin.

"You're not pregnant," she says. "Fuck you."

"What are you going to do?" I ask.

She takes a drag of her cigarette, her elbows propped on her knees.

"I don't think I really have an option."

"I'll help you," I say. I'm sure she would have helped me.

She leans against the wall and breathes in and out.

"We need to hide these tests first." I say, taking the teacup and cigarette away from her. "Then we'll find someone to do it."

She looks at me, confused.

"Maids must know some doctor, don't you think?" As soon as I say it I realize my mistake. The bathroom lights are white and Caroline's face looks ghostly.

"I'm not going to get rid of it, Iris." She scratches her knees and looks at me, defiant. I let my arms fall down the sides of my body.

"Alright."

Defiance gives way to helplessness. She stares at the floor and whispers, "Then what am I going to do?"

I hear myself say, "You have to win. So you can get out of here and have your child."

I go to the basement, the tests hidden in my pockets. The kitchen is mostly empty. There are only two older maids, dressing a big cake with strawberries, and Caroline's maid peeling potatoes in a corner, her hands quick and precise. She gives me an inquiring look when I enter and I shake my head slightly. She mustn't know.

"What do you need?" she whispers, looking around. The other maids haven't noticed me yet.

"I need to hide the tests. Is the garbage of the maids checked regularly?"

"No. And it wouldn't be the first time a maid's thrown out that kind of test anyway."

"That's good."

An older maid walks closer to us, wiping her hands in her apron. She has sad eyes and wrinkled hands.

"Iris," she says in a reverential tone, as if she was addressing a Leader. "Is everything alright?"

I fake a troubled face. "I just need a moment by myself. Somewhere people can't find me, just for a minute. What about where you keep the litter bins?"

The older maid seems hesitant, her hands clutched on her apron. "It's not a very nice place."

"I don't care."

"Of course. Just that door there then."

I reach the door feeling the maids' gazes on me and then close it behind me. The light bulb is broken and the feeble light comes from a dirty basement window. The bins are messy and stinky. Some pizza leftovers are in plain sight in one corner; the smell of fish coming from a green bin is unbearable. It strikes me that in a mansion like the Golden Palace a room like this exists, a hidden corner threatening to reveal the true nature of this place: foul, rotten.

I hide the tests carefully under dirty plastic containers, then leave the basement and hurry back upstairs.

The production studio is crowded. I move through the large room, between long tables and boards where pictures of Lovers and politicians are pinned. I see mine, in between Sebastián's and Theo's. No one notices me as I walk around looking for Adam. Everyone is either shouting or listening to bits of videos with headphones. I pass a young man who is looking at Victoria's grades on a tablet.

"Where's Adam?" I ask him. "The guy from the propaganda department?"

The man has a weird moustache and round earrings. He doesn't seem startled when he realizes it is me.

"Down the corridor on the left," he says, "in the meeting room."

I follow his instructions and enter an empty white room with a large screen on one wall and gigantic posters on the other. I look at the posters, amazed. There are the six Lovers chosen for Evaluation, our cheeks bright, our eyes big, our hair glossy. OUR GREAT ENTERTAINERS, the writing says under each poster. There is a large cross on Aura's.

"Sad, I know." Adam is standing by the door in the white light. He looks very tired. "I guess that's what the Leaders meant when they said they wanted to show the people that you're on our side. Anyway, soon the posters will be all around the city."

"I look like a doll."

"That's the kind of effect they wanted." He closes the door behind him and pushes a switch on his right. The lights on the cameras stuck to the walls turn red.

"You wanted to see me?" he asks, sitting on the table.

"We need to talk," I say.

"Go on. We're all alone."

I walk closer to him and he stares at my face, his eyes lingering on my split lip.

"Your meeting with Price was successful, I gather."

I snort. I don't know whether to be angry with him because he impregnated a girl and now doesn't have to pay the consequences, or to be sorry for him because maybe he really loves Caroline and pushed her away only because he knew they had no future together.

"Yes. But I want to talk to you about Caroline."

He looks annoyed. "Listen—"

I stop him before he can say things he will regret, "No, you listen. She's pregnant."

He examines his hands for a long time and I think that maybe he hasn't heard what I said. When he finally talks, his voice is cracked, "You're not serious." He looks away from me, as though by turning he could make me disappear.

"I am."

"I'm a disgrace," he says.

I didn't expect this reply. I expected denial, not shame or remorse.

"We need to find a way to help her," I say.

He makes a weird sound, exhaling a breath held too tightly. I notice there are no windows; dust swirls around the room.

"We need to help Caroline," I repeat, my mouth dry. "I've hidden the pregnancy tests, but she wants to keep the baby." It's hard to decipher Adam's expression but, for a moment only, he seems relieved.

"What can I do?"

"Wait for the scores. If Caroline's is not high enough, edit it. We need to make sure she wins and gets out of here."

"Get the score up," he repeats.

"Can you do it?"

"I'll try. I'm not in charge of managing the scores, but I know people who are."

"Good. That's good." I wait a second, trying to follow thoughts and words that wriggle like insects in my mind.

"What about my sister?" I ask. "Is she free?"

Adam stares at a point somewhere below my knees. "Not yet. Do you have the tape?"

"I do. But I told you I won't give it to you."

He frowns. "It will take a while before I manage to get your sister out of there."

I hold my ground. "Then you will have to wait for the tape. And in the meantime, you can upload the one you already have, and show everyone why Aura died." He doesn't say anything. "When will you upload that tape?" I insist.

"Soon."

"Soon is not enough, you need to do it now, before something bad happens again." He takes a flash drive out of his pocket, holds it in front of my eyes.

"This," he says, "might be your only way out. So give me time. It must be done in the right way, at the right moment." He puts it back in his right pocket again.

"This is the right moment!"

Adam slaps my arm and I turn around to see Jared opening the door, coming to a halt when he sees me.

"Hello, Jared," Adam says, nonchalantly. "The poster you asked for is almost ready."

Jared looks my body up and down critically, smiling slyly. He lingers on my swollen lip and bruised cheek.

"And Iris was helping you with it, was she? You aren't fucking her I hope, Adam?"

Adam snorts. "You know I like blondes."

I fake a laugh next to him. "I'll leave you to your poster then," I say.

Jared shakes his head and walks past me. In the few seconds his back is turned, I slip my hand into Adam's pocket and take the flash drive. He looks at me, bewildered, but before he can do anything I'm out of the door.

Now I have everything I need and if they want it back, they'll have to give me something in return.

THE LONGER WE WAIT, THE STRONGER THEY GET

I hide the flash drive and spy camera together in my room. In the early morning hours when I know cameras aren't working, I kneel by the wardrobe and examine the floor under it. I gather some boots, heels and sneakers and wrap the flash drive and camera in a paper napkin. I slip it into the toes of a boot, push it into the darkest corner and group the other shoes around it.

I think a lot about how to act with the least dangerous consequences, waiting for Adam to do his job and free my sister. I don't have many options. If I upload the tapes online and Lily's still in prison, she will likely get punished. On the other hand, if I don't share those tapes with the world, then sooner or later some other woman will get hurt.

"You should really upload them," Lily would say, giving me one of her serious looks. "These women deserve justice."

"What about you?" I would ask.

Her eyes would be reproachful. "We can't afford to be selfish now."

Still, I keep the tapes well hidden, ignoring the voices in my head. Every day I wake up early and sneak into the Dining Area before the other Lovers can join me, pouring myself coffee and stuffing my mouth with pancakes. Then I go and swim in the pool, letting my cold body float in the warm water. Water helps me relax, and when I'm relaxed my stomach also feels better. My lip is still swollen but soon it will grow normal again. Besides, I don't mind walking around with this bruise. It's a sign that says: look at what is happening here. Producers can't turn cameras off wherever I go, otherwise they wouldn't have cameras working at all. And yet, no one says anything. Maids and politicians look at me when I pass, then turn away, almost annoyed by the fact that I dare walk around without doing something about my face.

I keep checking on Caroline whenever I can. She eats and throws up a lot, but it's manageable because Lovers often do that. She doesn't talk about the baby, and yet I see that something's changed in her. She seems less reckless, more obedient. Fear does that to you. And it's easier to be fearful when you care about someone else, not just yourself. It's the people we care for that make us vulnerable.

Theo is good for wiping all thoughts away, like balm on cracked skin. I go to his room every day now, when the sun disappears at the edge of the city and the sky turns dark. We lie on his sofa and spend a lot of time in silence, me reading, Theo answering emails and calls. I wish he weren't so good to me. It's hard not to trust him. It's hard not being able to trust anyone.

It's nine in the evening and I'm lying in the bathtub, my head against Theo's chest. He must have fallen asleep because he's breathing harder than usual. I'm obsessing over the tapes, playing and replaying each potential scenario in my head, when he unexpectedly says, "Your lip looks much better." There's something in his voice, a wavering that makes me turn and face him.

"Yes," I say. He reaches out and touches it. I wince.

"Has Michael Price been bothering you again?"

"No."

"I should have never let you go to his father."

I'm about to say that it doesn't matter, that I wanted to go despite what he suggested, but Theo sits up and puts his face in his hands. I move away. Is he crying? I stand, wrap myself in a towel and go to sit by the window.

"Come to Europe with me when Evaluation's over," he says. I don't turn around but keep staring outside. I wouldn't know what to say otherwise. "I know you'll say that you can't, but you can. And I care for you, I don't want to lose you."

"You don't know me," I blurt out. I wish I could just erase his words.

"I never claimed otherwise. But you're unhappy, and I want you to be happy."

I keep my body still, wondering what'd be the right thing to say and coming up with nothing.

"Iris," he says. He has such a way with words that he can say just my name and yet it feels like he's said everything.

I turn, and we look at each other. It's as if there was a curtain between us, across my face, across my heart, but somehow he has seen through it. It's scary.

Back in my room, some time later, the floor is cold. The heating must not be working. I sit on the carpet in the cold darkness, feeling for tangles and knots in my hair.

What Theo said hurt me. It hurt me because it made me realize how incapable I am of loving. Something has been broken or drained from me and now there's no love left, only hatred, vengeance. It also made me realize that I think of myself as unlovable because as soon as Theo looked at me that way, I felt wrong, undeserving. Will I always be this way?

I hear a faint shuffling and panting from outside the corridor. Someone must be running. The steps come to a stop in front of my door. I stand, but before I can speak, Caroline rushes in, squeezes her eyes in the darkness. She doesn't bother to turn the light on but runs to me, horrified.

"What's happening?"

"Iris, we're fucked, it's over." She's trembling violently. She grabs my hand and her nails sink into my wrist.

"They found the tests. Someone found them in the basement and gave them to Victoria. It must be her maid, I don't know."

I freeze. "How do you know? Are you sure?"

She nods hysterically, the white of her eyes gleaming. "The maids are talking about it in the kitchen. What are we going to do now?"

I try to think straight. "Victoria has them?"

"And Margaret. I heard her in Victoria's room as I came here."

"They still can't know it's us. But you have to leave now. Find Adam, tell him what happened, he'll help—" I shut my mouth. Someone is knocking on the door, a violent knock.

"Fuck." Caroline pants.

"Just a minute!" I shout, but a guard storms into the room and the light of the corridor hits us like a bullet. Caroline catches her breath. The man is the same who drove us to Gildedtown weeks ago. He's looking into the room, then at me, dark against the light of the corridor. Another guard appears behind him, shorter, larger. They move forward. We step back.

"You need to come with us, both of you."

"Why?" I ask.

In one very quick motion he reaches out and grabs my arm, squeezing the inside of my elbow.

"What is this?" Caroline blurts out, as the other guard seizes her. "What's happening?" She twists in the guard's arms, her eyes mad.

As they lead us away from the Lovers' Area, I hear the doors of the corridor being shut quietly, each Lover barricading herself in her room.

"What are you going to do?" I say. "Are you going to get rid of every Lover in here?"

"That's not my decision," the guard replies.

I think of the tapes hidden in my wardrobe, and how stupid I was for not acting earlier. Theo was right. The longer we wait, they stronger they get.

CAROLINE'S MISTAKE

I'm in Price's suite. The guard who's brought me here is now standing behind me, his hideous smell, like cigars and bleach, making me sick. He's not touching me anymore, and yet I can still feel his hands all over me.

Next to me, Caroline is panting. Her skin is damp and greenish. She's doing everything in her power not to throw up, not here. I pray that she can hold it in, for both of us.

Victoria and Margaret are sitting in two armchairs. They were already here when me and Caroline were dragged inside. They were speaking in hushed voices but when they saw us they dropped silent.

"Traitors," Caroline hissed, loud enough for them to hear, but all Victoria did in return was smile. I'm sure she's enjoying all this immensely; she can finally be the best again. It must have been her idea to come here and speak to Price.

Still, how can they know it's us? Have they found our fingerprints? I know the president has a whole forensic team at his disposal but has the team already been called? Wouldn't they be here if they had?

To make things even worse, Michael is crashed out on the sofa, staring at me with a disgusting, complacent smile on his face.

"What have you done this time, Iris?" he asked when I was dragged inside, as if this whole thing was extremely amusing.

I can see every detail as if filtered through dirty glass: the silver eye shadow on Victoria's eyelids, Margaret wiping her hands on her jeans, Michael's smile, the gloss of Price's desk.

He's sitting right in front of us, but I'm not looking at his face. My head is lowered like the good, obedient girl he wants me to be. So all I see are the precious gemstones on his fingers.

For what feels like an eternity, he doesn't speak. He taps on his desk, slowly, and the gemstones scratch against one another. There is an oval mirror behind him, where a camera is surely hiding. Unexpectedly, Michael stands and walks to it. He feels the golden frame of the mirror with his fingers and switches a button. The camera is off. I catch my breath, as if punched in the stomach.

Price lifts his head. His eyes land on me.

"Iris," he says, flashing his shiny smile. He looks like a psychopath. "You signed a piece of paper when you came here, you remember that?"

"Yes."

"There were a few rules written on there. Just a few fucking rules, easy to remember." His body remains stiff and hard as a stone. But his smile doesn't falter; it looks as if a sculptor carved it like that by mistake. *He knows. He knows it's us.*

I say the rules out loud quickly, "We must not fall in love with another Lover, we must not get pregnant, we must not leave the Golden Palace, we must not reveal any classified information we overhear in the Resting Rooms."

Out of the corner of my eye, I see Margaret digging her nails into her thighs. She must be relieved that Price, for once, will take his anger out on someone else.

He walks past me, and I hold my body rigid and tense, ready for him. But then he takes Caroline's hand. She moans and I realize that he's crushing her fingers.

"Little Caroline," he says. "Did you forget the rules?"

"No," she says in a whisper.

"What happened then?"

Caroline suddenly understands that Price knows her secret, because she starts sobbing right in front of him. I didn't think of Caroline as someone capable of crying like that. Her knees give way and she falls onto the floor, her shoulders shaking. It's pitiful to look at. I hope she betrays Adam; it's her only chance.

Price raises his eyes to the ceiling. "Oh fuck, don't cry."

Caroline sobs even harder, hair sticking to her face, hands over her mouth.

"Get up!" Michael shouts. "He told you not to cry!"

"Let's try to keep calm everyone," Price says. He crouches down and faces Caroline. "Caroline, don't try to manipulate me. Stand up."

She stands, shaking, and breathes in and out quickly. I realize my left hand is clutched against my mouth. I let it fall down the side of my body.

"The president—" I start, desperate to distract Price. "Where is he?"

Price's smile becomes wider, more dangerous. "The president's a busy man. What he doesn't know won't kill him."

"What if he comes?"

"Shut your mouth, Iris. No one's here to help you."

I obey, my mind racing. *What can we do? What can we do?*

"Let's sort this out once and for all," Price says. "Victoria, who gave you the pregnancy tests?" He says the word *pregnancy* with revulsion.

Victoria smiles. She's fucking incredible. "Caroline's maid. She said Iris left the tests in the garbage and she saw that one was positive."

I close my eyes. How stupid of me to go Caroline's maid. I thought that, just because she gave us the tests in the first place, she wouldn't speak.

"One was positive," Price repeats. "And that's you Caroline, isn't it? You got pregnant and wanted to keep your baby?"

He takes Caroline's hand again, as if she could run away from him without warning. Caroline shakes her head, desperate, tears streaming down her cheeks.

"Because I went to see the doctor yesterday and guess what? He told me you didn't go to him, you didn't ask for any abortion. That was a mistake. A stupid mistake. Getting pregnant, hiding it from me, stealing the tests, trying to keep the baby." He inhales, his face red. "You insulted the Leaders. We need to fix that. We can't allow other Lovers to see how forgiving we are, given that there are only four fucking rules!"

Michael takes my arm. I try to free myself but his grip is tight. If only I could get closer to the wall and smash the mirror on his head...

"Did you think I wouldn't find out?" Price says. "And I'm sure Iris wanted to help... and not to confide in me. Another mistake." He's staring at me now, his gray eyes like blades. "I knew you'd be trouble from the day I picked you up from that shithole."

I feel Michael's breath on my neck. For a moment, no one speaks and the only sound is Caroline's faint sobbing, soft and painful like needles in the skin.

"The problem is," Price starts again, "if we let you have an abortion now, you'll still be here, all angry with us, all vengeful. And then you'll go home after Evaluation and what will you say? I'm sure you understand this is not the right time to insult the Leaders, with all those madmen protesting in the streets."

"I won't say anything," Caroline says.

"No," Price continues, ignoring her. "You'll be a hand grenade ready to explode at the first provocation. This is the only way."

The guard walks to Price's desk and opens a drawer. Next thing I know, he's holding a gun: small, black, glossy. Victoria gasps and Margaret jumps out of her chair, knocking over a vase. It drops and shatters on the carpet. I turn to Caroline just in time to see her faint. The sound of her body hitting the floor is like a scream.

This is it then. This is it. Michael keeps holding me tight, but where would I run anyway? I close my eyes.

The guard fires.

When I open my eyes I'm not dead.

The body that lies on the floor, dying, is Caroline's. Her eyes are looking at me, light slowly burning out. I lunge toward her. Michael pushes me back but I free myself and stumble onto the floor.

A body dying doesn't look like you think it will. The worst part of it is the noise it makes. It's a pitiful sound, barely human, more like a wounded animal. On the floor in a pool of her own blood, Caroline whines and whimpers like a sick puppy.

"What have you done?" Somewhere on my left, Margaret's voice is faltering.

"You did this!" I shout, pointing at her and Victoria. "You did this!"

Margaret opens her mouth like a dead fish. I look away from her and back to Caroline, small and bloody in my arms.

"I'm sorry," I whisper into her ear, crying, holding on to her. Caroline moves her lips, but no sound comes out anymore. Her silent words are beyond my grasp.

She dies as we lie parallel like two sisters in the same tomb.

Extracts from *The Silver Times*

"What Happened to Lover Caroline?"
by Peter Corbett

Last night the propaganda department of the Golden Palace announced that another Lover had to leave the competition for health reasons. Caroline was nineteen years old and had been in the Palace for no more than a year, and yet she was among the most popular Lovers. She entertained two high-ranking politicians before being chosen for Evaluation (one of the few Lovers to be chosen during their first year on the show) and spending time with European delegate Julian Bisset. Yesterday Caroline was escorted outside the Palace into a private hospital to take care of her mental health. The president has not yet spoken about this. Nelson Price gave one brief comment on the matter, claiming that Caroline "was probably too young to be under such a spotlight as Evaluation." According to sources from the Palace, Caroline's mental health problems had a negative impact on fellow Lover Iris, who has already suffered from anxiety and panic attacks. Thanks to the generosity of the Leaders, Iris has been given a two-day break to calm down and relax before entertaining again.

"Dangerous Agitator behind the City Protests Publicly Executed Last Night"

by Nicholas Cole

In response to inciting the riots and protests that have been destroying New Town and insulting the Great Leaders, a team of guards executed a 40-year-old woman yesterday evening in front of a large crowd of witnesses. The sentence was carried out in Golden Square, where new posters of our Evaluation Lovers have been hanged on the most popular spots. In the night after the execution, despite the strict patrolling of the streets, the posters of the Lovers were spray-painted and torn. The Leaders encourage anyone who knows about the people behind this act of vandalism to come forward.

CRACKS

4th week of Evaluation

They left no food in my room. There's only a small bottle of water, half-filled, but I'm not drinking any until I know when they will unlock the door.

The guards restrained me, while Michael told me to calm down. He was caressing my cheek, but he might as well have been slapping me. I didn't scream but they treated me like a madwoman anyway, dragging me back here "until you are ready for the cameras again," Michael said. He said they didn't want me to be seen in this state, otherwise they would be forced to do something about it. I wanted to strangle him. I never wanted anything so desperately. After they pushed me into my own room like it was a cell, they quickly closed the door and locked it from the outside. I screamed and banged my head against it but they were already gone.

I think I've been alone for two days already but I can't be too sure. How long will they leave me in here? Maybe they think that if they starve me I will forget. But I don't forget. Traumas are like shadows—they never leave you; they're always one step behind, but they are there, untouchable shapes.

I give up and drink some water. My throat hurts, as if bruised. It's beginning to get hot, but the windows are locked too, I've already tried them. There's not much I can do except panic. I bury my face into the bed, panting.

My cellmate in prison once said that the purpose of solitary confinement is to make you feel sorry. "For what?" I asked and she said, "For yourself."

I drag myself to the bathroom and take a red pillbox I have sworn never to touch. I swallow two pills without water, even though my throat is dry.

I don't want to be alone in this room.

Stars are scattered all across the sky when Margaret comes to see me. I'm counting them to keep focused and ignore my stomach pains. My mother used to make me count if I couldn't sleep. "Count stars, posters, buildings, anything. It always works." It's not working now.

Margaret closes the door behind her and clears her throat, but I ignore her. She hasn't even knocked. Guards don't knock when they open a prisoner's cell. She walks past me and sits on the bed.

I wait for her to say something but nothing comes out of her mouth so I turn and face her. She looks awful. Her skin is paler and more spoiled than usual; her lips are chapped. She's holding a tray with a sandwich, some blue pills and a lot of water. I consider smashing the tray onto her head but I need the water. Still, I must not show it to her. I must not have weaknesses for all she knows.

"You're a traitor," I say.

She looks down at the tray, takes one pill for herself and gulps it down with *my* water. Her hands are shaking a bit. She must be afraid of me, of what I could do to her. Why did she come here then?

"The cameras in your room are off," she says weakly. "They don't want you to say anything against them."

"Good," I say. "So I can insult you and no one will know." I move closer to the bed and take the water. I drink some. It's warm and my stomach rumbles.

"I made a mistake," Margaret says.

"You made many mistakes."

"When you came and talked to me about Price," she says, "I should've accepted your help. I should've—" she breaks off staring down at her hands. "But I hated you."

"Well, now I hate you."

I take the sandwich and I bite into it. Mayonnaise drops onto my shirt. I think of Caroline eating her hamburger before we went to the club, weeks ago. She had mayonnaise on her fingers and told me, "I'm never going to win."

Margaret stares at me while I swallow, which is annoying because I can't tell what she's thinking, while I feel like she can see my thoughts, my hunger. But then I realize she's not really staring at me. Her eyes are blank.

"I hated you because you made me look at myself and think that I was pathetic."

The sandwich is gone. I have eaten it too quickly. Now I don't have anything else to do while Margaret confronts me with her feelings, which I'm not ready for. I just want her to shut up. I can't answer that she's not pathetic because she doesn't deserve my compassion. I gulp down some more water. She waves her hand, as if pushing some thought away.

"Anyway, the reason why I came here is Aura."

This is unexpected. I fix my eyes into her. "Aura?"

"I think someone killed her because she would've never

killed herself. And that might be Price. After all he's done to us, I wouldn't be surprised."

"You believe that?"

"Yes. I said it to Price when he asked me two weeks ago."

"And what did he say?"

"He told me to shut up about it so I did."

"He said the same thing to me."

She stands up and touches her shaking hand to her throat. "Maybe if I had complained about what he did to us, if I'd said something, Aura wouldn't have died."

"Did Price beat Aura too?"

"Sometimes. Not as much as me."

I don't really know what to say to that.

"And if I'd told Victoria to ignore the pregnancy tests..." She looks at me with a pitiful expression and I feel grief coming over me in waves, drowning me. "But I wanted you to feel pathetic too."

"Caroline died because of those tests."

She makes a choking sound. "I know."

"What are they saying to the press?"

"They said she's left the Palace because she couldn't handle the stress of being on camera anymore. That production arranged for her to go into a private hospital to take care of her mental health. That she was getting too skinny and that—"

"Fame's not for everyone," I interrupt her. Price used to say this.

"Yes. But someone will be punished for this and we know it is you, me and Victoria because we were there when it happened."

"Price will force the politicians to give you and Victoria good grades."

She shakes her head. "You don't know him as well as I do."

She glances at the door as if expecting someone to be there. "Soon they'll let you out of here, I heard a producer talk about it today. They explained your absence by saying that Caroline's mental breakdown was too hard on you and that they're giving you time to relax."

"How thoughtful of them."

She picks up the tray and looks at the blue pills. "Aren't you going to keep these?"

I shake my head.

Margaret shrugs. "If anyone asks you what we talked about, tell them I just brought you food. I'll see you tomorrow."

She's gone as quickly as she came.

They let me out early in the morning, when the sky is of a pale yellow and the air is cold. I wash my face several times and brush my teeth until my gums are sore. I take one more pill, just one, then throw all the others into the toilet and flush. I take a look at myself in the large mirror. My lip is swollen and purple, my face strangely asymmetrical.

I take the flash drive and spy camera from the shoe under the wardrobe and hide them both in my pockets. No matter what happens, I will share these as soon as I can.

In the Chatting Room, Bella is having breakfast by herself. She looks me up and down as I pour milk into a large mug.

"Where were you?" she asks. "You disappeared."

"On vacation," I say, as sarcastically as I can. Is it possible she doesn't know anything about what happened?

"Why?"

I don't have time to answer because Margaret flings the door open. Her hair is as dirty as last night, the circles under her eyes as dark. She looks around as if she can't see us.

"Margaret?" I ask.

Victoria appears behind her. She walks up to her, grabs her arm and shakes it.

"We agreed to it, now keep quiet." Victoria hisses.

Margaret laughs hysterically. Her voice sounds too shrill, unlike her. She's losing it. "This is what you do, isn't it?" she says. "You keep an eye on the other Lovers for him, you find their secrets to make sure they're loyal."

"Shut up," Victoria says. "You don't know what he did for me."

"I don't care."

"I was homeless when my father lost his money. I was sleeping at friends' places, shitty places. But Lara found me in a fitting room and told me about Price. They helped me ever since. They gave me a home, they gave me money."

"And you gave them names."

"He offered me a way back to the life I had. But I don't expect you to understand."

"Fuck you," Margaret says. She comes to sit on the sofa next to me. She stinks of sweat. She's about to open her mouth again but I give her a nudge: the cameras have turned green. We all rearrange our features into pleasant expressions, all but Margaret, who hides her head in her knees.

Victoria takes a glass for herself, closing the glass cabinet loudly. I look at her and then back at my mug. Her skin is white and opaque, like the top layer of milk. It's hard to see too clearly beyond it. Yet, somewhere beneath this delicate facade there's something rotten, infectious swelling up under the skin. It makes me think about the dark room of the basement kitchen, with litter bins and overflowing garbage.

"Somebody turn the TV on," Victoria says. "The grades should be ready."

I grab the remote control and the screen turns bright. Instead of the usual profile with our grades, Michael's face appears on screen. He's talking about the news of Caroline's treatment in the hospital.

"Caroline will get better," Michael says staring into the camera. "Eating disorders are too common among girls and we must fight them. We must set an example."

Victoria rolls her eyes and pours herself another glass of juice.

"She was getting so skinny," Bella says. "Some people just can't handle it."

"Yeah, she definitely got stuck on the wrong path," Victoria comments.

But then the scores appear and she shuts her mouth. As Margaret predicted, the three of us get a five. Bella gets a nine.

I take a deep breath, exhaling all the panic that was stuck to my chest; I expected much, much worse.

Bella is frowning, both amused and confused. "Why are your grades so low?" she asks.

But she's not the only one to be taken aback. From the way she stares at the screen gaping, it's clear that Victoria expected only me to be punished. She thought her loyalty would be rewarded, but that's not how Price reasons. Margaret was right: all three of us paid the price because we saw what happened. This low grade is a threat and a reminder that he has her—and all of us—in hand. Victoria is punished now for seeing something forbidden, so then later, when she's rewarded, she'll be more grateful.

I look at her leaning forward in disbelief, with her golden robe and pretty face. I have learnt to see the cracks in this palace and its people. It's time that everyone else sees them too.

I know what I have to do now, but I can't do it alone. I need Adam's or Theo's help. Asking Theo would probably be the better option but after everything that's happened, I don't feel like seeing him unless he calls for me. I couldn't take his affection, or his pity. So I go and look for Adam.

I might be taking a stupid chance but I go to the production area. I wouldn't know where else I could find him. Weirdly, the room looks empty when I get there. A head pops up from behind a desk and a maid looks at me suspiciously. She's wearing white gloves for cleaning and has a mop in her hand.

"Hello, Iris."

"I'm looking for Adam."

She looks down and says shyly, "I don't know names. But there's a man in the restroom."

"What does he look like?"

"Blond curls, tattoos on his arms. He's been in there for a while."

I hurry in the direction of the toilet with an indescribable feeling rising inside me, like my body warning me of something bad about to happen.

"Maybe you want to wait outside?" the maid calls softly. I realize she's saying this because the toilets are for men only. Women don't work in production, of course.

"I don't like waiting," I say.

In the toilet everything seems quiet. I lean against the cold sink and wait until I hear the water flushing. Then, a faint sobbing.

"Adam?" I whisper. "It's Iris, open the door."

He bangs on the door from the inside, hard. I try to open it but it's locked.

"Open up, Adam, I need your help."

He bangs again, harder. "I can't," he says. "I can't."

I kneel down on the floor, trying to see from below the door. His black leather shoes are stained with drops of blood.

"Adam, open the fucking door."

He slides down into a crouching position. His hand comes into view, his fist clenched. His knuckles are bleeding, the skin raw and flayed. I enter the next stall and climb onto the toilet. I can see him from here. He has a wild look in his eyes.

"I'm going to jump in there," I warn him.

He doesn't respond. I grab the edge of the toilet wall and lift my body over it. I shift my weight and fall into his cubicle. I steady myself against the wall.

"We need to get out now," I say, "or they'll notice." I move to open the cubicle door but he grabs my arm and pushes me back.

"I can't," he repeats. He jerks his head back, banging it against the wall. I move forward to hold it in my hands when he takes a swiss army knife out of his pocket and shouts.

"They killed her!"

I back up. The knife looks sharp.

"I know," I say quietly. "I was there. Don't shout now, or someone will hear."

"How did they kill her? They wouldn't show me the footage, they wouldn't let me see!"

"She was shot. Under Price's order."

He wails, wounded like a beast. He points the knife at me, his eyes savage. "Back off," he shouts. "I swear I'm gonna hurt you if you don't."

I raise my arms. I can't step back because I'm already against the wall. "Please," I say. "Caroline didn't protect you for nothing. She could've snitched you out, but she didn't. She must have loved you very much. She must have thought you deserved it."

"I don't." He cries, choking on his own words. Tears stream down his cheeks and his face crumples. I've never seen a man cry like that. I move forward slowly and take the knife from his hand. He collapses against me and I feel his tears all over, soaking my shirt. His body is heavy on mine; his arms are shaking.

"They're going to pay for what they've done," he whispers.

"Yes. They will."

It hurts me to see him like this, to see that he cared. It would've been easier if he didn't have regrets, it would've been easier to hate him like the others. But men aren't all the same.

I'm called for Counseling at six in the afternoon. I arrive early, cleaned and brushed just like Dr. Brooks wants me to be.

"I have been told what happened in the vice president's room, Iris," is the first thing she says to me. Her hands are cupped around a mug of hot tea, smoke spiraling out of it towards the ceiling. I smile, feeling my lip splitting. It splits again every time, despite the balm that a maid has left in my room.

"I thought you would." I lick the blood and savor it.

Dr. Brooks looks at me, frowning. "Do you want to talk about that?"

"Of course," I say, "whatever you want." She used to drive me mad with her patience, her control. Now it's my turn. Let's see if she cracks.

"Why don't you start by telling me what happened?"

"I thought you said you knew that already?"

"Yes, but I want to hear—"

"You want to hear my *version* yes," I say, because that's what she used to say to me, as though my memories of abuse were dreams, hallucinations.

"This is what happened. I was dragged to the vice president's room together with Caroline. Once there, Margaret and Victoria watched as Nelson and Michael Price turned the cameras off, shouted at us, humiliated us and then ordered a guard to kill Caroline in cold blood. She died in my arms."

Her eyes glisten, raindrops against the cobweb-like lines of her face. She looks down at her desk, pretends to read some notes, then says, "Before that incident, you went to see Price to talk about Aura."

It isn't a question so I keep silent.

"I assume you now believe Aura was murdered too because you witnessed this incident with Caroline?"

"What incident?" I ask.

"You just described it."

"You mean Caroline's *murder* then."

"Yes."

I tilt my head to the side. "Why do you call it an incident?"

Dr. Brooks sighs. "Iris. Don't make things difficult. I know you're distressed."

"I'm not distressed. I'm just surprised by your choice of words, given your profession. I thought words were important?"

Dr. Brooks stands. In this office, she's always been seated and I've always been seated in front of her. This change of perspective surprises me, as though I thought that she would be glued to her chair forever.

"They do. Which is why you're being insolent. Does the word insolent appeal to you?" She still sounds calm, but I can sense distress growing underneath her façade.

"I think it's perfect."

"Good. You surely realize that being insolent won't work out for you?"

"During my first day in this office, you told me I could say anything I wanted in here, as long as I behaved outside of this room."

She scoffs. "Are you going to quote me back to make me sound incompetent?"

"Yes," I say. "You also said—and this was the *last* time I came here—that life is made of difficult choices and that choosing one thing or the other doesn't make us better people."

"I said that and I believe it."

"Of course you do. That's the only way to convince yourself that you are decent, which you aren't."

Dr. Brooks paces back and forth in silence, then stops under the poster of the Great Leader.

"You keep complaining, Iris, but you're too blind to see all the good that's been done to every girl in here."

"All the good," I repeat.

"Most of the young women who come here are desperate. Poor, or worse, homeless, unwanted children of violent parents, rejected by society, incapable of dealing with their past, their feelings. Bright, attractive women who would be wasted out there. But here they get clothes, food, money, fame. They only have to give something in return." She waves a hand at the poster. "But because you seem keen on complaining about how things work here, tell me, what would you change?"

"I would be free," I say. "I would start by changing that. I wouldn't be expendable."

She looks at me with placid eyes. "You're not expendable."

"But Caroline was?"

"Caroline got *pregnant*, Iris." She says this as if she was speaking of pedophilia, or aggravated murder. Then she looks at the clock. "Time's almost out. Should we do some meditation?"

"Of course," I say.

"Oh, and before I forget, Theo Droit has called for you," she says. "You are to go to him when we are done here."

"I will." I close my eyes and hold out my hands on the desk. Dr. Brooks sits back in her chair and starts tapping, her fingers heavy on my palms.

This time, I don't think about the past. All I think about are Dr. Brooks's crushed fingers, Bella's broken head, Price in a pool of blood. All I think about is violence and death. I've become a hateful person.

When I leave the studio, the Palace is more crowded than usual. Lovers stream past me whispering in small groups, and maids hurry around carrying clean bed linens and food trays.

When I get to Theo's room, he's seated at his desk with his hands in his lap, staring blankly at the poster of the president. He jumps when I come in and gives me a look of pity that makes me sick.

"You ordered dinner. Wonderful." I reach for a tray that's been left on the tabletop.

"Iris," Theo says.

"I'm starving," I say, stuffing food in my mouth. "Can we eat on the balcony?"

"Iris, listen to me."

I turn and say, "I'm listening."

"I'm sorry."

"What's done is done," I say, keeping my face straight.

He seems at a loss for words. Maybe that's what he was doing when I came in, he was thinking about what to say to me. I take the tray to the balcony and sit on one of the two iron chairs. Theo sits on the other and watches me eat. Around us, the sky is painted with orange and pink streaks, as the sun quickly falls closer and closer to the ocean.

"I won't stay tonight," I say.

"Why?" Theo asks.

I move over to his chair and sit on his lap. I let my hand slip inside my pocket, grab the spy camera with the tape of Price slapping me and close Theo's hands around it.

"I trust you with this."

His face is so close to mine that I can count every faint line around his eyes, every shade of his skin.

"Adam wanted it," he whispers.

"He can't have it now. He's lost control. Upload it as soon as possible, tonight if you can."

He nods imperceptibly and I go back to my chair.

"Remember last time I came here, when you said you cared for me?" I ask.

He grows rigid. "I remember."

"You didn't mean that," I say.

He watches my face for ten long seconds; I count the time in my head. When he finally speaks, his face is strangely expressionless. "No I didn't."

I feel a welcomed pain, which makes me feel ashamed of myself for a moment, as though I wanted his love.

The orange sky turns crimson.

I want the fading sun to burn me but its touch on my skin feels like water.

I go back to my room at midnight. After I've closed the door behind me, I drag the armchair in front of it, just in case. I sit on the carpet, feeling its softness under my fingers like rose petals.

I wait.

WHAT HAVE YOU DONE?

Waiting for something bad to happen is unnerving, but this time I'm the one bringing trouble and this is a consolation.

I look out the window until I doze off.

I dream about my father, which I haven't done in a very long time. I dream about his new family, a new woman with a bob of brown hair and new little children running around him. The children look nothing like me. They play and laugh and pull my father's sleeves to get his attention. But he's staring at a tall poster on the walls of a tenement building. I move closer, my body faint like a ghost. It's *my* poster, my face serious, my right hand raised in an ambiguous gesture. I might be calling for help or else saluting someone. My father stares at the poster without moving, his eyes sad.

"Dad!" I call, but he doesn't hear me. I'm a shadow and I don't exist for him, even though it's my dream. The children stop playing. They let my father's sleeve go, turn and lock eyes with me. They're angry.

"Leave!" they say. "Go away!"

"Dad!" I call again and this time my father turns, slowly, but the moment he's facing me I'm already fading away.

When I wake, a faint light is coming out of the water of the distant harbor. Dawn has come, shy but brighter by the second. I stand and smooth my dress. I leave my room and walk along the quiet corridors, passing every poster and chandelier, my soles silent on the carpeted floors.

I reach the post-production studio. The door is open and two maids are cleaning, one sweeping the floor, the other spraying the tables with a detergent. When I enter, they stop and look at me, their faces tired but cocked with curiosity.

"Are you alone here?" I ask.

They nod.

"Go back to what you're doing and stay here until I'm done. If you leave and warn someone, anyone, I'll call Price."

The maids share a fearful look, then start cleaning again in silence. I turn a screen on and wait. Thankfully, it requires no password. Whoever left it like that was working on the montage of the latest episode. I close the tab then open the official page of *The President*. When the page has loaded I try to figure out how to upload a new file. Under the question "who can access this content?" I select the option "everyone" then plug the flash drive in.

I upload the video of Bella and Price then press "share." It takes a minute to load. When it does, I catch my breath. I know that producers will delete it first thing in the morning, but I hope that a few hours will be enough. It only takes one viewer who saves the video and shares it to make it viral.

I look up from the screen. The maids are standing still with their spray and mop in hand, looking at me, incredulous.

"Wait until the sun is up to call anyone," I say. "When they ask you why you didn't call them before, say I threatened you."

The younger one clings to the table until her knuckles are white. "There's nothing that can free us of Price," she whispers.

"You're wrong," I say.

Soon it will be morning. In the corridor of the Lovers' Area I find a maid dusting the Leaders' portraits, her face still sleepy like a baby's. I tell her to go and wake Bella up. She is to meet me in the Chatting Room. The maid doesn't ask questions, just nods and scampers away.

In the Chatting Room, a lamp is turned on and it glows golden, casting a soft halo around. Nothing moves here, every object lies still, resting in this peaceful light. I try to be still too but my heart is beating too loudly, my whole body is shaking. Lights are beginning to brighten up outside, in the city.

I hear a click and Bella comes in, leaving the door ajar. Her face is bloodless, her thin hair uncombed. I move past her and close it.

"Iris," she yawns, "it's six in the morning." When she looks at me, her eyes seem unusually large, her pupils dilated like an owl's.

"Oh, I'm sorry, did I wake you up?"

She must notice the irony and meanness in my tone; she tries to come closer, but my look makes her understand. She must not dare to touch me.

"What's wrong?"

"Aura died." I say this calmly, because I want to give her a chance, a last chance to confess.

"Yes," she says, careful. "Weeks ago."

"How did Aura die?"

"She killed herself."

"Aura didn't kill herself."

"Why do you say that?" Her voice is suddenly dark with fear.

"Because *you* killed her," I say.

"Iris—"

"Say it. Say what you did."

"You're nuts."

"Say it!"

Her eyes fill with tears. I can't believe she's playing the victim.

"Don't you dare cry now."

She steps back towards the door, shocked. I move quickly to stand in her way. She won't leave until I'm done with her.

"You're the worst kind of person," I say. "A bad person who pretends to be good. Dr. Brooks called you 'an envious psychopath' in your file, do you know what that means?"

She tries to get through but I push her back. She stumbles.

"It means that you harm good people to feel better about yourself, that you think everyone around you is a threat."

"That's not true."

"It is. Everyone knows that. The politicians, the producers, all the ones you want to charm, they all know what you are. They keep you in here just because you're good for this stupid show."

"I didn't do anything." She says breathless.

"Liar. You killed Aura because she was better than you. Is this how far we've come? We just kill off one another, as if there's no space for us all."

"It's not like that."

"How is it then?"

"You have no evidence," she repeats, stubborn. "No one will believe you. They all think you're crazy."

"You made sure of that." I move aside and let her pass.

That was her last chance. She seems surprised and lingers for a moment.

"Get out of this room and pay the consequences of your lies," I say.

She stops at "consequences." She keeps very still in the feeble light and for a moment seems to be fading, like a dress worn and washed too many times.

"What have you done?"

I walk past her and leave the room before she can move or speak again.

"Iris?" She calls after me, panicked. "What have you done?"

THE BOMB

I wake up with a gasp, my stomach hurting like an open wound. Margaret is shaking my arm, mumbling something I can't catch.

I reach out for the stomach pills on the nightstand, swallow one. The chair I had moved against the door has been put back in place. I look at the clock next to the bed. It's ten in the morning. I've slept four hours.

"What have you done?" Margaret says. She looks terrible; her eyes are red, as if she's been given drugs. "What on earth have you done?"

"Did they censor the footage?" I ask.

"It's all over the news." She turns the TV on and lets me see for myself. On the morning news a reporter is speaking:

22-year-old Iris dropped a major bomb directly from the Golden Palace last night. The Lover uploaded a video of vice president Price and fellow Lover Bella as they plot Aura's death. Aura was found dead in Iris's bathtub three weeks ago. The mode of death was described by the producers as an inexplicable suicide. We still don't know if the footage Iris uploaded is a leak—

Margaret steps back from the bed and starts pacing the room.

"What were you thinking?" she mumbles, more to herself than to me.

I sit up. The pain in my stomach is so strong I feel like I won't be able to stand straight.

"You shouldn't be here," I say. "It's too dangerous."

She ignores me. "What will you do now?"

"I don't know. What's happening with the Leaders?"

"The protests are getting worse outside. Most guards are on duty around the Palace. Internet connection is gone. Too many comments and complaints have shut down the system."

"Where is Price? And the other Leaders?"

"The president's called some of them to the conference room. They're deciding what to do now. But Price's not there."

"Where is he?"

"He's not been called. He got mad and destroyed his office. He sent Michael away to his villa in the city, with guards to escort him."

"He'll come for me."

"Yes."

We give each other a meaningful look. Margaret has lost all color in her cheeks.

"What do you think will happen?"

"Price will be sent away."

"Why should he?" Her eyes are as big as eggs. "He's done many bad things before and no one complained. His lawyers are here now, I've seen them. Everyone says they're invincible."

"This is different. The people know this file is a leak. And there were protests outside long before this. The people are angry, they'll fight back."

Margaret stares at the poster of the president on the wall, looking helpless.

"Why do you think he sent Michael away?" I insist. "In that footage there's no mention of him, but he fears that more files will come out and incriminate him."

Something in her expression shifts. She takes my hand and pulls it over her sleeve. I feel something cold and sharp. A knife.

"I took this from the Dining Area," she says quietly. "I'll stay with you."

We sit on the bed, waiting. I wonder when Theo is going to upload the other tape. Maybe he will keep it to himself and wait until he's safely out of the Palace to share it. Maybe he'll betray me, sell me out to the Leaders. Or maybe he's already tried to share it, but the guards have caught him. Whatever the case, I'll find out soon enough.

The news keeps going on TV, but nothing more of the footage. Then, at midday, the reporter comes back with a shocked expression on his usually impassive face. I shake Margaret's arm and her eyes come back into focus.

There is yet another shocking piece of footage coming directly from the Golden Palace today. European politician and activist Theo Droit has uploaded a tape of Nelson Price slapping Iris in his apartments. How Droit came to be in possession of this file is yet unclear. In the tape, Price tells Iris that she is "stupid" and "a whore." We are waiting to hear from our Great Leaders yet, as they are currently deciding how to deal with these leaks in the conference room of the Palace. In the meantime, an unknown source from *The Silver Times* has published a list of names of

underage girls who declare they have been trafficked to Price and other high-profile producers and politicians.

"Did they force you to go to him?" Margaret asks me.

"They didn't force me to do anything."

"I didn't know you were working with these people."

"It doesn't matter. We're alone now."

We turn back to the news. They're showing a past interview with O'Hara, the president's and Price's attorney. A young man is asking him questions outside a huge white building.

- Mr. O'Hara, are you familiar with the criticism that many protesters share about your protection of some of the Leaders?

- I don't care about people's criticism. I do my job defending the Great Leaders and my job is to look for vulnerabilities in the Leaders' enemies.

- Does that include your defense of vice president Nelson Price's son, when he was accused of the rape of multiple underage girls and was given immunity from all federal charges both for himself and for any of the named conspirators?

- The outcome of that case was based on the lack of enough evidence to convict Michael. But whether people like it or not, Nelson Price didn't think the deal we made for his son was a good one. He thought we could have done better.

Margaret grabs the remote and turns the TV off. She stares into the black screen and says, "Fuck the Leaders."

Price comes for us hours later, when there's no news from the president yet. It's five in the afternoon and the cameras have just turned green. I'm trying to think whether this is good or bad for us when we hear the steps down the corridor. We look at each other first, then at the bed, where the knife is hidden under the pillow. There is a very long moment when everything is still and I think that maybe it isn't Price, maybe nothing bad will happen.

But then he throws the door open. He's disheveled, his tie is stained, his shirt creased. Anger warps his features; a vein throbs in his neck. He slams the door shut and fumbles for a cigarette in his pocket. I imagine him putting it out on my neck. The burn feels real.

"You weren't in your room," he tells Margaret, eyes fixed on her face. "So I figured, she doesn't have any friends, this crazy bitch, where could she be? With a traitor, of course." Margaret, next to me, stays very still. I turn to her and see that her face is yellowish.

"You're fucking pathetic!" Price shouts at her, his cigarette ashes burning the carpet. "Do you hear me?"

She looks down. "I hear you."

"Say sorry!"

"I'm sorry." Margaret speaks quietly, tears streaming down her cheeks.

Price turns to me. He's not breathing properly; he looks like a rabid dog. "And you… where the fuck do I even begin with you?"

The knife is just a few steps behind me, so I move closer to it. It wouldn't be the first time I stab a man.

"Michael told me you were a whore, told me you had to be eliminated, but I kept saying: give her a chance, brainwash her, she can learn. And that propaganda asshole kept defending you. But now I understand why the fucker wanted you. He wanted you to spy on me!"

I take one more step back. Before I can reach out for the knife, Price kicks me in the stomach. My breath is gone and for a moment I can't see. Margaret shouts and tries to push him aside but he punches her hard in the face. She drops onto the floor, her hands on her nose.

Price puts his hands around my throat. I can't swallow. He is shouting, "What the fuck did you do!" and I feel as if veins are exploding in my head. I try to reach the pillow but my arm feels dead. He is spitting as he shouts, and I think that Margaret will not stand, she won't take the knife.

But then she does something weird. She grabs the light bulb on her nightstand, pulls it and smashes it against Price's shoulder. Shards fly everywhere. In shock, Price lets me go for a second. I fall down, my head hurting, and take the knife before he can attack us again. I hold it to his throat. Margaret comes to stand behind me. Her hand is bleeding. I try to speak but I can't even breathe. My voice comes out cracked, hoarse.

"Stay away."

A shard of glass is stuck in his shoulder, blood smearing his shirt. He touches it, winces, then looks at his bloody hand, bewildered. When he raises his head, his face is disfigured.

"I will destroy you," he spits. "I will ruin every second of your bitch life. You're just stupid useless whores and you'll be treated like it."

I turn to face the cameras and shout with all the strength I can find, "Here's your privilege! Here's your great, generous Leader!"

Minutes later, when the guards come and take Price away, Margaret and I are holding on to each other and refuse to let go. Dr. Brooks and two maids escort us to the Infirmary and I see our faces in the mirror along the corridors: red, swollen and broken, but with a fierce pride in our eyes, and the relief that we did the right thing, for once.

THE WINNER

The bruise on my throat is purple and greenish, sickening to look at, but I haven't covered it. Foundation is a lie, especially if applied on bruises. Men don't cover their wounds when hurt, they carry them around as trophies. So let this bruise be my trophy.

The protests are raging outside. In the ballroom, the windows have been covered over, but we can hear the people shouting even from up here. When I was brought here before, straight out of the Infirmary, I looked out a window and caught a glimpse of the guards down by the gates. They had helmets with visors and gas-canister guns.

The four of us are waiting in a row in silence. My stomach rumbles and hurts and I wonder how much longer I'll have to keep standing. Bella is on my left and occasionally stares at me with so much hatred that the air thickens with it.

As soon as she joined us in here, she told me that I would go to hell because of what I did. She was yelling madly, I'd never seen her so unhinged. A guard had to restrain her and for a moment I thought of the look she had given me when the guards were dragging me away the day of my panic attack. If I go to hell, Bella will go too.

Behind us are four guards, one for each of us. There is no

trace of the European politicians. I wonder if Theo is safe, or if they have taken him.

My hands are folded; my feet are hurting in the tight heels. Lara forced me to wear them, so I imagine something formal will take place soon. My guess is it's either a celebration of my brave actions or an exemplary punishment. I'm more inclined to believe it's the latter. Women always pay for their crimes.

An assistant keeps walking around us under Lara's order, fixing our hair and dresses. When it's my turn to be fixed Lara steps closer to me, taking my chin in her hand and forcing me to lift my head. As she examines my neck, she says, "How could you betray him, Iris. Your Leaders did everything for you." Her voice is ice-cold. It's hard for me to pity her. She's involved in all of this after all, she chose to be involved.

"How could you sell all those girls into prostitution?" I reply.

She shakes her head and walks away, her assistant trailing behind her. The guards around us don't move so we don't dare move either.

We stand, wait and pray, doomed to hear the shouts of the people and the shots the guards fire to scare them away.

Dear God, I want to go home.

Please.

Finally, the president comes in. His suit is of a fluorescent yellow and there are dark circles under his armpits. Behind him, a few other politicians and a troupe of cameramen and journalists. How they were allowed entry in here, I have no idea. This must be a very special announcement.

The men set up the cameras, casting confused looks in our direction while a group of maids hurry to align chairs for the politicians. No chairs are brought for us, so we remain standing. The president sits in the middle while all the others take their places around him. Price isn't among them.

When journalists and cameras are all set, the president finally acknowledges us. He frowns at the sight of my bruised neck and Margaret's bandaged hand, as if our wounds were an affront to him. Then he takes a tablet out of his pocket and clears his throat.

"These are peculiar circumstances," he says, looking at the tablet. Has he written a speech? He crosses his legs and the fat swells his pants. "Very peculiar," he repeats.

On the president's right, Jared takes out a pair of glasses from his jacket pocket. They all seem tired, or embarrassed, I can't say.

"We have discussed the issue in depth," the president continues. "And even though the end of the week is still a couple of days away, we decided to announce the Evaluation scores today."

We all catch our breath. Journalists shuffle nervously on my left. The president pauses, looks down as if gaining some strength.

"But before I do, I want you to know that my long-time colleague Nelson Price will step aside as vice president."

Margaret gasps. I try not to look too euphoric.

The president feels the need to justify his decision. "The people demand justice. They don't accept a man who plots behind their backs, especially behind their Great Leader's back." So the president didn't know about Price. I turn and watch Margaret. She is leaning forward in disbelief.

"However," the president continues, "as Price's lawyers pointed out, there is no legal evidence that Price actively participated in Aura's murder. Until his position is cleared, he will remain in the Palace to prove himself loyal. He will lose every responsibility with the show and remain as a councilor only."

There's nothing that can free us of Price. If we don't win now, our lives will be hell. Margaret begins to cry. The president, visibly annoyed by her behavior, asks for some brandy. A maid quickly appears and pours it for him in a crystal glass. He drinks. I keep as rigid as possible.

"Some more news to share before Jared announces the scores. After the recent leak of a piece of footage that I personally wasn't aware of, I have decided that Bella is officially disqualified from the competition. She will be held on trial to decide whether the allegations against her can be proved or not."

We all look in her direction. Bella's expression turns from one of confidence to one of horror.

"It's not fair," she says. She struggles to find the right words, then blurts out, "Iris broke the rules as well. She revealed classified information."

The president seems to ponder for a moment. He didn't think about my transgression in these terms.

I raise my voice, "I wouldn't have needed to, if they didn't secretly murder Aura in the first place." I stare at Bella. We all stare, like a herd looking back at its weakest member devoured by predators.

The president wipes his forehead with his hand. "You will be escorted back to your room to meet with your lawyers, Bella. Whatever sentence the judge gives, you will never have a chance to take part in any other televised competition or reality TV of any kind."

Bella doesn't move. The president sits back in his chair, weighed down by all of his responsibilities, all the trouble we have caused him.

"Bella, you are dismissed," he says.

She is shaking with rage. "You will pay for what you've done," she hisses at me before the guard behind her takes her and leads her out of the ballroom.

I look away from her, listening to her heels clicking on the marble floor. I wait for some sick satisfaction to take hold of me, but I can feel nothing. Bella's finally gone and all I can think of is what Price will do to me if I don't win.

"Now," the president says, surveying the room. There are only three Lovers left. Jo Winters had told me. *They just wipe us out.* "Let's move on to the grades."

The journalists type frantically on their tablets. Jared takes the tablet from the president's hands.

"Victoria," he says. Somewhere on my right, Victoria steps forward. "You've done great on this show and the audience loves and roots for you. But times have changed in the past week and the stakes have become higher. You didn't adapt too well. You weren't able to play outside the rules." He stops to clean his glasses before finally getting to the point, "Which is why your grade is seven."

This still doesn't mean anything. Maybe Margaret and me have scored so low that Victoria has won. In the few seconds of silence that follow, there is so much suspense that I can hardly breathe. It's like running in thick fog.

Jared goes on, "Margaret, you earned a nine." Margaret takes my hand and squeezes it. "You were wronged and yet you never betrayed your Leaders, you never let us down. You were resilient."

Cameras are clicking madly now and the journalists start shouting questions. The president silences them with a flick of his hand.

"Iris," Jared says. He pauses for a moment and Margaret lets go of my hand. I can tell that whatever he's meant to say, it's costing him a great effort. *Go on, go on.*

"Iris didn't adapt to changing circumstances. She was the one who changed the circumstances." I don't know why he talks of me in third person. Maybe he's afraid. "Iris created the show, just like the audience wanted. That is why we decided to give her a ten. That makes her our winner."

Fifteen years ago, I watched Jo Winters win *The President* on a half-broken screen of my district. She was pretty then, nothing to do with the woman Aura and I saw on Serenity Lane weeks ago. Dark hair, freckled skin, luminous blue eyes. The scores were announced in the ballroom and Jo shouted "YES!" crying and hugging the president. There was another president at the time, not much different from ours.

They gave Jo something like a crown, a beautiful jewel with gems that she wore on her perfect hair. They took pictures of her and she looked so charming. I think that, back then, I even pictured myself in her shoes, as we often do when we watch stuff on TV. Like when you watch reality shows where contestants have to survive in the woods and you wonder, would I make it?

With Jo, I didn't ask myself the question: would I win, like her? I just stood there and watched her slender figure crying and smiling and wondered: how does it *really* feel?

My victory doesn't feel like Jo's. I'm sure it doesn't look like Jo's either. I'm too puzzled to say anything. While the journalists keep shouting questions, Margaret shakes my arm—"You won!"—and Victoria complains, outraged, "It's not fair! We were told to follow the rules! Why isn't Iris punished?"

And then we hear them. The shouts outside, louder than before, as if the protesters were tearing the Palace gates apart. We go to the windows, look down. The guards don't stop us, because they're busy looking too. It's hard to see, at first. Then my eyes adjust to the crowd. The protesters are trying to do something, climb like ants over the tall gates that protect the building. The guards keep firing them away.

But on the gate, tossed like garbage bags, there are two bodies already. They look curiously long, as if their limbs have been stretched out. No one does anything to remove them; the guards are all focused on pushing the protesters away. I catch a last glimpse of one body, swollen like a broken foot, before a guard takes me by the shoulders.

"Go back to your rooms. Now."

My room feels claustrophobic. I pant and try to open the window, but it's still stuck. The shots sound like firecrackers in the distance. I collapse on the bed, exhausted, thinking of those bodies on the gate and why no one moved them away. They looked like abnormal growths, like tumors.

Extract from *The Silver Times*

"The End of The President show? An Enraged Crowd and an Early Surprise Win"

by George Graham

Evaluation results have been announced two days early, after the recent scandal involving vice president Nelson Price and Lover Bella. Footage of Price plotting Aura's death and abusing Iris on the show has been shared by Iris herself and European politician Theo Droit. Whether Iris and Droit planned this leak together is still unknown. The Leaders have decided that Nelson Price will remain in the Palace after losing all of his responsibilities related to the show. Many feel like this decision is unfair considering the footage and the documents containing all the names of underage girls allegedly trafficked through his other properties. On the other hand, Bella has been removed from the show and is currently awaiting trial. In the last statement she released, she claimed that, "Iris was the one who deserved to be disqualified. She is manipulative, violent and dangerous. All I did was try to put her back in her place."

In one of the most unexpected plot twists of Evaluation of the last few years, Iris was instead named the winner. This was totally unforeseen considering that many found it a surprise when Iris was chosen for Evaluation in the first place. After her recent behavior, however, the audience seems more than willing to support her. But not only rich people have voted for Iris. A few protesters recently arrested in Chinatown name the Lover as the reason why they took to the streets. Will that put Iris in a precarious position with the Leaders?

More than one hundred men and women who invaded the street the morning after the leak have been taken to the CMP to be executed under the Great Leader's orders. Guards are patrolling every street of Gildedtown. Anyone who insults or offends the Leaders in any way will be arrested. European politicians who were guests in the Palace during Evaluation are being sent home.

ONE LAST THING

Five hundred thousand dollars. It's the amount of money I win. It's so much that I don't even know what to do with it. But the truth is, I don't really care about the money anymore. When I told Dr. Brooks this morning, she asked, "What do you care about then?"

"Justice," I said.

She gave me a pitiful look. "Not everyone gets justice in this world."

That made me think. I knew she was right of course, but it was, as always, the matter-of-fact tone of hers that annoyed me. I left Counseling without another word and went back to my room to pack my things.

I'm going home tonight. It feels dangerous to even think about it. I'm afraid that, as soon as I think about the word *home*, it comes into being and then someone can snatch it away from me.

Adam comes to bring me lunch. He looks well, just a bit tired perhaps. He closes the door behind him, saying that "too many people hate me right now," so it's better if I lock myself inside. When he's put the lunchbox on my nightstand, I ask, "Did you make me win?"

"The audience made you win." He smiles, looking at the

piles of clothes folded on the bed. "You're finally going home." My eyes drop to his hands: the knuckles are still reddened and swollen.

"You won't find just your mother there," he adds.

I lift my head. "What do you mean?"

"I got her out. Your sister's home, waiting for you."

I want to jump forward and hug him but my body feels static, unmovable.

"Thank you."

"Good luck," he says. "I doubt we'll see each other again."

"Are you leaving too? Price suspects you already."

"I have to stay. I'm needed in the Palace."

I nod. He reaches out his hand and I take it. It feels such a formal gesture after all that's happened that it makes me smile.

"Can I ask you one last thing?" I say. "Can you get me the keys to Price's apartment?"

When he leaves I lock the door as he instructed and lie down on the unmade bed, staring at the poster of the president. I think about all the things I said to the poster in my years in the Palace. How I pleaded for some help, some privacy, some mercy. All the pleading was wrong.

"Women can't always have what they want," Lara told me once.

Yes we can. And we don't have to ask the Leaders for it. We have to take it ourselves.

There is a bang and a scream. Someone is trying to take down my bedroom door.

"Open the door, open it now." Victoria, shouting like a spoilt child.

"I know you're in there," she hisses. "Do you even know what you did? I always knew you were a slut." She slams her fist against the door and cries.

"Go away, Victoria," I say calmly.

"*Slut, slut, slut,*" she cries.

"Leave," I repeat.

She starts shattering things, shouting. Sooner or later someone will take her to the Infirmary and give her pills, but because I have no intention of wasting my time listening to her, I start running a bath, so that the sound shuts her up. I lie down in the warm water and think about hugging my sister.

I meet Theo by the pool for dinner. Two guards come to escort me. I don't know whether it's because I'm a winner or just considered dangerous.

When he sees me accompanied, Theo says, "Leave us, we're fine."

I walk towards him and take his hands into mine. I examine his face but he seems unhurt.

"I was afraid they'd done something to you."

He gives me a feeble smile. "You do care about me after all."

"I do." I blurt out the words before my mouth shuts them down, but Theo doesn't react. Maybe he's given up on me already.

"They interrogated me and Adam for hours. But they had nothing to incriminate us. Adam has many friends: no one would speak against him. I told them I found the spy camera in my room and that I did the only sensible thing: to share its content."

"Good."

"I have to go back to Europe tomorrow. Price's lawyers are after me."

"This is a goodbye then."

He smiles sadly. I move forward to kiss him, just once, but he draws back. He's slipping away from me, and it hurts. Which is wrong because I was the one who pulled away in the first place.

I want to tell him that none of this makes sense, that we're strangers. That I can't talk about my feelings because they don't matter here, or anywhere else. That I still have a family and that's what's kept me alive all this time. That caring for me would be a mistake on his part because I'm wrong *inside*, hurt and patched up badly.

But I can't find the words so I keep silent. We look at the city together until it's time for me to go and leave him behind.

Margaret is in the shower when I enter her room to say goodbye. I wait patiently sitting by the window, two cups of tea in hand. By the time she steps out wrapped in a towel, water dripping from her hair, the tea is cold but she takes it anyway.

"You've come to say goodbye," she says.

"I'm leaving tonight."

"Of course you are."

"What will you do?" I ask.

She shrugs, plays with the sheets of her bed. "I think I will leave too. Dr. Brooks told me they would let me, after everything that happened."

"That's good," I say.

"I don't know." She smoothes strands of her hair away from her forehead. "I really don't know anymore."

Then she does something very unlike her. She stands and hugs me. Her arms around me feel like branches: hard and strong. I remain still for a moment, then I hug her back.

When I go back to my room the door is slightly open. Maybe Theo has changed his mind and come back. The hopeful expectation suddenly makes my stomach clench. I can barely breathe as I touch the polished knob and go in.

Theo isn't in there, but the president is. He is admiring his portrait on the wall, his bright blue suit flashing like a neon light.

My heart almost skips a bit. I don't think I've ever seen him in the Lovers' Area.

"Here you are, Iris." He offers me a chair even though it's my own room.

I sit. He remains standing, caressing his belly.

"The producers think that I can't let you go home without seeing you first," he says. "They would like me to handle you as I would handle a traitor or a madwoman, but I'm going to be honest with you. You seem smart after all."

"Thank you."

"You know what I mean when I say smart?"

"That I won't be difficult."

He smiles. "See, that's what I mean. You're not mad after all." He looks around, as if bewildered by the dimension of the room. It must seem miniscule to him. To me, it looked huge the first time I saw it.

"I understand why you did what you did, Iris," he says. "You wanted to go home, you were afraid of Nelson. And I'm not the only one who understood that. I'm sure many people at home voted, rooted for you because they saw you were scared and wanted to help."

"Yes."

"Unfortunately, others thought you were angry. All those protesters you saw in the streets, they think you're on their side. Your defiance gave them hope and that's a problem."

"I'm not on their side."

"I know, I know. But that's why I came here." He comes closer to me and caresses my face. His hand is sweaty. "I'll let you go home today Iris, but you have to cooperate. You have to swear you won't be defiant again."

"I promise."

He lets his hand fall. "Good girl."

I follow him as he heads for the door. He's almost out when he says, "By the way, I'm glad your sister's home safely. What a cute little rebellious family you are."

Then he shuts the door behind him.

A car will be ready for me in two hours. But first, there's one last thing I need to do. Adam has left a key card on my bed. I take it and make my way to Price's apartment. All cameras are off; the protests keep raging outside. Safe in my pocket, a small glass container filled with sleeping pills and anxiolytics, all those tablets that Dr Brooks wanted me to use so badly.

In front of Price's apartment there are two guards, chatting about the recent scandals. When they see me, they stop talking and give each other a worried look.

"Can I go in?" I ask, smiling.

They're young, I notice, younger than guards usually are. Maybe all the others are patrolling the gates, fighting the protesters.

"He's not here," one of them says.

"It's okay. I want to leave something for him." I raise my head, make my smile cheekier. "An apology."

The guard hesitates for a moment then, "We'll come with you."

I shake my head. "That wouldn't be appropriate after all that's happened, don't you think? I don't want to risk being *abused*, when a thousand people are screaming at the gates right now."

"Let her in," the other guard says.

They open the door and I walk past them into Price's living room. The lights are dim and the desk is messy, sheets half-torn covered in ink stains. The television set in one corner seems broken; there's a crack on the screen. I move past it and touch the handle of the bedroom door. It's locked. I try to force it, nothing. I take out the key that Adam's given me, try it. It works. The door opens with a soft beep.

I hurry inside. With the key card, I smash all the pills into a fine powder. I pour half of it into the water bottle by the bed and the other half into the bottle of wine on the desk. Then I hurry outside with a large smile on my face.

In the parking lot, my feet look small on the wet, cemented ground. Behind me, the Palace stands massive. Somewhere up there, Price will be drinking his wine and going to sleep. If he doesn't, Adam will make sure he dies. Soon, one way or the other, he will pay the price.

I'm about to get in the car when Theo appears, wrapped in a long black coat.

"I thought you'd left," I say, walking closer to him.

"I'm about to."

He cups his hands around my face and draws me to him. His lips on mine are soft as petals, and I let myself be kissed.

When he draws away, he looks me straight in the eyes and says, "You're very brave. Don't let the Leaders scare you."

I don't have the time to reply because the guards are taking me by the arms and guiding me to the car. I turn again and again and Theo keeps standing there, rooted to the spot, a beautiful expression on his face. It's something like pride.

The car doors close and I sit alone in the darkness, my hands folded.

It's done, it's over.

HOME

The city appears to me in glimpses. It's getting dark outside, the evening falling like a curtain, and the lights of signs and posters flicker feebly like distant stars.

In Gildedtown, everything seems quiet. Guards are patrolling every street, uniformed working women sweep debris from the sidewalks, a lonely man talks on the phone with his expensive-looking coat flapping in the wind. I wait patiently, the guards in the front talking quietly and smoking.

We cross a few residential neighborhoods, white facades and doors laced with ironwork, before Chinatown reveals itself in all its mess. I see everything in scraps. A homeless woman warming herself in front of a little fire in a trash can. A bar fight spilling out on the street. A girl with violet hair running quickly in her high heels. I see the posters of us Lovers on a wall. OUR GREAT ENTERTAINERS. My poster has been partly torn, partly spray-painted.

And then there's my district. The streetlights are lit, little moons shedding light on the puddles of watery mud. The fire escapes of the tenement buildings. The factory workers walking back home, mud stuck to their boots, cigarettes in hand. The bare tree branches. I try to crack the window but they've locked it, so I sit back again.

When the car finally stops and the guards open the doors,

the air stinks and it is wonderful. A soft and warm rain has started to fall and people hurry to get home, oblivious to us. I step outside with my bag. For a second, I'm conscious of my own brightness, my hideous neatness. The guards push me, impatient, but I shake my head.

"Leave now," I say. "I'm good."

When the car drives away, I stand all alone, dwarfed by the tenements. I can't move. I can feel the rain on my skin like a balm and look around me, instinctively.

Someone moves on the other side of the street. A girl, with a jacket too large for her body, and hair tucked under a cap. She is looking at me and her eyes are shiny with tears.

I start walking quickly in her direction, rain falling on my face, drenching my hair. On the other side, Lily starts walking too. I drop my bag, and I'm running now because nothing else matters, no cameras, no protests, no Leaders' threats, nothing.

This is what it feels like not to run away from something, but to dive headfirst into it. It is the best run of my life.

Extract from *The Silver Times*

"New Shocking Truths on The President Cause the Reality Show to be Cancelled"

by Marlowe Garcia

The President show has been cancelled. After twenty-five years of mounting success, the Great Leader has announced the end of the show this morning during a conference in the Palace, "Today we announce the cancellation of *The President* after receiving many allegations concerning the nature of our Lovers' treatment at the hand of some of our politicians and producers. Many decisions have been taken to make sure justice is served. Our former Secretary of Defense has stepped down after being accused of abusing non-consensual Lovers. Our former producer Jared Lerner and stylist Lara Rocher are currently being held on trial for soliciting prostitution and sex trafficking. I hope the public will appreciate the efforts that the Great Leaders are making to restore justice."

After the mysterious death of Nelson Price in his apartment, his son Michael is fighting to get justice for the former vice president, while more evidence keeps being unearthed in Price's villas in the city, with hundreds of nude photos and lists of names of underage girls taken from the poorest districts of New Town and lured into prostitution.

Former Lovers Iris and Margaret detailed various abuses at the hands of high-profile figures in the Palace, and also the murders of fellow Lovers Aura and Caroline.

When Iris was interviewed this morning after the president's conference, she said: "Some people have been held accountable for what they did, many others haven't. I'm amazed that Michael Price is not only free, but currently being considered for the position of New Town Mayor." When asked about why she decided to share classified tapes and fuel the revolts, Iris replied: "Once I read that politics is like dogs barking. The people who make noise are the ones who are listened to the most, while the patient ones get drowned in the clamor. Better to be loud, don't you think?"

ACKNOWLEDGEMENTS

Thank you to my parents, from whom I learned to love books and stories. Their love and belief in me are the greatest gifts a daughter can wish for.

I am also grateful to Michelle Meade for her early developmental edit and for saying that I had "an immense talent" after reading this novel. That comment gave me the strength to keep going.

Thank you to Tina Morganella for her proofreading and Alexa Whitten at The Book Refinery for putting the book together.

To my boyfriend, who read the first draft of the book and had only words of encouragement.

To my friend Anna, who shares this writing journey with me.

Finally, thank you to Sophie Parsons for her wonderful illustration.

About the Author

Costanza Casati was born in 1995 in Texas, USA, and raised in Northern Italy. She holds a BA in English and Film from QMUL, a Masters in Writing from the University of Warwick, and currently works as a freelance journalist and screenwriter. *The President Show* is her first novel.

Made in the USA
Las Vegas, NV
08 April 2021